Acclaim for the works
of MICHAEL CRICHTON!

"Michael's talent outscaled even his own dinosaurs of Jurassic Park. He was the greatest at blending science with big theatrical concepts…There is no one in the wings that will ever take his place."
> —*Steven Spielberg*

"Intricate plotting and flawless pacing…you won't be able to put it down."
> —*Time*

"Crichton keeps us guessing at every turn."
> —*Los Angeles Times*

"A fascinating, splendidly documented thriller."
> —*New Yorker*

"One gorgeous read."
> —*Boston Globe*

"Irresistibly suspenseful."
> —*New York Times*

"Will keep you turning the pages."
> —*Forbes*

"Compulsively readable."
> —*National Review*

"Completely brilliant."
>—*Daily Mail (UK)*

"An exciting story…in the hands of a master storyteller like Crichton, it's good entertainment."
>—*Sunday Telegraph (UK)*

"Wonderful…powerful…"
>—*Washington Post*

"[Crichton] marries compelling subject matter with edge-of-your-seat storytelling."
>—*USA Today*

"Crackling…mysterious…"
>—*Entertainment Weekly*

"Every bit as informative as it is entertaining. And it is very entertaining."
>· —*Wall Street Journal*

"One of the great storytellers of our age…What an amazing imagination."
>—*New York Newsday*

They came to the temple, huge and empty in the sun, and walked under the colonnades to get out of the heat. There were hieroglyphics everywhere, depicting scenes in the life of Hatshepsut. She had been a strong, domineering queen, one of the most famous women in Egyptian history—perhaps the most famous after Cleopatra and Nefertiti.

"Tell me," Lisa said. "Why are you so interested in the tomb?"

Pierce shrugged.

"Do you need the money?"

"No."

"Then what is it? The challenge? It isn't a game for you, a way to kill time. I've watched you; you're serious about this, more serious than anyone else."

"Maybe it is the challenge," Pierce said. "A chance to prove something, to do something concrete."

"And dangerous?"

"I suppose."

They stopped at a pillar, and she leaned back against it. He kissed her, pressing her against the warm stone, feeling her breasts against the rough cloth of his shirt. She did not draw back. He kissed her again.

"You know, I think you're much nicer than you act," she said.

"Oh, I'm mean and tough."

"I wonder," she said...

Easy GO

by Michael Crichton

WRITING AS JOHN LANGE

A HARD CASE CRIME NOVEL

A HARD CASE CRIME BOOK
(HCC-MC3)
First Hard Case Crime edition: October 2013

Published by

Titan Books
A division of Titan Publishing Group Ltd
144 Southwark Street
London SE1 0UP

in collaboration with Winterfall LLC

EASY GO™
by Michael Crichton writing as John Lange™

Copyright © 1968 by John Lange;
Copyright renewed, 2005, by Constant c Productions, Inc.

"John Lange" and "Easy Go" are trademarks of
The John Michael Crichton Trust, used under license.

Cover painting copyright © 2010 by Glen Orbik

ISBN 978-1-78329-120-5

Design direction by Max Phillips
www.maxphillips.net

Typeset by Swordsmith Productions

The name "Hard Case Crime" and the Hard Case Crime logo are trademarks of Winterfall LLC. Hard Case Crime books are selected and edited by Charles Ardai.

Printed in the United States of America

Visit us on the web at www.HardCaseCrime.com

"What secret was ever kept in Egypt?"

— HOWARD CARTER, DISCOVERER OF
THE TOMB OF TUTANKHAMEN

PART I *The Plan*

PART II *The Search*

PART III *The Last Tomb*

EASY GO

PART I: The Plan

"Everything forbidden is sweet"
—Arab Proverb

1. Barnaby

The Great Pyramid of Cheops filled the horizon. It was titanic, a giant mass of yellow-brown stone stretching wide and high, staggering the imagination. Harold Barnaby stood near the base, in the vast shadow of the pyramid, talking to a guide.

"I want to go up," he said.

The dragoman looked at him wearily, then shrugged. "Okay, boss," he said. "I show you."

"Good."

Barnaby looked up the facade to the top. From a distance, the pyramid appeared to slope gently; up close, it seemed almost sheer. A group of tourists were coming down. They were small specks, barely visible from where he stood.

"You are alone?" the dragoman asked. He was a short fellow, very dark, wearing baggy trousers, sandals, and—incongruously—a black suit coat, on which was pinned his brass license.

"Yes," Barnaby said. "I'm alone."

"Okay, boss. We go now. You do what I do, okay? Feet like mine, hands like mine. I show you." He started off, Barnaby following closely. Barnaby would have preferred to climb by himself, but the police required a guide. Now, as they began the ascent, he understood why. The blocks were immense, three or four feet high and sometimes six feet long. In many places, there was no more than a foot of ledge between tiers, and the path had been worn treacherously smooth by the tread of countless tourists before him.

Climbing was hard work; the guide set a quick pace. He seemed adept at scrambling over the four-foot stones, but Barnaby was cautious. The ground was very far away. Taxis and camels were minuscule. As they climbed the southeast edge, he soon found that he could see all of Cairo, fifteen miles away. Though it had been stifling hot on the ground, the wind blew strongly up here, tugging at his clothes.

The guide stopped to wait for him.

Barnaby was moving carefully now, for his hands were covered with fine dry sand, and he did not trust his grip. He heaved himself up, over block after block, until he reached the guide.

"Okay, boss?"

"Sure," Barnaby said, winded. They were standing halfway up, with the desert and the Nile and Cairo spread out before them. He could not see the other pyramids of Giza or the Sphinx—the Great Pyramid blocked their view.

"Pretty, yes?"

Barnaby nodded. He very carefully did not look down. He was painfully aware that they were both standing on a narrow ledge not wider than two feet.

"Let's go on."

"Okay, boss."

They climbed.

Now it began in earnest: the wind whistled in his ears and blew sand in his eyes. He noticed the names of tourists cut into the huge stones; he forced his mind to read them, trying to forget the height. The way was steeper still, and once the guide had to stop to find the path again. Barnaby found he was sweating.

He cursed himself for wanting to do this, and paused to wipe his hands on his pants—one hand at a time, always holding onto the rock. And yet he knew that he had to climb the Great Pyramid. He would never forgive himself if he came to Egypt and did not try it.

Quite suddenly, they reached the top. Barnaby, who had

resigned himself to climbing forever, was startled to see a flat space some ten feet square. The guide bent over and helped him over the final block.

He stood on top of the pyramid of Cheops, or Khufu. He felt his legs shake from relief and excitement and sat down quickly to admire the view. From his vantage point, all Cairo lay spread out at the head of the green Nile Delta. He could see the radio tower, the mosques, and the citadel. To the south, on this side of the river, were the scattered pyramid fields of Saqqara and Dashur. And behind him—he turned to see them—were the two small pyramids of Giza, the burial chambers of Khafre and Menkure.

He recalled standing atop the Pyramid of the Sun at Teotihuacán, outside Mexico City, and looking across at the smaller Pyramid of the Moon. It was a similar feeling, but this was different. Egypt imbued the view with a heavy sense of mystery and foreboding. He reached into his pocket for a cigarette, turning his thoughts to his problem.

For the first time in his life, Harold Barnaby, 41, associate professor of archaeology at the University of Chicago, was contemplating dishonesty on a grand scale.

Barnaby was an Egyptologist, and his particular interest was hieroglyphics. He was an astute linguist, a talent that had been evident from childhood. His interest in language, in obscure writings, and difficult grammars had led him in college to study the languages of the Near East—languages both living and dead. It had been the purest chance, the taunt of a fellow graduate student, that had started him on Egyptian hieroglyphics. Now he could read the characters almost as rapidly as he read English.

While a student, he had become fascinated with all aspects of Egyptian life as revealed by the writing.

And slowly, he had come to understand that much that had been translated was wrong.

It was this knowledge that had first brought Barnaby to Cairo, six weeks earlier. He had a grant to study previously translated papyri, for it was his contention that such a study would radically change all existing notions of life in the dynasties of the Middle Kingdom—an era of Egyptian history characterized by the spread of empire, fabulous wealth, and vast armies.

The day after his arrival in Cairo, he had met the proper people—the curator of the Egyptian Museum, the director of the Antiquities Service of the United Arab Republic—and had been established in a little room in an obscure corner of the rambling building. The room was bare, consisting only of a table, a chair, and a lethargic guard. One after another, the precious papyri were brought to him, and he checked the manuscripts against the translated texts. He read of the military engagements of Thutmose III, seventeen times conqueror of the Hyksos; of the court machinations of Hatshepsut; of the glories of Ikhnaton. He reviewed, like an auditor, the messages, dispatches, and bills of pharaohs dead 3,000 years. A whole new world came to his eyes as he read —he forgot the guard and his foul-smelling cigarettes, forgot the heat and dust that streamed in through the open window, forgot the clanking noise of Cairo outside.

He was completely immersed and completely happy. Until two days ago.

Barnaby had been reading a document recovered from one of the Tombs of the Nobles, the rock-cut chambers in the cliffs of Thebes, Deir el-Medinet, across the river from modern Luxor. It was the tomb of a court majordomo, a vizier named Butehi, who had served one of the many kings who succeeded Tutankhamen in rapid succession—just which king was uncertain; the history of the period was confused.

This particular papyrus had been originally translated as pertaining to the procurement of firewood for the queen's hot baths and the disposition of slaves to attend her majesty. Now, rereading it. Barnaby was disturbed. It had been translated from right to left, which made some sense, but very little; the original translator had squeezed the grammar into his own conception of the meaning.

Translating from left to right was not much improvement. He tried reading the hieroglyphics vertically, top to bottom (the Egyptians wrote all three ways), but still no success. It was frustrating.

He began to wonder about this innocuous little passage. He was about to put it aside as not worth the effort when he had a flash of intuition, the result of long years of translating such manuscripts. He suddenly, instinctively, sensed it was important. He looked at it again and tried working from bottom to top. Still nothing.

There were no cartouches in this particular passage. That was odd. Also, the spacing of the hieroglyphs was irregular, the arrangement suggesting some kind of trick. Was it a code? If so, he was lost—it would take as long to break it as it had taken Champollion to discover the clue to deciphering the hieroglyphics in the first place.

He played with the message, rearranging the symbols, testing simple replacements. He got nowhere. He sat back, lit a cigarette, and thought about the character of the man who had caused this passage to be written. What could have been so important that it required a departure from normal writing patterns?

This man, this vizier, would no doubt have access to many secrets of the pharaoh be served. He would also be vain, as was Rekhmire, who was the vizier of Thutmose III. Rekhmire had said of himself that there was nothing he did not know, in heaven, in earth, or any quarter of the underworld; he had inscribed that on his own tomb. But the viziers were important —in their own times, they were the second most powerful men in the world.

Yes, he would be vain. And he would wish to inscribe on his tomb the deeds he had accomplished, the successful administrative acts he had managed.

Staring at the papyrus, Barnaby finished his cigarette and still had no answer. He stubbed out the butt and pushed aside the ashtray. When he looked back at the rows of symbols, he suddenly saw it, clear as day.

Diagonals.

The passage was to be read diagonally. That was what the spacing hinted at. He tried, from top left to bottom right, and got nothing. Then he tried top right to bottom left and found that it read,

> *My majesty, lord of east and west, over all things ruler, commanded*

He worked on the next diagonal, but it did not follow directly. It said something about a dwelling-place eternal, but he could not get the syntax correctly. Perhaps it was necessary to skip a diagonal and then come back.

Barnaby studied the manuscript for two hours. He found that there was no regular arrangement in the order of lines, but that the whole could be fitted together to make a reasonable statement.

> *My majesty, lord of east and west, over all things ruler, commanded, and I have made for him a place that may be satisfying to him therewith, forever and ever. I have built [my] majesty, my father, a rest for the heavens, a dwelling-*

place eternal, which no one knows and which not shall be found. My architect, my son-in-law, shall be nameless as the dwelling-place, known to no [man].

Barnaby glanced over at the guard in the corner, who was half-asleep, chair pushed back against the wall. A fly buzzed aimlessly around the room.

In deep the rock, a work of fifty men, is located the place, final rest, of [my] majesty, lord of east and west, ruler of the peoples. Not where many kings have been disturbed, but near; not so low, but high; in the north, where only by this may it be known. From the arcade of the woman-king, half-way, and north 6 iter, 1 khet, to the high cleft where fly the birds, for they draw near to [heaven] even as my majesty, in eternal rest. The fifty slaves lie near the dwelling-place, and my son-in-law watches over them. I have done this myself, and only I know the place. It was a great work that I did there, and my wisdom shall draw praise for ages after.

It was incredible. Barnaby read it again, and still again. He could not believe what he saw, though it was beyond doubt. This was the record of an official who had made the tomb of an unnamed 19th-Dynasty pharaoh and who had personally murdered all those who had worked on the tomb, including his own son-in-law. And yet, the man could not restrain from recording the deed for posterity in his own tomb. It was, Barnaby thought, typically Egyptian—kill fifty people to guard the secret, but announce it blandly for all to see on your own tomb.

But was it so bland?

He looked again at the original translation. Read right to left, the passage did make some sense. Perhaps that was why the vizier had felt secure—he had hidden his secret within another statement that could be interpreted as a common-place record. It was clever.

Barnaby stood up and walked to the window. The guard stirred, looked at him, and relaxed again. Barnaby stared out at the city, turning yellow-red in the afternoon light. A streetcar rumbled past, crammed with passengers, bearing an advertisement for Aswan Beer.

It was a staggering opportunity, he realized. With this information, he had a reasonable chance of finding the tomb —and there was a reasonable chance that it would still be intact. Most tombs of the 18th–20th dynasties had been robbed, usually a few years after the pharaoh's death. But if the preparations had been conducted in such ruthless secrecy, and if the official was as cunning in all things as he had been in the manner of telling the secret, then there was a chance.

Harold Barnaby could become famous overnight, the discoverer of a tomb to rival Tutankhamen's. He could have a full professorship in archaeology at any university in the world. His name would become a household word, as common as King Tut's was now.

There would be secret passages, of course, and dead ends, and a great deal of hard, dusty work, but if he were successful....

Professor Barnaby. He tried the name on his tongue, silently. Professor Barnaby, the first man to break the seals on the door and enter the underground sepulcher, the first man to see the sarcophagus and the fabulous treasure stored with it. The first man in 3,000 years to gaze at all this, as the flash-bulbs popped and the newsreel cameras whirred.

He smiled, and then his eyes narrowed, and he frowned. Something had occurred to him, something tempting and horrifying. At that moment, staring out of the window of the Egyptian Museum, the conflict was established—a conflict that was still not resolved.

It was growing late; the sun hung low and angry in the sky. It would fall quickly now, Barnaby knew. He stood atop the pyramid and beckoned to the guide.

"Okay, boss? We go now?"

"Yes," Barnaby said. "We go."

It was silent in his hotel room. Barnaby lay on the bed, smoking a cigarette and staring up at the ceiling. His mouth was dry from smoking so much, but he could not stop; he lit each cigarette from the glowing butt of the last, mechanically, his mind elsewhere.

Every instinct, every bit of training and inclination argued against him. It was so fantastic an idea that it became illogical, almost absurd. He should dismiss it outright.

He sighed and swung his feet onto the floor. He walked across the threadbare carpet and looked at himself in the mirror over the washbasin. Brooding eyes stared back at him. Forty-one years old, he thought. Most of that time spent hunched over books. In retrospect, his efforts seemed excessive, the rewards too few. Egyptology was a dying interest in archaeological circles, particularly in America. Even if he did make a world-famous discovery, he could expect nothing better than a full professorship—*sixteen thousand dollars* a year, perhaps. Six weeks ago such a prospect would have thrilled him beyond measure. Now, he was not so sure.

His face was still youthful, but the hairline was receding, the eyes growing weaker, the shoulders beginning to slope. His youth was departing, and he could imagine himself as an old man. He would be lonely, as he was now—he had never found time for women before. Egypt was his mistress and had been for many years.

On the airplane, coming over, there had been a girl, but he had not approached her. They had exchanged glances, and he had looked away. Timid. Afraid.

He had no idea how to carry out his plan—perhaps it could not even be done. Perhaps he was indulging himself, wasting energy on an appealing dream that could never be materialized. He doubted his own strength to carry out a feasible scheme, should he arrive at one.

He looked at his eyes. "You haven't got the nerve," he said aloud. "Stupid ass."

But nerve was only part of it. He needed contacts, finances, organization. These could only be obtained in a world that was unfamiliar to him.

Yet, there must be a way.

2. Pierce

Robert Pierce sat in the bar of the Semiramis Hotel, thinking he had never been so bored in his life. He watched the bartender, a big Nubian with a wide face and a red fez, mix drinks for the only other people in the bar, a Midwestern American couple who looked tired. It was 10:00 A.M.

The bartender came back to him. "Drink all right?"

"Fine."

The bartender bent over behind the counter and washed glasses. Down the counter, Pierce heard the American man say, "Nasser. I wouldn't mind it, except for Nasser."

"Yes, dear," his wife agreed. "Dulles was right."

The bartender clinked the glasses as he dried them. Pierce turned to him and said. "Is it always this hot?"

"September," the bartender said. "September is always hot." He spoke English with a slight British accent.

Pierce nodded. He had been here four days, and each day had been over one hundred degrees. Fortunately, the Italian engineer had been right on schedule, and Pierce had done most of his interviewing in the air-conditioned hotel. Now he could get out of Cairo. He had his plane ticket for the evening flight to Athens.

"Have you seen the pyramids?" the bartender asked.

"No," Pierce said. "I'm here on business." He finished his gin and tonic and pushed it across the bar. "I'll have another."

The Nubian mixed it. "You should come back in the winter," he said. "It's better in the winter."

"So they tell me." Pierce thought about his bags. He would

have to pack. He hated packing. The flight left at nine the next morning. He could get stinking drunk tonight.

The bartender handed him a fresh drink. He sipped it. Perhaps he wouldn't wait until evening. He reached into his pocket and drew out an oval Papastratos cigarette. He liked Greek cigarettes. He would have to remember to buy more in Athens.

What else was there to do in Athens?

Another man came into the bar, looked quickly around, and took a stool near Pierce. Pierce watched him, playing a game he often tried at times like this. It consisted of guessing nationality and occupation; in his years of traveling, Pierce had become quite good at it.

This man, he decided, was American, judging from his clothes: button-down shirt of oxford weave and hopsacking sport jacket—rather collegiate attire, considering the fellow's age. Pierce put him at a weary forty. The man's eyes were bloodshot and his face haggard. Physically, he was nondescript —medium height, ordinary looking. Except that he was very nervous.

"Whiskey," the man said. "On the rocks."

He looked over at Pierce. Pierce smiled. "Hot, isn't it?"

"Yes." The man took his drink and swallowed it in a gulp. "I'll have another," he said to the bartender.

Pierce watched curiously, then said, "Allow me," and nodded to the Nubian.

"Thank you," the man said slowly. "You're most kind." He looked suspiciously at Pierce.

"My name is Robert Pierce."

"Harold Barnaby. How do you do." He did not offer to shake hands. If anything, he seemed more nervous than before.

"What brings you to Egypt in September, Mr. Barnaby?"

"My life's work," he said, in a rather disgusted voice. "I'm an Egyptologist. And you?"

"A writer. I was sent to interview the engineer in charge of the Italian construction firm moving Abu Simbel."

Barnaby nodded. For an Egyptologist, he was peculiarly uninterested. "Been here long?"

"Four days."

"Seen the pyramids?"

"No."

"I don't blame you. Christ." He wiped his neck with a handkerchief.

"Are you excavating here?" Pierce asked.

"No. Translating. I read the stuff, you see."

"You mean hieroglyphics?"

"Uh-huh." He finished his drink abruptly. "My turn. What're you having?"

"Gin and tonic." Pierce was fascinated by this man. His gestures were so abrupt, so edgy—something was definitely on his mind.

Barnaby signaled to the Nubian, then looked at Pierce. "Have we ever met before?"

"I don't think so," Pierce said.

"You look familiar."

"I travel a lot, on various assignments."

Barnaby shook his head and lit a cigarette. Then he said, "Korea?"

"Just during the war."

Barnaby thought about this, biting his lip. When his drink came, he turned the glass around in his hands, staring at it.

"Pyongyang?"

"Yes," Pierce said, startled. "Company B."

"You were a captain," Barnaby said.

"Yes." Pierce said, "And you…"

"I was a captain, too. The zenith of my life." He laughed tensely.

"I don't think I remember you," Pierce said. "I don't recall a lot from Pyongyang. I was only there a week."

"On your way out," Barnaby said.

"That's right." And heavily sedated, because the pain from the bullet-shattered bones in his left forearm was severe.

"I have a good memory," Barnaby said. He sipped his drink. "You've been a writer ever since?"

"Yes." Strange fellow. He was practically twitching with a kind of inner excitement.

"And you travel a lot?"

"Yes, I've been traveling almost constantly through Europe for the last ten years."

"Know many people?"

Pierce shrugged.

"Must be an interesting life," Barnaby said, finishing his third drink. He had a peculiar way of beginning slowly, then drinking more and more rapidly. "You know any *rich* people?"

"Some." Pierce signaled to the bartender, who brought two more drinks. Pierce now had three gin and tonics lined up in front of him, two untouched.

"I mean really rich. Terribly, stinking rich."

"I think you could say so, yes."

"I see." Barnaby dabbed at his forehead with the hand-kerchief and said nothing for several minutes. Then he lifted his glass. "Cheers."

Dutifully, Pierce drank. "Cheers."

"Going to be in Cairo long?"

"No. I'm leaving tonight."

"Another assignment?"

"I wish I had one. Actually, I'm just going to Athens to be

near the water. I may spend a few days on Crete until something turns up. I understand I may be sent to Bonn after that."

"You're leaving tonight?"

"Yes."

Barnaby set down his empty glass. "Just time for one more," he said. The bartender set up a final round. Pierce managed to finish his gin and tonic, so there were only three fresh drinks sitting before him.

Barnaby was sluggish, red-faced, and sweating heavily. He looked at Pierce's drinks. "Come on. Bottoms up," he said, "I must be off soon."

He gulped back his own drink swiftly and set the glass down. Then he made small, embarrassed shifting movements on his stool.

"Well," he said, "it's been a pleasure." He stood rather unsteadily and smiled. "A great pleasure."

He started to walk out of the bar, then stopped, and looked back. "You were a pretty rough customer in those days, weren't you? Silver Cross, as I recall."

Pierce nodded. Barnaby smiled again and stumbled out. Pierce turned back to his three gin and tonics, arranged in a neat line before him. He picked up the first and sipped it slowly.

Strange fellow.

Pierce finished packing his typewriter, locked the case, and walked to the window. He looked out on the Nile, a broad muddy river in the yellowing afternoon sun. A small sailboat traveled gently downstream; he saw the traffic on the Kasr el-Nil Bridge. Directly below him was broad Maspero Street, named for a famous director of the Cairo Museum. It was a tree-lined boulevard, with flags flying in the light breeze.

Little black and white Fiat taxis hurried up and down, weaving, honking.

Pierce watched, his mind a blank. He hated inactivity, hated passivity, and had spent the last twelve years of his life moving around the world on assignment after assignment, deadline after deadline.

He dreaded the occasional times like this—moments between stories. It had nothing to do with the money; he had more than enough. It was simply the time that hung so heavily upon him.

Lately, it had been getting worse. When he was not working, the glamour of his job, the excitement of the travel and the women drained away before his eyes, and he could find nothing behind it all. Nothing but a bored, tired man standing in a hotel room, living out of a suitcase.

He sighed. The Italian engineer, Mannini—now there was a busy man, totally preoccupied with his work, completely satisfied by it. The project he had just finished was quite incredible: lifting the entire monument of Abu Simbel and relocating it on a new site two thousand feet higher, clear of the lake to be formed by the Aswan High Dam. The giant statues were cut from friable limestone; they had been sawn into sections and had been rejoined after raising. The project had taken nearly ten years and cost thirty-six million dollars.

He sat down on the bed, forgetting Mannini, and wondered whether he could fall asleep. The easiest thing would be to nap until he went to the airport.

Just as he lay back, the telephone rang.

3. The Proposal

He picked up the receiver. "Yes?"

"Mr. Pierce?"

"Speaking."

"Harold Barnaby here."

"Yes, Mr. Barnaby."

"I hope I'm not interrupting anything," Barnaby said quickly.

"No. I was just resting."

"Oh dear." A pause. "I wanted to speak to you."

Pierce laughed: "Speak away."

"It's a private matter," Barnaby said, lowering his voice.

"Then come over, and we'll discuss it in my hotel room."

A very long pause, then: "Why don't you come over here?"

Pierce shrugged. "Where are you?"

"Gresham House. Suleiman Pasha Street."

"All right. I'll be there shortly."

He replaced the receiver and thought for a moment. Probably, he would be treated to a tale of woe concerning Barnaby's maiden aunt. Drink was called for. He went down to the bar and said to the Nubian, "Will you sell me a bottle of Scotch?"

"It's not allowed," the bartender said.

Pierce pushed a five-hundred piaster note across the counter. The Nubian looked at it, and wrapped a bottle for him.

The Gresham House was a small *pension* occupying the two top floors of an office building right on Suleiman Pasha. It preserved a faintly British colonial atmosphere, with dark wood paneling, huge bathtubs, faded watercolors of Windsor Castle and Ely Cathedral on the walls, and occasional little signs. One quotation, framed in cracking gilt, read: "Please understand there is no depression in this house, and we are NOT interested in the possibilities of defeat. They do NOT exist—Queen Victoria."

The corridors smelled of kerosene, used to keep down the dust. A short man in a fez directed Pierce to Barnaby's room.

Pierce entered and coughed. It was hazy with stale smoke. Barnaby sat on the bed, hands on his knees. "It was good of you to come."

"Not at all."

Washbasin in the corner, with glasses. Pierce broke open the bottle and poured out two stiff drinks. "What's on your mind?"

"I have a problem," Barnaby said, drinking and wincing. "Warm Scotch. Christ."

"What kind of problem?" Pierce dropped into a chair and lit a cigarette.

"Well, you see—" Barnaby broke off and gave him a strange, direct look. He twisted his hands and said nothing for several moments.

"Go on."

"Well, you see, my problem involves…a lot of money."

Pierce remembered the questions about rich men. "You're in debt?"

"No, no. Nothing like that. This involves money which is— well, *available.*"

Pierce drained his glass on that. Barnaby seemed suddenly frightened, as if he thought Pierce might leave, but he remained seated.

"How much money?"

"I don't know. A lot."

"Give me a rough estimate."

"You don't understand," Barnaby said, almost whining. "It's difficult to say." He finished his drink and held out his glass for more. "Twenty million, maybe fifty million."

"Dollars?"

"Yes."

"That," Pierce said, refilling both glasses, "is a hell of a lot of money to be available."

"Yes."

With a journalist's mind, Pierce ran over the great robberies of the past. The largest in recent history had been the British train robbery in 1962, but that had amounted to only seven million dollars. But twenty million! Where in the world was that kind of cash?

He began pacing up and down the room. "Just how available is this money?"

"I don't really know."

"Who has it?"

"Nobody, at the moment. At least, I don't think so."

"You're not being very helpful," Pierce said. The man's nervous secretiveness was tiresome. "Why don't you just tell me the story from the beginning. When did you first find out about this money?"

"Two days ago," Barnaby said, then hesitated. "Are you interested in the possibilities?"

"Interested? Yes. But not committed. Frankly, I don't have much experience with robberies, but I'll listen to anyone who's talking about twenty million dollars."

"Robberies? Who said anything about a robbery?"

"Oh, for Christ's sake," Pierce said. "Are you going to tell me, or not?"

Eventually, nervously, Barnaby told him.

❉

Pierce stared. "You're kidding," he said.

"No."

Suddenly, Pierce began to laugh. His whole body rocked, and tears came to his eyes. He sat on the floor and clutched his aching stomach.

"What's so funny?"

"This tomb—you want to rob it?"

"Yes."

This threw Pierce into another uncontrollable fit of laughter. He rolled helplessly on the floor, knocking over his chair and his drink. Barnaby watched him solemnly.

"I don't think it's particularly funny."

Pierce got up, wiped his eyes, and poured himself another drink.

"Neither do I," he said at last. "I think it's the most brilliant thing I've ever heard."

Barnaby found talking with Pierce an enlightening, if uncomfortable, experience. As they began to discuss actual procedure, he realized that the gaps in his thinking and information were vast.

"Whose tomb is it?" Pierce asked.

"I don't know. The inscription does not name the king. After Ikhnaton died—he was the monotheist, the heretic— the country declined, and several kings followed in rapid succession. First was Tutankhamen, then a man named Ai. After him, several whose names we do not know until Ramses II. It was a period of turmoil in the country—invading armies and a corrupt bureaucracy. Rapid changes of power, that sort of thing."

"Where exactly is this tomb?"

"In Thebes, along the banks of the Nile three hundred miles

south of here. Most of the pharaohs of the 19th and 20th dynasties were buried there, in and around the Valley of the Kings. Sixty-two in the valley itself, which is a little niche set back in the cliffs on the west side of the Nile. But most of those tombs have been found, and nearly all had been robbed before they were discovered by archaeologists. Supposedly, there are two more tombs which lie in the valley and have never been found, but I wouldn't bet on it."

"This tomb isn't in the valley?"

"Apparently not. It lies to the south, high in the cliffs. The inscription gives coordinates for its location, and knowing the Egyptians, they are probably quite precise coordinates. They were sophisticated mathematicians."

"Have you looked for it?"

"No," Barnaby said. "But it wouldn't have proven much if I had. Finding that tomb will be a major undertaking. It would require several men living in the area for months. One man on his own couldn't do anything."

Pierce accepted this. "What makes you think it hasn't already been robbed?"

Barnaby explained about the diagonal code, which read in both the normal and secret manner. He explained, too, about the philosophy of the times.

"There is a progression in Egyptian tomb-building. In the earliest dynasties, the kings erected pyramids, designed to protect their bodies after death. Unfortunately, the pyramids didn't protect anything—they merely signaled the presence of great wealth, and attracted robbers. By the time of the Middle Kingdom, one thousand years later, all the pyramids had been entered and robbed. So the kings of this period changed tactics.

"The first to break with tradition was Thutmose I, who

ordered a rock-cut tomb near Thebes, which was then the
capitol of Upper and Lower Egypt. Thutmose did this because he wanted his resting-place to remain secret. It didn't,
and later pharaohs, though following the rock-cut tradition
in the Valley of Kings, made no attempt to hide the location
of their tombs, but relied on guards to protect them after
death. That didn't work, either. The guards could be bought
and the priests could be bribed. Whether the location was
secret or known, the tomb was plundered all the same. And
usually, it was an inside job—the robbers seemed to have
known the precise location of the tomb, which passages were
false, and so on. Somebody must have told them.

"But the progression was there, a tendency toward more
and more secrecy. After Tutankhamen, it isn't surprising that
the pharaohs would begin to conceal completely the location
of their tombs and build elsewhere than the Valley of Kings.
This particular tomb was built, and afterward, the architect
and all the workers were murdered. If the inscription is true,
only the vizier knew the location—and he kept his secret."

"None of that proves anything, of course," Pierce said.
"The tomb may still have been robbed."

"I know," Barnaby said, "but I don't think so. It's funny—
when you've been reading the manuscripts and vicariously
living the life of the people for as long as I have, you begin
to develop an instinctive feeling for what you read. You can
tell when something is a lie or an exaggeration, or when
someone is puffing up his ego or degrading an associate. It's
just a feeling, that's all."

"How are you going to go about the robbery?"

"To tell you the truth, I haven't any idea." Barnaby sighed.
"It may be impossible. You can't formally excavate, or you'll
have the government all over you, watching like a hawk.

Nothing of importance gets out of Egypt anymore—not if the officials can help it.

"And even if you found the tomb and loaded it all onto a caravan of trucks, there would be other problems. Checkpoints on every road, frequent checkpoints. Hotels register you with the police each night, and they hold your passport. All in all, it's a very effective system for keeping track of anybody in the country."

"Why couldn't we get five or six people together, check into a Luxor hotel, and then excavate during the day? That's a start, anyway."

Barnaby shook his head. "Doesn't work that way. Luxor is a little town, and there are only three hotels. No restaurants, except for those in the hotels. No self-respecting tourist would stray far from them. Also, no self-respecting tourist would spend more than a week in the town; there isn't a lot to do there. We'd be spotted as phony right away."

Pierce paced up and down the room for several minutes. It obviously wasn't going to be easy—and quite clearly, Barnaby wouldn't be much help in making plans.

"All right," he said at last. "Meet me in my hotel room tomorrow night at seven. Until then, keep this under your hat."

"What are you going to do?"

"Think."

"You're not going to Athens?"

"No," Pierce said. "I'm not going to Athens."

4. The Plan

Pierce was waiting in his room when Barnaby knocked on the door and entered.

"Sit down," he said. "Make yourself a drink. I spent the day in the library of the American University here. I also talked to a few people—on general matters—and have come to several conclusions."

"Yes?"

"First, it can only be done one way—as a straightforward, legitimate archaeological expedition."

"But I told you! They'll watch us every minute—"

"Not if we're smart," Pierce said. "Our expedition doesn't have to be searching for the tomb, does it?"

Barnaby was silent.

"We will need a reasonable cover," Pierce continued. "The expedition will have to be approved by the Cairo Museum staff and the Department of Antiquities, and probably by the UNESCO liaison. I'll count on you to devise a project that puts us near the Valley of Kings for credible, if unexciting, reasons. Can you come up with something?"

"I suppose so."

"All right. Second, we will need money. I understand from my friend Dr. Aliopoulous at the American University that few foundations are putting money into Egyptology anymore, except for saving the flooded Nubian monuments."

"That's true."

"So we need a benefactor, a person of eccentricity and wealth. I know just the man."

Barnaby began to feel a certain sense of helplessness. What had been, just a few hours before, his idea was no longer his. Pierce was taking control of everything. He was both grateful and resentful.

"Go on."

"Third, we will need help. Obviously, native laborers are out of the question, though they are traditionally employed. We must put together a team of capable and strong people to do the manual work involved. Naturally, they will have to know the secret and share in the eventual profits."

Barnaby frowned.

"Well, did you expect to do the digging all by yourself, on weekends?"

"All right," Barnaby said. "What else?"

"We must have a method of removing the treasure and transporting it elsewhere. Now, the whole operation as I see it works like this."

Pierce spread a tourist map of Luxor out on the bed.

"You will begin thinking of an excuse for an archaeological expedition. When I contact you that we have our patron, you will work your way up the bureaucratic ladder, bribing where necessary. Once you have a concession, start collecting provisions for the expedition. We'll need a Land Rover, a half-dozen tents, sleeping bags, food for six or seven. Try to think of a project which will give us an excuse for batteries and lights, for night work.

"I will recruit all necessary personnel—paying my own travel expenses—and collect them in Athens, where I will brief them. We will meet you in Cairo and proceed to Luxor.

"This expedition, like the man who sponsors it, will be highly colorful and eccentric—I believe the term is a 'party dig.' We will all be out for a good time and a bit of adventure. You will be the patient, long-suffering scientist who has to endure our buffoonery in order to gain access to our money."

Pierce thought to himself that it would not be a hard part for Barnaby to play.

"The rationale of our approach is based on the assumption that government watchdogs will be off-duty at night. The tombs, as I understand it, are over here—" he pointed to the map "—on the other side of the Nile from the town of Luxor. Anybody who is assigned to keep track of us, and somebody is sure to be sent along, will return to Luxor each night. After all, why sleep on the ground when you can have a nice bed? And there is little chance of our escaping with anything large. Any of us who leave the dig, which is out in the desert in the middle of nowhere, will be watched carefully. Any packages we mail, any letters we write, will be opened—we can expect that. They will think that it is impossible for us to get anything of value out of the site and so will watch us casually."

"Won't they be right? The road is on the other side of the river, remember—the only road back to Cairo."

"We won't move the stuff by road," Pierce said.

"By air? The airfield is also on the other side."

"Not by air."

Barnaby paused. "The railroads are out of the question. Completely out of the question."

"Quite right."

Barnaby took a long drink, put his glass down carefully, and looked at Pierce irritably. "You're crazy," he said. "I thought of going overland by truck, too. We could make for Libya and try to ship it out from Tripoli. The Libyans wouldn't suspect anything. But it's hundreds of miles of desert, with only two large oases in between, El Kargeh and El Dakhel. Even in Land Rovers, it would be one chance in a hundred that we'd reach civilization alive."

"That's true." Pierce folded his hands quietly.

"Then how?"

"I have worked it out," Pierce said. "There is only one way that it can be done, the only really logical possibility....But actually, moving the contents of the tomb is not our greatest problem."

"What then? Getting it out of the country?"

"No," Pierce said, making himself another drink. "The greatest problem is selling it."

"What do you mean?"

"Did you ever wonder how we are going to convert this treasure into hard cash?"

There was a silence. Barnaby puffed his cigarette. Pierce had hit a question that had not even occurred to him. The treasure was certainly valuable—priceless, literally—but the actual value of its gold and gems, taken apart, melted down, would not be so great. Much of the treasure of Tutankhamen's tomb had consisted of gilded wood statuary, most of the intrinsic value lay in its beauty and historical value, not the costliness of the materials.

"Sell it to collectors, I suppose. There are a lot of collectors around who wouldn't mind buying illegal stuff if it's genuine. It happens in paintings all the time."

"True, but how are you going to find all these unscrupulous collectors? And how long will it take you to unload fifty million dollars worth of treasure?"

Barnaby threw up his hands. "All right, how?"

"Ah," Pierce said. "That's a secret."

"You mean you won't tell me?"

"More or less."

Barnaby stood up. "Forget it," he said. "Forget the whole thing. If there's no trust between us—"

"Of course there's no trust. Now sit down." Pierce took

an envelope from his breast pocket "This is a plane ticket. Tomorrow I am leaving for Europe, to find people for the project. Shall I cancel it?"

Barnaby hesitated, then sat down. He reviewed what he knew of the plan and decided it was good. If Pierce had figured it out this far, perhaps he could go all the way. He had a better chance than most.

"No," he said. "Go ahead."

"There are a few conditions, however," Pierce said. He smiled easily.

Barnaby waited.

"First of all, I'm running this project. I will be the boss, and I will make the decisions. If anybody wants to do something —if they even want to go off and pee in the rocks—they have to get my permission first."

Barnaby squirmed. In a sense, he had been expecting this all along, but not so blatant, not so forthright. Perhaps it was best in the long run. There would be no time for squabbles and angry scenes. "Agreed."

"The money will be distributed as follows: for you, twenty percent of the gross; for me, twenty percent; for our bene-factor, twenty-five percent; the remaining thirty-five percent to cover expenses and the other people on the project."

Barnaby hesitated, then nodded.

"If we do strike it rich, no one is to touch his money for two years. The lump sum will be conservatively invested in Geneva, and any interest will be proportionally distributed before the final division. Everyone must agree to spend what-ever portion of their own money is necessary to arrange a credible explanation for their sudden wealth. A man in your position, for instance, might not be noticeable if he suddenly received fifty thousand dollars. But ten million is a different animal. It's damned hard to conceal."

"Does everyone else have to agree on all these points?"

"Absolutely."

"Okay," Barnaby said. "It's a deal."

They shook hands.

Pierce raised his glass. "To the tomb."

Barnaby smiled. "You know," he said, "it's funny. Every archaeologist who has worked at the Valley of Kings has left convinced that he has uncovered the last tomb to be found in the valley. Belzoni said it, Davis said it, Maspero said it. But perhaps this time it really will be the last tomb."

"All right then" Pierce said. "To the last tomb of the pharaohs."

"To the last tomb."

5. Grover

They sat at a corner table, looking out at the dancers moving frantically on the tiny floor. The music was loud, pounding the walls.

Lord Grover leaned over and spoke into Pierce's ear. "I like it here," he said. "Better than digitalis."

Pierce smiled. "You don't take digitalis."

"Oh, but I do, you know. My heart is terribly weak, and I subject it to such mighty strains." Lord Grover threw an affectionate arm around the blonde seated alongside him. She smiled at Grover—an animal grin, earthy and anticipatory.

"She doesn't speak much English," Grover said, "but she has the strongest, flattest stomach you have ever seen. It is quite remarkable. In all my experience, I cannot recall—oh say, look at that."

He nodded toward the knot of dancers. A new couple had joined the throng on the discotheque floor, now shaking in wild abandon as the Rolling Stones screamed for satisfaction. The man was uninteresting, tanned and greasy-looking, but the girl was startling. She was barefooted, with long legs and a hard figure ensheathed in a shimmering white dress; her platinum hair was cut short and contrasted sharply with her tan.

"Quite nice," Lord Grover remarked, after a moment of observation. "I must look into her—in a manner of speaking, that is." He laughed, a deep rumble.

Lord Grover, fifth earl of Wheatston, was a huge man. He was nearly six feet tall and weighed over two hundred pounds. As he approached his mid-fifties, some of the physique of a fine athlete was softening and sagging, but he remained a formidable figure. His manner was vigorous and masculine, assertive in the way that only those born wealthy can bring off. He would have been an obnoxious, perhaps boorish man were it not for his face, which was extraordinarily childlike and constantly smiling, as if concealing devilish thoughts.

At the same time, he was nobody's fool, and he did not lack nerve. During the war, Pierce knew, he had parachuted into France to coordinate resistance groups for the coming Normandy invasion; Grover had volunteered simply because he regarded it as an important job that he thought himself best fitted to do. He never mentioned it. Pierce had found out from a mutual acquaintance.

"You are probably wondering why I suggested we come here," Grover said.

"Yes," Pierce said. A discotheque on Capri hardly seemed appropriate.

"It is quite simple. I wish to relax before you involve me in gruesome discussions. I assume it concerns money?"

"Yes."

Lord Grover sighed. "It always does. Can I persuade you to stay at my villa for a few days?"

"I would like that, but I will be rather busy—"

"But Robert, I am arranging some entertainments for you. I really must insist."

Pierce hesitated. The thought of Grover's entertainments —undoubtedly weird, and possibly practical jokes—did not appeal to him. On the other hand, he did not want to insult the man.

"I accept with pleasure."

"Good, good. Let's go to the villa now, shall we?"

They all stood, and Grover led the way out, holding the girl by the hand. It occurred to Pierce that he was probably lonely and wanted company for a few days—but the thought was fleeting. He was watching the girl's hips shift as she walked.

The villa was small, on a promontory near Marina Piccolo, but it had its own private beach. The house was white-washed, a cheerful little place with three guestrooms, a master bedroom, a dining room, and living room. Nearby were servants' quarters for the maid and cook.

They came into the living room, and Grover dismissed the girl with a kiss on the forehead and a pat on the bottom. When she had gone, he turned to Pierce and laughed, as if ashamed of himself.

"What will you drink?"

"Nothing, thanks. You want me coherent, after all."

"Precisely. How do you expect to order your thought without a drink? Scotch?"

"Thank you."

"A sober man is a depressing man." Grover walked to the bar and mixed it quickly. Then, he produced four bottles with strange shapes and unfamiliar labels. "I'm off Scotch, myself. Too dull. Have you ever had a vampyra? Fabulous. I believe it is of Rumanian origin. It calls for slivovitz, grain alcohol, and a shot of absinthe. Horrible, you say—but I must tell you it changes a man utterly."

"Hence the name?"

"Superstitious people, the Rumanians," Grover said, as he prepared his drink. "Or possibly they just hold their liquor badly." He finished and brought both glasses over, handing Pierce the Scotch. "To money."

Pierce grinned and drank.

"Now then," Grover said, sitting down. "Let's have it. I must warn you that my finances are in a rather poor state at the moment. You can't expect miracles. What's on your mind?"

"I have a proposition for you," Pierce said. "A little investment which will give you rather remarkable returns. Something on the order of, say, two and a half thousand percent. Can I interest you?"

Grover sighed. "You Americans. So clever in business. What's the initial outlay?"

"Fifty thousand dollars."

"Hmmm." Grover got up and walked to the bar. He mixed himself another drink, though he had hardly touched the first. "You must excuse me," he said. "I often prepare a second drink beforehand. After the first, it is sometimes hard to get the right proportions. Do I understand you to be talking about twelve and a half million dollars?"

"Approximately."

"Hmmm." He returned to his seat and began patting his pockets. Then he stood, went to a cabinet, and searched through several drawers, muttering "hmmm" at intervals. He looked back at Pierce, frowning. Then he walked to the door, calling "Maddelena? Madd-e-lena?"

A maid appeared, fortyish and matronly. "Signor?"

"Where is my damned marijuana? I seem to have misplaced it."

She went to the cabinet and opened the lowest drawer, removing a small packet that she handed him without a word. Her glance was sympathetic but still disapproving. She left silently.

"You'd think she was my goddamned *mother*," Grover said, watching her go. "Now where are the blasted toothpicks?" He rummaged again for a while and finally found them at the bar. He licked one, rolled it in the packet of marijuana, and held it up to the light, critically inspecting the little ball of clinging powder. Then he popped it into his mouth like a thermometer.

"Hmmm," he said, and sat down again. He propped his feet up on the coffee table. "Old custom, you know. They used to do it in Elizabethan times—you absorb it right through the gum. Saves wear and tear on the lungs. You were saying?"

Pierce smiled. "I made you a proposition." Inwardly, he was thinking that Lord Grover was perfect, just the man he needed. Pierce was aware that this little act had been performed for Pierce's benefit, to convince him that Grover was an unreliable man, hopelessly debauched. But Pierce had watched the eyes, which were alert, looking for a reaction.

"So you did, so you did. A very interesting proposition. But I must tell you something: I will not countenance illegal actions of any sort except for my own amusement."

"Who said it was illegal?"

"Robert, you are a dear boy, but nobody ever made a profit like that legally."

"All right," Pierce shrugged. "It's illegal."

"Terribly illegal?"

"I'm afraid so."

"Dangerous?"

"Possibly."

"Can I be in on it, or do you simply want my wallet?"

"No, as a matter of fact, your presence is essential."

"Hmmm." Lord Grover sipped his drink. "I think this is going to be amusing after all. Shall we discuss it more fully?"

It was three in the morning when Pierce finally went to bed. Lord Grover had heard the whole plan—with certain deletions—and announced he would make his final decision in the morning. Pierce had climbed under the covers completely exhausted and was instantly asleep.

He awoke smelling perfume. Something was tickling his ankle. He raised his head from the pillow and looked into a pair of very blue eyes. "Hello," the girl said. She was lovely, with long blonde hair and a deep tan. She was getting undressed.

"Hello," he said.

"Hello," said another voice. He looked over and saw another girl, also blonde, also undressing. Pierce glanced from one to the other.

"What's going on?"

"Entertainment," said the blonde at the foot of his bed. She smiled deliciously.

"At this hour?"

"Oh, *le petit pauvre.*" The other girl leaned over and kissed him softly on the cheek.

"Yes," said the girl at his feet. "Lord Grover thinks highly of it. He says it improves your appetite for breakfast."

"I am pleased," Lord Grover said, as they sat at breakfast on the terrace overlooking the sea, "that you are eating well. There is nothing so distressing to me as a man who does not consume a hearty breakfast."

Pierce nodded, eating his fourth poached egg. He sipped the coffee and looked out at the beach. It was a beautiful day. The sea was clear and deep blue.

"Have you reached a decision?"

"No," Grover said. "Not yet. I find the whole idea intriguing, you understand—but I should not like to end my days in a miserable Cairo jail. Even this—" he gestured to the villa "—is preferable to a jail." He laughed.

"Take your time," Pierce said. "There's no rush. I don't have to leave until tomorrow morning."

"That will be fine. Meanwhile, if I were you, I'd spend the

day on the beach. This is one of the last nice days we shall see this fall on Capri."

"Egypt will be pleasant for the winter."

"It has occurred to me."

They were silent.

"Tell me," Pierce said. "I've never known you to hesitate before. Why are you stalling now?"

Grover laughed and lit a cigar. As he shook out the match, his eyes gleamed delightedly. "I should think you'd have guessed. I'm having you investigated."

He swam hard for fifty yards, straight out to sea, then turned and swam back. When he threw himself down on the brilliantly white sand, he felt winded and good. The sun was hot and high in the sky; he relaxed and closed his eyes. Egypt seemed very far away now, and the whole scheme rather improbable, like a dream. He slept.

When he awoke, he looked up at the villa. Someone was on the terrace, watching him. He could not see who it was from this distance. Pierce turned away.

The water was calm, peacefully lapping at the beach. The sun was dropping in the sky. He pulled on a sweater, lit a cigarette, and sat there thinking.

"You know," Pierce said later that day, "I really should be annoyed with you. We're old friends, after all."

Grover blew a cloud of cigar smoke. "Nonsense. I would lose respect in your eyes if I hadn't checked up on you. You know it. Old friends make the best con men."

"Did you get your answer?"

"Yes. When do you want the fifty thousand?"

"A week from today. We will meet in Athens."

"I have a friend who owns a villa in Khifissa. Will that do? He's not using it this time of year."

"Fine." Khifissa was the diplomatic suburb of the city, a hilly, elegant village north of Athens. It was secluded and discreet. "Give me the address. We will all meet at eight o'clock, September 29."

Grover got up to jot down the address. As he wrote, he said casually, "How many girls am I allowed?"

"One," Pierce said.

"You're joking, surely," Grover said. His voice sounded genuinely horrified. "We might be out there for months. One girl?"

"One," Pierce said firmly.

"Three, at least."

"Sorry," Pierce said. He already knew they would settle on two. Perhaps it was not so unreasonable. After all, Lord Grover did have his image to maintain. One girl would hardly be proof of debauchery in the eyes of the Egyptians.

"Two," Grover said.

"All right."

"Now, a final point, which I forgot to mention last night. I am afraid I cannot—simply cannot—travel for any length of time without my personal secretary, who is now in Naples. I do have my finances to maintain, you know."

Pierce frowned at this. He did not like bringing an extra man along, but Grover might seriously need him. "What kind of fellow is he?"

"Fellow? Don't be silly. She's a girl."

So that was it. Lord Grover was having three girls after all.

"No," Pierce said.

"I know what you're thinking," Grover said, hastily raising

his hand. "Demeaning thoughts, unworthy of you. Do you honestly believe I mix business with pleasure?"

Pierce laughed. It was impossible not to; Grover's face was so childishly innocent.

"Well then, it's all settled," Grover said. "Where shall we eat dinner?"

"Sorry, but I can't stay. I've just time to catch the last hydrofoil back to Naples."

"But you can't leave! I've planned some entertainment."

"Frankly, I find your entertainment exhausting."

"Just as I suspected," Grover said. "Out of shape. Sickly. Too much fast living. You're a wreck." He looked at Pierce slyly. "Where do you go from Naples?"

"Somewhere else."

"I knew it," Grover said, chomping down on his cigar and puffing like a steam engine. "You don't trust me."

"That's right," Pierce said.

They shook hands.

6. Conway

"Would you pass the cucumbers in peanut sauce?" Mornay asked.

"Of course," Pierce passed it.

"I am very partial to this particular dish. Watch that curry —it is murderously hot."

Pierce was dining with Roger Mornay at the Bali on the Liederstraat. Mornay assured him it was the finest Indonesian restaurant in Amsterdam, and Mornay should know. As an expert in diamonds, he had lived in Amsterdam most of his life.

They were eating rijsttafel, the national dish of Indonesia, which consisted of dozens of separate dishes, each to be mixed with rice in a large plate and then eaten. The waiters, in white jackets and brightly colored headbands, first served a series of hot, curried foods, then a number of sweet and sour dishes. Then vegetables, spiced and bland. Pierce found himself feeling exhilarated, and slightly ill.

"More beer is what you need," Mornay advised. He ordered it, then said, "What is on your mind?"

"I want to hire you."

Mornay laughed. "Impossible," he said.

In the morning, they walked through the Rijksmuseum. There were a half-dozen excellent Vermeers on display, and Rembrandt's "Night Watch." The painting never failed to annoy Pierce. He disliked the large room where it was hung, with the benches all around and the deathly, funereal air. The picture itself did not seem to justify the overblown solemnity of the setting.

They sat down. "I don't like it," Pierce said.

Mornay shrugged. "Of course. You like nothing today. I cannot help your disappointment."

"I think you're being foolish. You could be wealthy."

"At my age? I do not care. I have money enough now—and so do you."

"Shhhh," said a guard in the corner.

They walked down the narrow, crooked streets of the port, listening to the seagulls caw. It was a disreputable section; girls posed in picture windows. The first leaves of autumn were falling into the canals.

"I don't know how to make you understand," Pierce said. "This is a chance in a lifetime. But you see my position—I can't explain it fully if you are not interested."

Mornay shook his head sadly. "You are stubborn, Robert. I will say that for you. Perhaps it is a virtue, particularly in this undertaking of yours. I want to hear no more about it. But I do have a suggestion."

Pierce raised his eyebrows.

"Let us go to my office."

A cramped room on the third floor. The windows were dusty, yellowing the afternoon light that filtered through. Papers, invoices, and receipts were stacked high on Mornay's desk. He sat back and pushed his rimless spectacles up on his forehead and looked at Pierce.

"Robert, let me be honest with you. Twenty years ago—even ten years ago, perhaps—I would have found your offer exciting and attractive. Now, I feel nothing but fear. I am too old for intrigue, too tired, too slow. My nerves are not good. I know all this, though I do not like to admit it." He scratched the back of his neck. "I am afraid because I might accept, despite my better judgment. So I have an alternative for you, which may satisfy us both."

Pierce waited.

"There is a young man who came to me from South Africa some time ago. He is young and strong and may be the man you want."

"I would like to meet him."

"Of course. He is living in Paris."

"You have his address?"

"No, just his name. Alan Conway."

As they pulled onto the Pont Neuf, a taxi cut them off. Alan Conway honked his horn and screamed, *"Merde!"*

Sitting alongside him in the two-seater Alfa roadster, Pierce smiled. The taxi driver looked back, and Conway shook his fist and shouted, *"Espèce de con!"*

Then he turned to Pierce and grinned. "You gotta do that. Otherwise you spoil the natives."

The car turned onto the Quai des Tuileries and sped past the gardens toward the Place de la Concorde. Conway drove very fast, weaving among the other cars, but in perfect control.

Pierce had liked him from the start. He was a muscular Negro with an engaging smile and an offhand manner that belied a perceptive mind.

"Who put you on to me?"

"Roger Mornay, in Amsterdam."

"Oh yeah. He's a good fella. He helped me out once, when I was in a jam."

"So I understand."

Conway smiled, a slow, bemused grin. "And then you came all the way to Paris to meet me, right?"

"Right."

"You must think I'm pretty important." Abruptly, he stomped on his brakes and honked the horn. They missed a Mercedes sedan by inches. "French have no idea how to drive," he said. "The other day, I watched a nice little girl—sweet little girl —take off her heel and pound it into a fella's head, just because he stole her parking place."

"What happened?"

"The fella asked her for a date," Conway laughed.

"Just like that?"

"You shoulda seen the girl." He whistled and cut right into the traffic streaming around the obelisk in the Place. "That's Egyptian," he said, nodding toward it.

"I know."

"I know you know, man. Where's it from?"

Pierce frowned.

"Temple of Luxor," Conway said. "Now you see, you learn a little something every day."

"How do you know it's from Luxor?"

"I ought to. I'm an archaeologist."

"You're what?"

"An archaeologist. Didn't Mornay tell you?"

"No. He just said you were South African."

"Uh, well. I'm afraid that's what I told him. A little white lie to expedite things in a moment of stress. Covering up my tracks. As my grandpappy said, 'Hide-um trail from pale-faces.'"

"You're kidding."

"Honest to God. My grandpappy was a red-blooded Sioux. His name was Walk-on-Water, and I always appreciated that. It comforts me. In times of stress."

"That's interesting."

Down the Rue Royale to the Madeleine.

"Right now," Conway said, "I am probably asking myself, what are you doing here, talking to a simple fella like me?"

"It's a long story."

"I'm not going anywhere," Conway said, swerving left up the Boulevard Malesherbes.

"You look like you are."

"That's just the impression I give. Strictly for the foreigners."

Pierce smiled. "I could have sworn you are as American as I am."

"That depends on how American you are. Were you born in Cincinnati?"

"No."

"Then you can't be very American."

"Were you born in Cincinnati?"

"From the moment I laid eyes on you, I thought to myself, now there's a bright fella." He sighed. "But I'm wasting your time. Here you came all this way to talk to me, and I'm not letting you get a word in sideways." He glanced at Pierce.

"I have a business proposal."

"Will I make money or lose money?"

"Make money, I hope."

"You're getting warmer."

Past the Eglise St. Augustin, through the Place Malesherbes, toward the Boulevard de Courgelles. The leaves were falling, giving a red-brown color to the city. Girls sat sipping and talking in the open-air cafes. It was midafternoon.

"Why did you tell Mornay you were South African?"

"Pressure of circumstance. I had some things to sell."

"Diamonds?"

"More or less."

"South African?"

"Well, you see, I spent one summer—of course, it was winter, down there—working with Raymond Dart in the Transvaal. He's a big man with australopithecus, the fossil ape-man. They have an unusual archaeological situation; they excavate with dynamite. Only place in the world where they do things that way."

"And?"

"Well, uh, on one of my little excursions to Johannesburg, I happened to come across some diamonds. They were lying in the street, you see. I thought, if I take these to the police, the officer will say they're his, and he lost them, and he'll pat me on the back and send me away. Or maybe he'll throw me in jail. So I just sort of slipped them in my pocket. You know how it is. I remember I used to tell my mother I found things in the street. She never believed me. You know. Mothers and cops—they're all in cahoots."

It took Pierce a few moments to realize what Conway was saying. "You mean you smuggled them out of South Africa?"

Conway shrugged modestly. "We do our part, you see. The place is not the nicest for a young fella like myself. I often had the distinct feeling—and I don't want to sound prejudiced, but it's true—I often had the distinct feeling that they didn't like me down there."

Pierce could imagine. "Why'd you go in the first place?"

"You mean, being Negro?" He laughed. "I went to study under Dart and to steal as many diamonds as I could find. It was a hard period in my life. I had been living in France for three years and had built up a powerful list of creditors. They were thirsting for my blood. So I hotfooted it out and came back a new man. Little tense, you know, but not too bad considering."

"Considering what?"

"Hundred thousand dollars."

"Very nice."

Conway was headed toward the Bois de Boulogne. "I was proud of myself. I just wished my daddy coulda seen me. He would have been tickled pink. He always said to us kids, 'Kids, take care of yourself.' We'd get beat up, and come home all bloody, and he'd say, take care of yourself."

"Do you have a police record?" Pierce asked.

"Just parking tickets."

"Think Interpol has a file on you?"

"What're you trying to do, build up my ego? 'Course not."

"Then perhaps we can do business."

They were parked in the Bois de Boulogne. Pierce had explained the plan, and Conway had listened silently.

"Left a few things out," he said, at last. "How do you get it out of the country? And how do you sell it?"

"That's all arranged," Pierce said. "I'll explain it later."

"You're all twitchy," Conway said. "You oughta relax more. Now why don't I fix you up with a nice little girl who'll get your circulation back to normal, and then we can meet tonight, and you can tell me the whole thing. Right?"

Pierce shook his head. "You'll just have to wait."

"Well, uh, I'm a bad swimmer."

"So what?"

"So I never jump into the water unless I know how deep it is."

"Sorry."

Conway sat behind the wheel and thought. Then he scratched his head and looked up at the sky; eventually, he began cleaning his fingernails with a toothpick.

After a long silence, he said, "You know, you missed your true calling. You shouldn't be a writer—you should be a pusher."

"Hooked?"

"Afraid so."

They shook hands. Conway reached into the glove compartment and brought out a bottle of cognac. As he pulled off the cork, he said, "You know, I must be out of my mind to do this." He sighed. "My mother always said I'd come to no good, and she was right." He passed Pierce the bottle.

7. Níkos

Pierce sat in his room in the Istanbul Hilton, thoroughly exhausted. The constant traveling had worn him down, especially the two fruitless days he had spent in Beirut. He munched a sandwich and waited for the call.

He was almost finished now. It had taken six days, but he had most of the group. Only one man remained, the man he had sought in Beirut. The man who was possibly the most important of all.

The phone rang. He picked it up.

"Hello?"

"This is Pedro."

"I'm glad I found you," Pierce said.

"So?"

"I want to meet with you."

"So?"

"It involves big money."

"Big money, big risks. I am a simple man. Do not tax my brain."

"There is several million dollars in it for you."

"You are crazy," the voice said. "I am not surprised you went to Beirut looking for me. I have not been in Beirut for six years."

"So?"

"I think we will meet," the voice said. "The Suleiman Mosque, in an hour. No games?"

"No games."

Click.

*

The Mosque of Suleiman the Magnificent, the warrior who made pyramids of human skulls, was located on the opposite shore of the Bosporus, overlooking the Golden Horn. Pierce arrived ten minutes early. He thought it prudent—if his man were really worried, he could observe Pierce at a distance first. He entered the mosque, slipping off his shoes and stepping onto the carpet. He was disappointed; the inside was ugly, cavernous, and uninspired. He wandered around for several minutes, hands in his pockets.

"You are early."

Pierce turned to face a man of medium height, chunky and muscular, with a handsome though unshaven face, and eyes as cold and deadly as he had remembered.

"Hello, Pedro."

"You can call me Nikos now," Nikos Karagannis said. "I have a taxi outside. Shall we go?"

They drove through the winding streets of the old quarter, past the seraglio and the fringes of the *kapali,* the vast bazaar. Covering nearly a square mile, Istanbul's open market was the second largest in the world after Hong Kong. It was a busy, teeming, colorful section of the city; vendors had set up portable displays on the sidewalks, and the stalls sold everything from luxurious brocade and Meerschaum pipes to Gillette razors. The streets were jammed with buyers, the air thick with dust.

Nikos directed the driver to a side alley, and they stopped near the end, entering a narrow, dilapidated house. He led the way up rickety wooden stairs.

"This belongs to a friend," Nikos explained. "Not here now."

They came to a hallway, and he opened one door. It was a small room with a small table and unmade bed. A girl sat on the bed, combing her hair.

"I told you to go," Nikos said.

She looked up, eyes large, mouth pouting. She was a big girl, voluptuous in a tight red dress. Her hair was as black as her eyes and very glossy. "I know," she said. "You told me."

Nikos looked at Pierce and sighed. "I try to be a gentleman," he said. "It was always my wish, as a boy. To be a gentleman."

Abruptly, his hand flashed out, and he smacked the girl across the face. She gasped, more from the suddenness of the move than the pain.

His face blank, Nikos held the door wide and nodded toward her. She was struggling to control her features and maintain her dignity. She stood, threw her shoulders back, and walked out. Nikos shut the door softly behind her.

"I have only ouzo," he said, going to the desk and removing a bottle. "Will that do?"

"Yes," Pierce said.

"You are agreeable today, my friend," Nikos said, pouring two glasses of the liqueur. "Do you need me very badly?"

"Of course not."

"Good. You know, I have never killed a man before." He stared reflectively at his glass. "It rubs me wrong, killing."

"No killing."

Nikos sighed. "I am relieved. Great money is always such a temptation; principles often suffer. You are sure no killing?"

"Yes."

"Then we can talk further."

Pierce sat down on the bed. "What is your nationality these days?"

"Greek. I have been Greek for the last six months, since my Lebanese passport expired. New passports are so expensive now. I had a good Turkish one, but it was stolen. Can you imagine? Something stolen from me?" He laughed.

Pierce laughed with him. It was really a ludicrous thought, for Nikos Karagannis was a superb thief. He boasted that he could steal anything from anybody, anytime. He had stolen a Ferrari from the Aga Khan, in Rome, to win a twenty-dollar bet. (He had later returned it for a sizable reward.) He had stolen the Golden Lions from the Venice Film festival three years ago. He had stolen four Rembrandts, three Copleys (during a brief visit to Boston), and a Giorgione during his career. He liked his work and was good at it.

He was handsome in a rugged, gruff way. His smile was broad, his manner open, and his mind unfailingly sharp. He was a natural athlete, with quick reflexes and fine coordination.

"I need an Egyptian," Pierce said.

"Impossible," Nikos said. "A decent Egyptian passport will cost you a fortune. They are very hard to find and must be well done—the government checks them carefully."

"No passports, just nationality. Can you pass for an Egyptian do you think?"

"I was born in Alexandria."

"That was a long time ago. How is your Arabic?"

Nikos snorted. "Better than your English."

"Could you pass as an Egyptian among other Egyptians?"

"Such trifles." He lit a cigarette. "Please do not insult me. How much money is involved?"

"For you, five million dollars."

"How much in total?"

"Fifty million."

"That is a great deal of money. It is by far the greatest robbery in history. You are ambitious."

"I suppose."

"Do not be modest," Nikos said, waving his hand. "The

Americans have always fascinated me. You, for instance—
I did not think you were dishonest, my friend."

"I wasn't."

Nikos shrugged. "Naturally. Who was ever dishonest until
he saw the opportunity?"

"Are you interested?"

"Do you think I am a fool? Of course I am interested. But
let us understand each other well." The eyes, cold and gray,
stared at Pierce. "Among ourselves, we will be honest."

"Of course."

"Do not say 'of course.' Say, 'yes.'"

"Yes."

From nowhere, the knife appeared and whished across
the room to stick in the door, quivering. It happened with a
speed that Pierce could not believe.

"No games?" Nikos asked.

"No games," Pierce said, his eyes on the knife.

"Good."

8. Athens

It was raining in Athens. Pierce could hear the drops spattering on the window of his hotel room. Distant thunder rumbled softly, and there was a flicker of lightning. He stopped to shake a cigarette out of a packet, then stopped and put it back. He had been smoking too much lately; his mouth was raw, his tongue numb. The constant traveling, the tension, the drinking had left him feeling uncertain and depressed.

Only a week ago, he had been a bored freelance writer sitting in a Cairo bar. His biggest problem was whether or not to spend the evening drinking or chasing women.

And now?

He sighed and lay down on the bed. Now it was all different: he felt like a new man—new goals, new interests, new fears. Mostly, it was the fears that he noticed. He was planning a robbery. Unbelievable, yet true. Almost in desperation, he looked at his watch, hoping it was time for dinner. It was.

In the restaurant, he sat at a corner table. It was still early in the evening; the only other people there were tourists, looking forlornly at each other and wondering where the Greeks were. Pierce knew that no self-respecting Greek would sit down to dinner before 9:30.

Perhaps, he thought, that is why they do it—to avoid the tourists.

After twenty minutes, a swarthy man carrying a newspaper joined him. He set the newspaper down on the table and signaled to the waiter.

"How is it?" Pierce asked.

"Not bad," the other man said. "It will do."

"When does it expire?"

The waiter came over, and the man ordered mousaka and a bottle of Fix Beer. When they were alone again, he said, "In five years." He smiled. "It's brand new."

"The name?"

"Robert Sevrais."

"French?"

"No, Brazilian. Born in Chicago, U.S.A. An expatriate."

"That sounds fine," Pierce said.

A slightly hurt look. "I thought it was masterful. What about the money?"

Pierce stared out at the room. "My right pocket."

The man also stared out at the room as he reached into Pierce's pocket, took the money, and slipped it into this own pocket without looking at it.

"Two thousand?"

"Exactly."

"Good. The picture looks rather like you, by the way."

"Excellent."

"Sometimes it is hard to arrange."

Pierce laughed. "All right, Giorgo. I'll see that you get another two hundred in the morning."

"*Efaristo.*"

"My pleasure."

The waiter returned with the food, which was cold this time of evening, but they ate anyway. When they left, Pierce took the newspaper with him.

It was, he thought, one of the advantages of being a writer and knocking around Europe so long. By now, he knew where to get an abortion, where to get heroin, marijuana, or opium, where to get a girl or a boy in any city of the world.

A passport, a visa, even immigration papers were relatively simple.

It was all a matter of money—and contacts.

He found the villa with some difficulty. Khifissa is a hilly suburb north of Athens, facing onto a hot valley and beyond, Mt. Parnes. The town itself sprawls in the foothills, the villas secluded in pine groves.

The evening was cool as he took the road out of town, past the Gropius-designed American Embassy and up around a row of high-rise apartments, glass-walled and impersonal. Several new buildings were being erected, and he was struck, as always, by the absence of steel in the construction. The Greeks had virtually no metal in the country—a problem since Homeric times—and so built almost exclusively with reinforced concrete.

It took him forty minutes to reach the outskirts of Khifissa and another twenty to find the villa. It was pleasant, surrounded by flowers and built on a slope giving a good view of the valley and the mountains. When he knocked, Lord Grover opened the door.

"How nice to see you," Grover said. "What will you drink?"

"Nothing, thanks." He entered the room to find that it was spare and modern but comfortable. The ceiling was high, giving it an airy spaciousness.

"Nothing to drink?" Lord Grover seemed appalled.

"It's been a long week, and it's going to be a long night."

Grover shrugged, as if to say that fools must be tolerated. "I have put all the women to bed," he said, "and no one else has arrived."

"The money?"

"Barclay's Bank transferred twenty-five thousand pounds to Cairo four days ago. That will cost me some money in the exchange, but it has the advantage of scrupulous honesty."

"Twenty-five thousand pounds is more than enough," Pierce said. "Twenty would have been ample."

"I suppose," Grover said. "But I do so hate to run short. Terribly vexing, really."

"Have it your way." Pierce walked around the room. There were two other doors; one led up a flight of stairs, the other into the kitchen. He shut both, then sat down. "How long have you been here?"

"Two days. The house belongs to a Spanish diplomat who returns to Madrid every so often. I suspect he goes back to pick up a medical report on Franco—wouldn't want to be caught out in the cold, you know, and the Spaniards can be very secretive. I'm glad we're not doing this in Spain. Spanish jails are dreadful."

"Don't tell me about it."

He had said that rather quickly, Grover thought. It's been on his mind, poor devil. That's what comes of taking this seriously.

For himself, Lord Grover did not for one minute believe that a tomb would ever be discovered. It was, to him, an entirely preposterous undertaking—and therein lay its fascination. The prospect of making a vast sum of money was not particularly appealing; he already had more than he could spend in his lifetime, and he had no children from his three marriages, only that dreadful frumpy cousin in Lancashire who spent her time knitting and hoping he would die of cirrhosis of the liver. And there were death taxes, of course. They would gobble it all up, unless he gave it away to charities.

Before he did that, he would go round to all the pubs in the West End and buy five drinks for every man he laid eyes on. Anything, anything at all, but charities. They were so viceless, that was the trouble. Charities.

A knock on the door. He answered it and faced a rather ferocious man, really, though handsome in his way. He was dressed in a dinner jacket, which did not conceal his animal power and strength. Capable of brutality, very self-assured, with cold gray eyes and a wide smile.

"I am Lord Grover," he said, extending his hand.

"Nikos Karagannis." The grip was dry and hard. "What are you offering me to drink?"

"A man I like," Grover said, turning to Pierce. In fact, he was not sure about this Nikos-whatever person at all. Behind those eyes, the brain could be thinking anything. He could smile happily while he strangled you.

"Scotch is acceptable," Nikos said, dropping into a chair. He did not shake hands with Pierce.

"Coming up."

"Good trip?" Pierce asked.

"Very good. I drove."

"You drove? Why?" In order to drive, you had to go all the way north toward Thessalonika, then south again to Athens. From Istanbul, it was much more direct to fly or take a boat.

"I drive my car to Turkey each month. It is a way to avoid the tax. In Greece, cars are taxed monthly—so I cross the border once a month and am free."

"I see," Pierce said. "What kind of car do you drive?"

Nikos seemed surprised. "A Cadillac."

Grover handed Nikos his drink.

"Your health," he said, raising his glass. He looked at Grover coldly. "So you're the wallet of our group."

"That's right" Grover said, returning to the bar for a drink of his own. "And you're the muscle, I presume?"

"Not quite," Pierce said. "I asked Nikos to join us because he can pass as an Egyptian and because he has had experience in this kind of thing."

"Robbing tombs?"

"Just robbing," Nikos said.

"You're a thief?"

"Isn't everyone?"

"Hmmmm," Grover said. He turned to Pierce. "Why do we need an Egyptian?"

"The boat."

Grover snapped his fingers. "Of course. You're moving the treasure by boat. How stupid of me."

Nikos said nothing, but his eyes had widened slightly.

Another knock at the door. Grover opened it to see a huge Negro, really gigantic fellow, but intelligent-looking. That was reassuring.

"Alan Conway."

"Do come in."

The meeting could now begin.

Pierce ran it quickly and well. The talk was precise, to the point, clear without repeating anything.

"We are the entire group," Pierce said, "with the exception of Barnaby and the women. A total of five working people—not very many, but our avowed project will not be ambitious. Our real project will tax us all, particularly since Lord Grover must leave after a few weeks—any decent millionaire would be fed up by then. Furthermore, we have only a limited amount of time; six months at the maximum. We could work a longer season if we wanted, since most of our real work will take place at night, but it would look strange. Nobody digs at Luxor in summer.

"So *if* we don't find it in six months, we have to knock off until next year. By then, our enthusiasm may have diminished considerably, and we will want to go our own ways again. For practical purposes, we have only half a year.

"We start in two days. Lord Grover will fly to Cairo with

his girls tomorrow. I will arrive three days later, after it has made the newspapers. I am coming as a reporter and photographer and will be asked to join the expedition; the rest of you are friends of Barnaby, called in to help him with his modest but interesting project. Alan, you have your documents?"

"Sure man." He reached into his pocket and drew out an envelope. "Letter of introduction to Cairo authorities from André Maurice of the Louvre; Professeur Derain of the Sorbonne; François Bordes, Director of Prehistory in France."

"All real?"

"Real as your mamma's apple pie."

"Good. Nikos, I have certification for you from the Italian School in Athens, stating that you are a trained draftsman with experience in classical digs in Sicily and Turkey. Better read it over."

He handed him the envelope.

"You will fly one week from today, and Alan, nine days from today. Lord Grover will meet you at the airport; introduce yourselves formally—you've never met before, remember."

He gave each man a plane ticket and looked around. "Any questions?"

Nikos snorted. "Of course there are questions. Isn't it time you told us how you intend to dispose of the treasure and get it out of the country?"

"Cairo," Pierce said. "Wait until Cairo."

9. A Project of Interest

The stencil on the door said DIRECTEUR DES ANTIQUITIES, with a translation into Arabic below. All the doors in the Egyptian Museum were titled in French; it was a tribute to Auguste Mariette, the Frenchman who worked in the late nineteenth century to stop the pilferage of Egyptian antiquities and who was responsible for the founding of the Egyptian Museum in 1857. His statue stood outside, in a little garden, but few tourists noticed it, and those who did found the name unfamiliar and passed on.

Harold Barnaby drew himself up straight, breathed deeply, and knocked. "Come in," said a voice in Arabic. Barnaby entered.

Ali Varese was an old man with a slim face and pure white hair, a rarity among Arabs. Actually, he was only half Arab; his father had been French, and he had been raised and educated in Paris. Despite the government's hostility and suspicion toward foreign-born Egyptian officials since 1952, Varese had kept his post. There had, in fact, been no argument about it—he was clearly the best man, and it was unquestionably an important job. At least, it had been until the wars with Yemen and Israel; prior to June, 1967, tourism was the largest industry in Egypt, far exceeding all other sources of income. It was vital that the tourist attractions be preserved for the half million visitors who arrived each year.

But as for finding new antiquities, there was little enthusiasm and less money. Military and economic projects, particularly the Aswan High Dam, had priority.

So Varese was a watchdog, and a fund-raiser, and the man

responsible for directing the reclamation of flooded monuments, particularly the titanic temple of Abu Simbel, near
the Sudanese border. He was not pleased with this turn of
fortune, but he had that passive acceptance of events that
is particularly developed in Egyptians and which allowed
him to look ahead and hope for more dynamic projects in
the future.

Barnaby knew all this; over lunch several days before,
Varese had explained his position. Barnaby had countered by
saying that he had a small project of some interest and that
money might be forthcoming if a government concession
could be obtained. Without hesitation, Varese had asked—
almost begged—for a resumé of the expedition's purposes.

"Please sit down, Mr. Barnaby," Varese said. He rang a
bell on his desk and told the boy who answered to bring
mint tea. Barnaby suppressed a smile; this habit of serving
drinks during any sort of business transaction was deeply
ingrained and practiced by everyone from the lowliest
hawker in the bazaar to the highest officials.

"Now then," Varese said, shifting to Arabic. "I have good
news for you. I have met with the Board of Antiquities, and
at my recommendation, your project has been accepted. I
had hoped to be able to help in the financing—if only a
token donation—but I fear that will not be possible. Can
you arrange for the moneys yourself?"

"I believe so," Barnaby said. His heart was pounding. So
Varese had bought it! At last, they could begin work.

"I know something of your patron, Lord Grover," Varese
said. "Everyone does. I hope you will be able to…keep matters
under your control."

"I will try," Barnaby promised. He knew what Varese was
saying: watch out for this millionaire, he is a kook, a pleasure
nut, potentially irresponsible. He knew that Varese pitied Bar-

naby for stooping to this man for the money, but he also knew that Varese was a practical man and understood the necessity.

"I mention this," Varese said, "because our country is now passing through a phase of acute self-awareness. Any publicity which adversely affects the antiquities reclamation projects, or which seems to indicate that we are treating our historical resources badly, will force us to cancel your expedition. It would be unfortunate, for example, if the *Daily Telegraph* published a photograph of Lord Grover sitting on the shoulders of the Colossi of Memnon, waving a gin bottle. It would leave me no alternative."

"I understand."

The tea came, glasses of liquid with mint leaves floating inside. The hot glasses were placed in copper frames to allow the drinker to hold them. Barnaby dropped in two lumps of sugar and stirred slowly.

"There is only one other point," Varese said, sipping his tea without sugar. Sugar was scarce, in a country that produced vast quantities of sugarcane. It was all exported. "You have requested to place your camp in the Valley of Kings. This will not be possible; the current concession is held by the University of Heidelberg, and we cannot have two digs there simultaneously. I have suggested that your camp be situated near Deir el-Bahri; you could work on the Tombs of the Nobles first, or else travel to the valley. Have you funds for a car?"

"I believe a Land Rover has been obtained."

"Ah, well. Then there is no problem."

Later, when Barnaby had gone, Varese remained at his desk, staring down at a blank pad of paper, tapping it with a pencil. He felt strangely disturbed, though he could not put his finger on the trouble.

Barnaby was an odd fellow, he thought. So narrow in his goals, so limited in his vision. With big projects waiting all over Egypt, he had requested permission to enter the tombs of the nobles and kings in Luxor to retranslate certain hieroglyphics which had never been copied, only translated on the spot.

It was true that Barnaby was a superior linguist, and his previous retranslations were illuminating. It was true that he also planned to make a large photographic atlas of the paintings and hieroglyphics of the region, a definitive work which would be of scholarly importance—and which could be edited to make an excellent, expensive volume for American coffee tables. It was true that he talked, in a vague way, of finding clues to the lost tunnel which connected the Valley of Kings with the outside world.

But still, despite the implications and minor hopes, it remained a small project. How could he be so enthusiastic about it? When Varese had talked with him, the man was nearly trembling with excitement.

Varese did not understand. He himself was trained as an archaeologist, and the only sort of project which excited him was a dig. That was an adventure—scooping into the desert sand, uncovering walls, buildings, monuments; watching the discoveries come to light, fit together; awaking each day with tense expectation, waiting to see what would be brought forth.

He sighed. He had not found time to join a dig for twelve years.

And why had Barnaby chosen Lord Grover as his benefactor? Varese could hardly imagine a more unpredictable, eccentric, and bothersome source of funds.

No doubt, Barnaby had filled Grover's head with a lot of nonsense about the lost tunnel and the mystical curses and incantations hidden within the hieroglyphics. Probably, he had reminded Grover of the fame of Lord Carnarvon, who had worked with Carter on Tutankhamen's tomb.

But still, why Grover? And why such an unambitious project? Varese shook his head: Harold Barnaby was a very strange man.

Harold Barnaby sat in his hotel room, half drunk, exhausted, and exhilarated. He was trying to compose a telegram to Lord Grover. Something properly blasé, which would indicate that he had expected official approval all along.

In fact, Barnaby had been terrified for a week. To him, the project seemed full of loopholes, riddled with inconsistencies. He was certain that Varese would see through them and realize something phony was going on. He had counted on Varese's frustration about new digs and fresh information on ancient Egypt. That sort of bias could be blinding.

Varese had bought it. Lock, stock, and barrel, he had been completely fooled. The last major obstacle had been removed from their path.

10. Documents

EDITED TRANSCRIPT OF NEWS BROADCAST BY BBC-TV, 30 SEPTEMBER, ALSO TAPED FOR USE BY BBC II RADIO.

Hugh Gowling: Today, the tradition of British participation in the excavation of ancient Egypt was renewed by the arrival of Lord Grover, fifth earl of Wheatston, in Cairo. Lord Grover is financing and participating in a new dig recently approved by Cairo. Our correspondent, Jeffrey Constable, interviewed him as he arrived in the United Arab Republic.

(Film clips of airport interview)

Constable: We are here at the Cairo airport with Lord Grover, fifth earl of Wheatston, a gentleman well-known to many of our viewers at home. May I ask you, Lord Grover, what exactly do you expect to find?

Grover: Well, as you know, the dig will be located in Luxor, near the ancient city of Thebes. It is a rich and famous region, archaeologically speaking.

Constable: Have you any particular thing you hope to discover?

Grover: (gesturing) Palaces…empires…perhaps nothing. Whatever the unwilling earth yields.

Constable: How long will this dig be running, sir?

Grover: It is impossible to say, and I shouldn't like to make an optimistic prediction, since any prediction is most likely wrong.

Constable: If in fact you discover something of major importance, will it go to the British Museum?

Grover: (sternly) My dear fellow, this project is being conducted with the kind cooperation of the government of the United Arab Republic. The decision as to the disposition of any artifacts must remain in their knowledgeable hands.

Constable: (undeterred) I understand preparations for the dig are in full swing. When will you begin work?

Grover: (fanning his face with a newspaper) Not until it's cooler, I hope!

Constable: Will you remain with the project throughout?

Grover: I should like to very much, but I am not sure it will be possible.

Constable: I see that you are accompanied by several young ladies—

Grover: Close family friends.

Constable: Will they join you at the dig?

Grover: It is my devout wish. It should be an excellent educational experience.

Constable: On the eve of this exciting adventure, do you have any final thoughts, hopes, or fears?

Grover: Oh yes, fears, lots of fears.

Constable: What, specifically?

Grover: The curse of the Pharaohs!

(Laughter)

Hugh Gowling: Lord Grover, in point of fact, would not disclose the precise nature of the expedition, but reliable sources have indicated that he hopes to find the lost tunnel which connects the Valley of Kings to the funerary temples along the Nile. There is considerable controversy among authorities here as to whether the tunnel actually exists, and Lord Grover may settle speculation once and for all.

Sir Roderick Thorpe-Trevor, Curator of Egyptian Antiquities, of the Ashmolean Museum, said: "I wish them all the luck in the world."

LETTER RECEIVED BY ROBERT SEVRAIS AT AMERICAN EXPRESS, SYNTAGMA SQUARE, ATHENS, UPON PRESENTATION OF PASSPORT:

> Banque Nationale
> Geneve, Suisse
> 28 Septembre, 19—

Mr. Robert Sevrais
c/o American Express
Athens, Greece
Grèce

Dear Mr. Sevrais:

Following your directions, an account has been opened in your name. We shall await further instructions from you. Please be informed that we have waived the rule that single transactions in excess of two million dollars U.S. will require personal presentation of suitable identification. Fully handwritten letters will be accepted in lieu of this for deposit transfers only.

Trusting that this meets with your approval, I am,

> Georges Lemarc,
> for the Banque Nationale

CONTENTS OF SAFE DEPOSIT BOX NUMBER 423–88,
NATIONAL BANK OF GREECE, AS RENTED BY ROBERT
PIERCE, U.S. PASSPORT NUMBER D098177:

One Brazilian passport in name of Robert Sevrais.
Rental for three years beginning 29 September, paid in
advance.

30 SEPTEMBER 19—
FOR IMMEDIATE RELEASE

TRANSCRIPT OF STATEMENT BY DR. ALI VARESE,
DIRECTOR OF ANTIQUITIES SERVICE, EGYPTIAN
MUSEUM, CAIRO, U.A.R.

It is with great pleasure that the government and people
of the United Arab Republic support the expedition of
Dr. Harold Barnaby to survey the tombs of the Nobles
and Pharaohs in Luxor. Our heartfelt hopes for a successful undertaking go with the entire group.

The history of Egypt is a monumental step in the history
of all mankind, and all men must share, as brothers, in the
excitement at the start of such a project. It is significant
that at the same time men are working at the Aswan High
Dam for the betterment of humanity in the present, others
are working in Luxor for a better understanding of humanity in the past.

PART II: The Search

"Evil is of old date."
—ARAB PROVERB

1. Cairo

The modern traveler's first view of Egypt is appropriate: Cairo airport, set out in the flat, brown sand of the desert stretching away in silent heat for miles. It is a landscape that communicates, quite distinctly, a sense of agelessness, unchanging, interminable.

Pierce flew in from Athens on a Polish airlines turboprop —a dirty, grumbling airplane that bounced down onto the Cairo airstrip in a disgruntled way and discharged its passengers into the late summer heat. The airline had only recently begun service to Cairo, and then only for a particular reason: to bring Russian technicians into the country to work on the dam.

The airport was handsome, almost splendid, with that faintly overblown quality that distinguishes many modern Egyptian buildings, dwarfing the people, contrasting with their poverty. The marble floors were polished and the friezes were monumental, but the baggage delivery was inefficient and the customs officials lazy and carping. He was glad he had already obtained a visa for his first visit. Travelers who had planned to buy them at the airport were obviously in for a long wait.

He stopped at the bank on the way out and changed some traveler's checks for Egyptian pounds. The bank was short on small change—a characteristic of all banks in the country—and he was paid his last few piasters in stamps and advised curtly to send some postcards home.

He looked at the money. The bills were not bad, but the coins had digits written in Arabic. He had not understood the denominations before, and he did not understand them now. They all looked the same to him. He walked outside and caught a taxi into town.

It was a half-hour ride along a straight highway. The sun was setting, turning the sky pink, then red, then suddenly black. There were no clouds, and the sunset had a rather cold quality. The driver told him in excellent English how the desert in this region had been a huge British bivouac during the war. Pierce did not listen.

The land was flat, desolate, windy; there was no vegetation, no sign of life.

They entered the outskirts of town, passing down broad avenues lined with elegant mansions built in the Victorian style. Date-palm trees swayed gently in the evening breeze. Traffic thickened into a weaving swarm of black-and-white Fiat taxis, most of them battered. There were few private cars.

At length, they were deep in downtown Cairo, a brawling, noisy, dusty city. The sidewalks were jammed with pedestrians —businessmen in suits, traders and shopkeepers in the native *galaba,* a striped garment like a nightgown. Everyone was talking, gesturing, active. It was a masculine crowd; Pierce saw only an occasional woman, mostly foreign.

They drove down Suleiman Pasha Boulevard, past the statue of that man, a Frenchman named Ferrier, who modernized the army of Mohammed Ali. They came into the central plaza of Liberation Square, renamed after the revolution in July, 1952. Here, fountains played in the evening air; streetcars clattered, and buses grunted in a cloud of gray exhaust. Above the buildings facing the square were bright neon signs, in Arabic and English, advertising TWA, Rolex, LOT (the Polish airline), and Aswan Beer.

The taxi drove up the ramp of the Cairo Hilton.

He was back.

*

"Robert Pierce," he said at the registration desk.

A short, pudgy man smiled pleasantly. "Passport, please."

Pierce handed it over.

"Sign here, please." The man pushed across a form and called a bellboy, who came up. The man handed the passport to the boy, who left.

Pierce did not blink. He knew what was going on: The boy was taking the passport to register it with the police. On his first visit, he had gotten excited.

"Hey," he had said, "where's he going with that?"

"To the police. You must be registered. He will bring it back."

"He'd better," Pierce had said.

Then, the man had said, "That will be one Egyptian pound, please."

"Why?"

"Cost of registration. The hotel does this as a service to our guests. If you do not wish to pay, you can register yourself. But the lines are long, and—"

"Never mind," Pierce had said, handing the man a pound note.

Now, he dug into his wallet and passed the pound note across the counter without being asked.

"Ah," the clerk smiled. "You have been in Egypt before?"

"Yes," Pierce said. "I have."

His room was impressive. There was a good view of the riverfront and the Nile; looking south, he could see the other two large hotels of Cairo, the Semiramis and Sheperd's. They were both faintly gaudy, reminiscent of Miami Beach.

A knock on the door. A boy entered and gave him his passport. Pierce thumbed through it and found a small stamp on page 13, beneath his U.A.R. visa. There was Arabic writing, then in English, REGISTRATION WITHIN THREE DAYS, followed by more Arabic. He shrugged; it was no different from the stamp he had received on his first visit.

The telephone rang.

"Hello?"

"Robert? Grover here, in 452. Come on up, will you?"

Grover opened the door. "Robert, how good to see you."

Pierce frowned. There was something funny going on; instinctively, he looked past Grover's shoulder, wondering if someone else were in the room. It was empty.

"Do come in, my boy, come in." The voice was falsely jovial. "Drink, of course."

"Of course," Pierce said, still frowning.

"I made quite an odd discovery," Grover said, "which I thought might interest you."

"Really?"

"Yes." He mixed the drink. "You see, this archaeological thing is quite newsworthy—oh damn, I'm fresh out of ice."

Pierce looked at the bucket; it was still half full. He was about to say something, when Grover put his finger to his lips and shook his head.

"Before I tell you about my discovery, let me ring down for more."

He went to the telephone, lifted it, and turned it bottom upward. Pierce saw a small black object attached to the undersurface.

"Room service? More ice for 452, please. Thanks awfully." He hung up. "It's on the way. Now, about that discovery. I wondered—"

"I can't talk business without a drink," Pierce said. "Let's hold off for a minute." He took out a pad and wrote, HOW LONG HAVE YOU KNOWN?"

"Whatever you say, Robert. Have you admired the view? My room is higher up than yours, I believe."

Grover took the pad. YESTERDAY MORNING. NOTHING SPILLED, BUT ALMOST.

Pierce got up, the pad in his hand. "It is a beautiful view. This is my second visit to Cairo. I think it's a marvelous city." SURE IT'S LIVE?

"Oh quite, quite."

"I'm eager to explore it further."

"My dear boy, we must. It is an absolute necessity." HOW'S YOUR ROOM?

HAVEN'T CHECKED.

"Perhaps we should wait until November for a thorough exploration of the city. It will be cooler then."

"You may be right." LET'S JUST CHAT.

"I think so," Pierce said. "How are preparations coming?"

"Wonderfully. We will be ready to leave in about a week's time, I think. It's very exciting."

"Yes, it is."

There was a knock on the door. That would be room service with the ice. Pierce gathered up the notes and stuffed them into his pocket while Grover answered the door.

"I have no damned idea what's going on," Grover said. They were walking toward Barnaby's hotel. "I simply cannot imagine."

"It's strange," Pierce agreed. "They didn't bug my room. Do you think the government suspects you?"

"I don't see why. In any event, if they've been snooping, all they'll hear are a lot of suggestive noises. I've been preoccupied with my girls," Grover said.

"Well, don't touch that mike, whatever you do," Pierce said. "Just play it straight until we get out of here."

"My feelings, exactly."

"Welcome," Barnaby said. "Nice to see you've arrived, Robert. Pleasant trip?"

"Very." Pierce took out his pad and wrote, GROVER'S ROOM IS BUGGED. IS YOURS?

Barnaby read it and shrugged. "Come in and make yourself comfortable. Not the Hilton, I'm afraid, but it will have to do."

"What have you got to drink?" Grover asked. He was walking around the room, looking behind the pictures, beneath the windowsill, over the door, under the washbasin. There was a faint smile on his face.

He likes this, Pierce thought. It's all a part of the game to him.

"Just a little bourbon."

"*Bourbon?*"

"An American drink."

"How ghastly. I thought they stopped drinking bourbon when they killed Wild Bill Hickok. Isn't that the one that tastes like Scotch and molasses?"

"Take it or leave it."

"I'll take it, of course. The room is all right, by the way. So perhaps our cover isn't blown."

The spy-talk irritated Pierce, but he said nothing.

"Why do you suppose they picked on me?"

"I don't know," Pierce said. "Maybe you don't have an honest face."

"Do you think so?" He gave a pleased little smile.

✿

Nikos came in, followed a few minutes later by Conway. Greetings were brief. Pierce took out a map of Luxor and spread it on the bed.

"You're all familiar with the first part of the operation. Now you want to know what we do with the stuff once we find it." He glanced at Lord Grover. "You guessed it, the other night—we float the treasure down the Nile in a boat. We can load in darkness and send it off; in the morning, if the government inspectors come around, we'll be lily-pure and empty-handed."

"Where do we get the boat?" Nikos asked.

"Upstream. We'll steal a fisherman's *felucca* in Aswan and sail it down. Nobody would ever connect us with a boat stolen 200 miles away. The Egyptians are always stealing things, I understand, and wood is scarce."

Barnaby was listening, shaking his head.

"What's the matter?"

"Do you know how large those boats are? Not very large, I can assure you. And when Tutankhamen's tomb was discovered, the treasure from the anteroom alone filled five railroad flatcars. You'll need a whole fleet of little boats."

"No," Pierce said. "We have to think of our second problem: how we convert our treasure into hard cash." He looked around the group. "Barnaby suggested selling it to private collectors. That's too difficult, and besides, word would be bound to leak out. Nikos undoubtedly could find fences, but we'd lose too large a percentage of the total value. So what do we do?"

He paused dramatically.

"All right, for Christ's sake," Grover said, puffing a cigar. "What do we do?"

"We sell it to the party that wants it most."

"Egypt?"

"Of course. We send them a note, a few photographs of the tomb, and a trinket or two—worth 20,000 dollars, perhaps. We announce to them our discovery and give them forty-eight hours to pay fifty million dollars into a numbered Geneva account, which I have opened. We might mention in passing that after forty-eight hours, the treasure will either be melted down or offered for sale *in toto* to the museums of the world. First choice, I think, going to the museum in Tel Aviv."

Dead silence in the room. Then Conway began to laugh, "Beautiful," he said, "just beautiful."

"In forty-eight hours," Pierce continued, "the government will have no time to search out the treasure themselves. They will have no time to hunt the tomb robbers. They will have no time to do anything except scrape up the dough and get it off to Geneva. We can arrange transfer of the money from there by letter. We cannot be traced. It will be done as cleanly and anonymously as you could wish."

"All right," Nikos said. "But you still haven't explained how we get the stuff out of the country."

"But that's the point—we don't. *The treasure will never leave Egypt.*"

There was another long silence, and then Barnaby said, "But won't they know? Won't they know—as we do—that it is almost impossible to get it out of the country? When they get the letter, won't they assume that it must still be in Egypt?"

"Would you, in their place?" Pierce shook his head. "I don't think you'd take that chance. Not faced with the prospect of having it melted down on the one hand or displayed in Israel on the other. So long as they are perfectly assured that a treasure exists—and we will take great pains to assure them —then they must act as we wish. They have no choice. The stakes are enormous."

Barnaby stood and walked up and down the room. He finished his cigarette in silence, turning the plan over in his mind. It was clever, as clever as the original hieroglyph. Somehow, the continuity of cunning appealed to him.

"Okay. What do we do?"

"We load part of the treasure—not all—onto a boat and sail it down to Cairo. We take only the most valuable and choice pieces. This will be our insurance against backfire of the plan. Should the Egyptians decide not to pay, we will have something to show for our efforts. The likelihood of their acting that way is minute, so minute that I considered not removing anything from the tomb. But I think it is best to be prudent, even if it is troublesome to us.

"Once in Cairo, we hide the treasure either in the city or in the desert outside. It should not be difficult to find a place. When it is secure, we will send off our letter. By that time, we will have returned to Luxor, where we will continue to dig innocently for another few months. The Cairo government will recover the treasure, and there will be immense publicity. We will feel foolish working diligently on a narrow-minded project when such grandeur was practically under our noses the whole time. But we will shrug and talk vaguely of the advancement of science by unspectacular steps. Six months later, we will all be rich men."

Pierce smiled. The others smiled back.

"Do you have final clearance from the antiquities people?" he asked Barnaby.

"Yes. All set to go. The Land Rover has been loaded with everything we need. Nikos is driving it to Luxor in the morning. We can fly down the day after tomorrow."

2. Lisa

Pierce was sitting alone at breakfast the next morning when a girl came up and joined him. She wore a blue linen sleeveless dress that fitted smoothly over her breasts and narrow waist. Her long dark hair was loose around her face; her eyes were an incredibly deep blue.

"Would you call the waiter?" the girl asked. She looked directly at him. "I hope you don't mind company. I wanted to meet you." Her accent was English.

"Not at all," Pierce said, lighting a cigarette. "My name is Robert Pierce."

"I know," she said. "I'm Lisa Barrett."

Then he remembered: Lord Grover's personal secretary. Count on Grover, he thought. He let his eyes run over her while she ordered coffee and eggs. When she looked back at him, he said, "Lord Grover has excellent taste."

"Is that a compliment," she asked, "or a slur on my character?"

"I'm wondering myself."

"I thought you were the man with all the answers."

"Only some of them."

She spread her napkin across her lap. "Well, you can keep wondering, then."

"Do you like men who have all the answers?"

"Never met any," she said. "That's why I wanted to meet you."

He watched her eat. She had a strong face, dark eyebrows leading to a fine, straight nose, and a proud mouth. High cheekbones. She looked rather Egyptian, he thought.

"Would you care," he said, "to accompany me on a tour of the city?"

"Yes," she said, without hesitation. "I would like it very much."

They took a cab to the citadel, on the eastern edge of the city. The mosque of Sultan Mohammed ibn Qualawun rose magnificently behind the high, ochre walls of the fortress, which still housed troops. Pierce walked with Lisa through the mosque and out onto a terrace where they could see all of Cairo spread out before them. In the distance were the gray hulks of the pyramids, disrupting the horizon.

She stood next to him at the railing, looking out. "It's awfully big," she said, "I never expected that."

"It's the largest city in Africa and the tenth largest capital in the world," Pierce said. "Three and a half million people. That makes it bigger than Paris."

"You've been doing homework," she said. She pointed to a nearby mosque. "What's that?"

"The mosque of Sultan Hasan."

"And over there?"

"The mosque of Ibn Tulun."

"You really know what you're talking about." She walked along the railing. He liked to watch her walk.

"Is that Giza out there?" She pointed to a group of pyramids to the south.

"No, that's Saqqara. Giza is over there."

He had the feeling that she was testing him in some peculiar way, examining him. Often, he noticed her watching him closely; she had been doing it all morning. He wondered about her age. It was hard to say—twenty-four, twenty-eight, perhaps even thirty. She pushed her dark hair back from her face.

"Do you have a cigarette?"

He gave her one and lit it. She really was an astonishingly beautiful girl. There was a wide-eyed look about her which he liked.

Suddenly, from one of the minarets came the sound of the muezzin, the warbling voice calling the Moslem faithful to prayer.

The call was picked up in one mosque after another. It floated over the city, soft and gentle, mingled with the wind.

"My God," she said, "that's an incredible sound. It's so... foreign."

He nodded. He was thinking of what Barnaby had said in a moment of drunken exhilaration: Cairo—the city of a thousand minarets, where the call to prayer had been heard five times daily for a thousand years.

"Have you been here before?" she asked.

"Yes, once."

"You travel a lot." It was a statement.

"Yes."

"Do you enjoy it?"

"I suppose."

He felt uncomfortable.

They walked down a side street, looking at the faces in the crowd. The variety was remarkable: pale Europeans in business suits; native Egyptians with dark skins and straight noses; black-haired, lighter-skinned men of Turkish or Persian extraction; stocky, purple-black Nubians from Lower Egypt and the Sudan; an occasional slim Negro from the Nilotic tribes of deeper Africa. There were women in veils and women in tight skirts, makeup, and high heels; and there were children everywhere, running up to clutch at your clothes, palms extended, asking for baksheesh.

In the Egyptian Museum, they stared at the mummies,

all collected in one room. A guide explained to them about each pinched, drawn face. Pierce found it a strange experience, looking at the features of men of power and majesty dead three thousand years and more. Some of them still retained their regal appearance.

For instance, there was Sekenre, who united Egypt about 1550 B.C. and drove out the invaders. He was the subject of a folktale for centuries afterward; his mummy showed the scars of battle, a horribly mutilated face and skull.

But the most impressive was Ramses II. The skin was black from exposure to air, the hair tufted, the body shrunken. Even in death, the firm chin and tight mouth indicated unmistakably that this was a man to be reckoned with. Ramses II had built the mighty temple of Abu Simbel; he had ruled Egypt with a strong hand for sixty-seven years and had sired 150 children. He had been the pharaoh of Biblical oppression, and he had ruled with an iron hand, one of the most famous kings in a civilization that continued for thousands of years.

Later, they walked through the galleries displaying the contents of Tutankhamen's tomb. It seemed to go on forever: case after case of jewelry, gold, lavish ornaments. Then, when they went outside, they passed a woman squatting on the street, nursing her child, her eyes hollow as she stared forward. Flies crawled on the baby's face.

"It's not fair," Lisa had said.

The air-conditioning hummed softly in his hotel room. The shutters had been drawn against the afternoon light, giving the room a warm yellowish glow. But it was cool. Pierce sat in a chair watching the girl sleeping on the bed. She had fallen asleep sitting upright while they had talked after lunch. It was his own fault, he thought—talking too much, as usual.

He had made her lie down. She mumbled protests but

was soon asleep again. Her skirt had been pulled up slightly, showing a firm thigh above a dimpled knee. She slept soundly, innocently.

A funny girl. More than anything else, she seemed to have been confused by their exploration of the city. Well, he thought, it was a confusing city—so vast, so poor, with so many sharp contrasts and contradictions.

He must have fallen asleep himself, because he dreamed of a huge wall of gold, then a room, then a vast cavern the size of a football field, all dull yellow. And he saw, drifting before him in a jumbled fog, a leering face above quivering breasts and the leering tanned faces of the crowd, which merged with the face of an old hag, missing most of her teeth, her jaws wrinkled grotesquely. Then a one-eyed man, staggering down a street, and a man on crutches. And the noise of an airplane, a humming, a droning.

He opened his eyes and heard the air-conditioner. Lisa was sitting up on the bed, looking at him.

"Feel better?" he asked.

"Yes," she said, standing up. "But my dress is all wrinkled. How long did I sleep?"

"I don't know. I fell asleep myself."

"It was all that sun," she said, walking into the bathroom. "Where did I put my purse?"

"By the lamp." Pierce felt oddly happy. The fact that they had fallen asleep together gave him a feeling of unexpected intimacy which was pleasant. He watched her retrieve the purse and go into the bathroom. He followed her. She was combing her hair.

"I think I'd like to know you better," he said.

"There's plenty of time for that."

"How about dinner?"

"Sorry, I have a dozen letters to get off before we leave Cairo tomorrow. I'll have dinner in my room."

"Are you serious?"

"Absolutely." She put the comb in her purse and snapped it shut. "I'd better get started now."

You're in a rush to leave, Pierce thought. You felt the same way I did.

He accompanied her to the door.

"Thanks for the use of your bed."

"Quite all right. I'm sorry it couldn't have been more—"

"It couldn't have been. See you in the morning." She smiled again, and was gone.

He went back and sat down on the bed, thinking about her for longer than he realized.

About ten that night, as he was packing for the airplane, a girl entered his room without knocking. He recognized her as one of the girls on Capri—a short blonde with short hair and a firm little body. She had a pixie manner and arched her back to thrust forward her breasts as she dangled the bottle of champagne in one hand.

"Company?" she asked.

"No thanks," Pierce said. He was working on a way to pack his shirts so they wouldn't wrinkle. In all his years, he had never quite learned how.

"Wouldn't you like some champagne on our last night in civilization?"

"You're nice," he said, "but I'm not in the mood."

"That's all right," she said brightly. "I can fix that." She began unpeeling the wrapping around the cork and loosening the wires. "Do you have any glasses?"

"Please," Pierce said. "I'd rather be alone tonight."

The girl shrugged and left. A few minutes later, he got a call from Grover, who sounded hurt.

"Listen," Grover said, "don't you believe in Santa Claus? I don't often have Communist impulses, you know."

Pierce felt nothing but exhaustion. He sighed and said, "If I didn't believe in Santa Claus, I wouldn't be here."

"I know what the problem is. You think *you're* Santa Claus. You're getting a complex, my boy."

"Go to hell."

"Dreaming of gold, are you?"

"See you in the morning," Pierce said, and hung up. He sat down on the bed and lit a cigarette.

Tomorrow, they would be in Luxor.

3. Luxor

The first thing anyone buys in Luxor is a little whisk rather like a feather duster. The going price is twenty-five piasters, or roughly fifty cents, and it is worth it.

The flies in Luxor are very bad.

In the following days, Pierce learned to do everything one-handed—take pictures, eat and drink, draw charts, and write up notes. With his other hand, he used the whisk to keep the flies off his face, away from his eyes and mouth. It was something you learned quickly in Luxor.

There was no wind at the airport, only dry, wavering heat that shimmered from the sand, distorting the red limestone cliffs on the horizon. They caught a cab into the center of town and said little on the way in.

Lord Grover appeared thoroughly disgusted. Sitting in the back seat between his two girls—the blonde and a dark-eyed Malaysian—he watched the dusty buildings go by, smelled the dung in the streets, saw the traffic of donkeycarts, chickens, dirty people on battered bicycles.

"Luxor," he snorted, "the jewel of the Nile."

Conway smiled. "Well, look at it this way. What's good enough for the pharaohs is—"

"Never mind."

It was a small town, though it had once been the largest city south of Cairo. That had been three thousand years ago, when Cairo was called Memphis, a city of splendor, boasting a huge sphinx of pure alabaster. Luxor was Thebes, the fantastic necropolis of the Empire, the "hundred-gated Thebes" of Homer.

Pierce looked out and saw a boy turn his back to the road and urinate against a building; another man walked by with a crate of birds balanced on his head—doves, or perhaps chickens.

"Animals are sold live here," Lisa said, thinking aloud.

"No refrigeration," Conway said. "If it's dead, it spoils."

Lord Grover sighed.

They passed down the single main street of the town, past the dilapidated railroad station toward the Nile. Here, along the river, was a large temple—the temple of Luxor—and the three hotels that Barnaby mentioned earlier. One was new and modern, with air-conditioning units protruding from every window. It looked inviting.

"Winter Palace?" the driver asked. He had assessed his passengers and had concluded they would be booked in the best hotel.

"No," said Pierce. "We are crossing the river."

"But first to the hotel?"

"No, to the river."

"Now?"

"We're archaeologists," Conway explained.

The cab driver's mouth dropped open, and he seemed about to laugh. Then he shut his mouth and nodded. He turned and drove down the river, away from the hotels.

As they followed the Nile, the cab passed flaking signs announcing the Ramses Casino, or the Luxor Casino. Pierce guessed that it meant cafe-nightclub and not a gambling establishment. Grover looked and groaned.

They reached the ferry; the driver carried their bags down and put them onto the boat. The other passengers, all tourists, watched with curiosity—they knew the only hotels were on this side of the river. Grover paid the driver and they all boarded the boat, which puttered slowly across the Nile.

The trip took longer than Pierce expected. The water was smooth, like a lake; the bow ripped cleanly forward. There were a number of native *feluccas* drifting by, under sails that had been patched, repatched, and patched again.

"How wide is the river at this point?" Grover asked Pierce.

"I don't know. Five or six hundred yards, maybe."

"Four hundred fifty," Lisa said.

"You've been doing homework," Pierce said.

Approaching the far shore, they saw women in black who had come to the river to draw water. They carried earthen jugs on their heads, balanced beautifully. Pierce took a picture. Some of the women saw him and shouted angrily, drawing their veils high across their faces.

"They don't like having their pictures taken," Barnaby said. "Like many superstitious people, they feel that something may be robbed from them by a man who captures their image. That's the way they look at it—capturing something which is theirs."

They disembarked on the west bank and loaded their bags into another cab. This one was really old, the kind of car Pierce associated with gangster movies. It had been painted several times over and was now a fetching mauve. The inside was reupholstered in a green synthetic material. It smelled musty.

"Where do we go now?" Grover said, wrinkling his nose.

"Valley of Kings?" the driver asked. "Valley of Queens? Tombs of Nobles? Temple of—"

"Temple of Hatshepsut," Pierce said.

"Ah, Temple of Hatshepsut," the driver repeated. He spent several minutes cursing his car, stamping on the ignition button, until it eventually rumbled to life, shaking like a man awaking in the cold.

They started off.

The road passed through green fields of sugarcane. Camels ambled awkwardly along, loaded down with cane. Small boys drove them, waving long sticks. The car swirled up dust. Pierce watched the camels with interest—he had never really seen one except in a zoo. Here, they were everywhere and accepted by the people as a natural means of transportation.

"Aren't they funny?" Lisa said. "So stupid-looking, but dignified. It's because they look down their noses at you."

They crossed an irrigation canal, the canal El Fadleyah according to the driver, and took a new road which paralleled another, smaller canal. In the green fields were waterwheels driven by patient, lumbering water buffalo. Other wells were operated by hand.

Soon, they left the fertile area along the Nile banks and came out into the desert. There were a few scattered herds of sheep and goats, but that was all.

"What kind of car is this?" Pierce asked. He had to repeat the question several times before the driver understood.

"Nineteen thirty-two Chevrolet," he said, pronouncing it "Chevro-let." He beamed proudly. "My car. I own."

He tooted his horn happily, although there was nobody within miles. The horn button had long since failed, and he worked it by touching a wire to the metal dashboard. He was adept at this and could flick his finger rapidly, producing a kind of machine gun effect which he obviously enjoyed.

To stop the noise, Pierce offered him a cigarette.

As they came farther into the desert, approaching the mountains, the land became hilly. The driver would go to the top of a rise, cut his engine, and coast down. He seemed to know exactly what he was doing—how far he could coast and when he had to start up the engine again. Gas is expensive, Pierce thought.

"One of these times the damned thing won't start up," Grover said, "and we'll be stuck out—my God, what's that?"

Up ahead, alongside the road, were two seated figures in stone, gigantic things, badly ruined. The faces had been shattered, the hands and legs broken away, leaving only the outlines of the body. Somehow, it was majestic and sad.

"The Colossi of Memnon," Conway said.

"But they're just out here, in the middle of nowhere," Grover said.

"That's where they were found. They used to stand at the entrance to a temple, but it's gone now."

The earth had turned gray, dry and cracking. They passed several ruined temples. The driver ticked them off: "Temple of Merneptah…Thutmose IV…Ramses II…Amenhotep II… Thutmose III…"

"Where's the damned place we're going?" Grover said. "I need a drink." The girls on either side of him said nothing, but their eyes were wide, staring out at the countryside. Pierce smiled: it wasn't exactly Capri.

They passed several small villages of crude mud huts, built under the cliffs. And then, quite abruptly, they saw the Temple of Hatshepsut. It had a Grecian look: a long colonnade, three tiers rising upward, set near the base of the mountains that shot up behind. A long ramp ran upwards to each tier. A straight road, perhaps half a mile long, led to the ramp and the temple.

Alongside the road, a Land Rover was parked. They saw it some distance away, and Pierce tapped the driver. "Stop by that car."

"You want rest house? Not there. Rest house—"

"No, just stop by the car."

They stopped.

Nikos was in the driver's seat, a cowboy hat pulled down over his face, his feet sticking out the window. They walked over to him. He was asleep.

The driver helped load the bags into the back of the Land Rover, and they got in. Pierce woke Nikos, who grinned and laughed broadly.

"Welcome to paradise," he said.

"Very funny," Lord Grover said. "How hot is it here?"

Nikos reached into his shirt pocket and withdrew a small thermometer. "I bought this," he said, "for laughs." He turned to Grover. "In the shade, 105 degrees."

Grover stared disconsolately out of the window. "God."

They started the Land Rover.

"Take us to the drive-in," Conway said. "I want a hamburger and an order of fries and a strawberry frappe."

"What's he talking about?" Grover said to Pierce.

Pierce smiled and looked around the car. They made an odd crew; nobody except Nikos seemed to fit the boxy utilitarianism of the Rover. Lord Grover wore a light blue sport coat and a Navy ascot, now limp with perspiration; the girls wore sandals and scoop-neck sundresses of cotton in pastel shades. Conway, a flamboyant dresser, had on a pink striped shirt, dark pants, and, incongruously, a straw boating hat.

In contrast, Nikos wore olive fatigue clothes, the pants tucked into heavy boots, the shirt unbuttoned halfway down, exposing a dirty undershirt. Only his hat, a broad Stetson, was clean.

They left the road and set off across the desert. The car ground forward, bouncing and tight-sprung, but did not falter for a moment. They passed another small adobe village and came into a stretch of fairly level ground near the cliffs. Up ahead, Pierce saw a cluster of white tents.

"You've been working, I see."

Nikos spat out the window. "Nothing else to do."

Conway's eyebrows went up. "No good movies?" He turned to Grover's Malaysian girl and said, "That was a joke."

The girl looked at him, not understanding.

"She speaks very little English," Grover said. "Only the essentials."

"Isn't that nice," Conway said. "If you pat her back, does she say da-da?"

The girl sat there silently, her face beautiful, composed, blank.

"Not exactly."

"Oh. She says something else, huh?"

Pierce said to Nikos, "When did you arrive?"

"Early this morning."

"Good drive?"

"Miserable. There are checkpoints every eleven miles. At each checkpoint, documents must be examined—all documents, very slowly. Sometimes, they want to look at our supplies; they think we have guns—it shows on their faces. If I did not speak Arabic, we would still be eleven miles from Cairo."

As they came closer, Pierce saw that the camp had been pitched at the base of the cliffs, in a little U-shaped depression. Up against the rock was a sort of awning; next to it was a large tent, which he guessed held supplies. The awning would be for the Land Rover—you couldn't leave it in the direct sunlight; the tires would crack, and the paint would peel. Arranged at the open end of the U was a line of five tents; they would sleep there.

Nikos parked beneath the awning. Everyone got out.

"We have to put the car and the food near the cliffs so

nothing will be stolen," Nikos said. "Would you like a guided tour?"

"Fine," Pierce said.

They stepped out from beneath the awning.

The heat struck them, and Pierce gasped. He felt as if he were suffocating; he sucked hot air into his lungs and coughed, his mouth dry and stiff. They had been moving all day, he realized, and only now were they standing still, at noon, when the sun was reaching its fierce zenith.

It was blindingly bright. For a moment, he thought he had taken off his sunglasses, but no, they were still in place —just not doing much. A hat might help.

The girls rubbed their bare shoulders and glanced up at the sun.

"This way," Nikos said. He led them to the first tent. "The white fabric helps. It is twenty degrees cooler inside. This first tent is for myself and you, Robert. Inside, they are all the same." He opened the gauze flap to expose two cots, sleeping bags, and a Coleman lantern. "The next tent, for Barnaby and Alan."

"Where's Barnaby now?"

"In Luxor, arranging with the hotels to provide supplies. We cannot store more than two weeks' food here."

They walked to the third tent. "For Lord Grover." Grover bent to look inside, sniffed, and straightened.

"The next tent, for his two charming companions—" he smiled at the girls "—and the final tent for Miss Barrett."

"Why isn't she sleeping with the girls?" Pierce said.

"My orders," Grover replied.

Pierce was about to object, but caught himself. It was Grover's money; he could do what he wanted with it.

"We cook in the Land Rover," Nikos said. "A portable kitchen can be installed easily."

"Who's cooking?" Pierce asked.

"I am," Lisa said.

"Photographic equipment is kept in the supply tent. Pictures can be developed at night. The darkroom is complete." Pierce nodded. "Now we'd all better change clothes."

Later, wearing khaki trousers, boots, and a short-sleeve khaki shirt, he went to inspect the supplies. They were neatly stacked on slatted boards and ranged from Campbell's tomato soup to a case of gin and two cases of Scotch. A gasoline-powered generator provided enough electricity to maintain a small freezer for meats and ice.

The photographic equipment was set out on a portable table. Three developing trays, a tank, and rows of bottles—fine-grain, high-speed chemicals, well chosen. The film was stored in the freezer, in moisture-free packages. They would do their own black-and-white work, including some enlarging; the color plates would be shipped back to Cairo.

He turned to the excavating equipment. There were small boxes containing camel's hair brushes, dental picks, and tiny trowels; there were also shovels, flashlights, ropes, and a case of extra batteries for the flashlights.

"How does it look?"

Lisa came into the tent. She was dressed in the same clothes, all khaki, but her boots were soft suede, and she had a bright red kerchief at her neck.

"It looks very attractive," he said.

"I mean the supplies. Do you know you're sometimes very corny?"

"I'm bad with compliments," he said.

A car pulled up outside. She looked and said, "Visitors."

They went out to see a Land Rover with Arabic writing on it. Beneath was stencilled "Antiquities Service, U.A.R."

Barnaby climbed down; there was another man with him.

Barnaby smiled bleakly. "I'd like you to meet Hamid Iskander," he said, nodding toward the second man, a darkly tanned Arab in a *galaba*. "He's with the Antiquities people and was kind enough to bring me back."

Lisa looked at Pierce questioningly.

"Mr. Iskander has brought his own tent," Barnaby continued. "He'll be with us awhile."

A fly buzzed around Pierce's ear. He swatted it away and tried to smile.

4. Iskander

"I am pleasure to be here," Iskander said, pumping Pierce's hand. "I wish you always."

"Thank you," Pierce said, trying to withdraw his fingers.

"Whatever you will wish, you will ask."

"Thank you."

"I can do whatever."

With that, he dropped Pierce's hand and stepped back. "Cigarette?"

"Yes, thank you."

Iskander shook a pack from his robes and gave one to Pierce, who lit it and inhaled while the Egyptian watched carefully. It tasted strong and sour. "Good."

"Yes. Good. Egyptian." He held up the pack so Pierce could see. Then he frowned: "Are you Holland?"

It was a moment before Pierce understood. "No, American."

"American. My congratulations. I hope you will be very happy." Abruptly, he grabbed Pierce's hand and began shaking it again. He was a nervous, fluttery little man, constantly in motion. Even when standing still, he shifted from one leg to the other, swaying slightly.

"Thank you."

The handshake seemed to go on forever.

Barnaby watched it all with a sad expression on his face. Poor bastard, thought Pierce, he's had to put up with this all the way from Luxor.

"This women," Iskander said, turning to Lisa. "We will not introduce you."

Silence.

Barnaby nudged Pierce.

"Oh. I'm sorry. Mr. Iskander, Miss Barrett. Miss Barrett is Lord Grover's secretary."

With a bow, the Arab grabbed her hand and delivered a long, fervent kiss. "I am charming."

"Pleased to meet you," Lisa said.

Iskander straightened, stepped back, and looked at her critically. "Very beautiful," he said, and made a loud clucking noise. "She is…" he broke off and pointed toward Pierce, then back to Lisa.

Lisa reddened.

"No, no. She is Lord Grover's secretary."

"Yes? I know." He smiled, showing several brilliantly gold teeth. *"Very."*

"I hope," said Barnaby, clearing his throat, "that you will enjoy your stay with us, Mr. Iskander. Would you like to see the rest of the camp?"

"I have with me my tent."

"Yes, but I thought perhaps you would like to see our arrangements."

"Yes?" He seemed very surprised.

"Yes, I think so."

"I think so," he repeated doubtfully.

"Well then. If you will follow me—"

Abruptly, the Arab whirled and faced Lisa. "Are you Holland?"

"No."

"Oh. Yes I see."

And with that, he followed Barnaby through the camp.

They stood in the supply tent, leaning on crates, talking. Everyone was tired; the barrage of new impressions, the heat, and the attempt to adjust had exhausted them. Grover's two girls were asleep in their tent. Iskander had pitched his own tent a respectful distance from the camp and had retired early.

Outside, it was dark—dark as only a desert can be, the sky clear and starry, untinted by the lights of the city. It was also cold. The temperature dropped sixty degrees when the sun went down, and everyone wore sweaters.

Barnaby was talking.

"We begin tomorrow," he said. "We'll start with the Tombs of the Nobles in the hills all around us. You may have noticed them—they're just little holes in the rock, high up."

A few of them nodded. Barnaby went on, "The Tombs of the Nobles aren't really tombs. They're memorial chapels built in honor of various court officials—the vizier, the royal gardener, the vintner, the gamekeeper. Nobody was actually buried in them, and they're small places, usually just a single room. We'll photograph the paintings and mind our own business. Mr. Iskander is a pleasant fellow, but he has a young lady in Luxor to whom he is very much attached. I don't think he'll stay with us long."

He took out a map of Luxor, printed on fine cloth, very detailed. On it he had drawn several fine lines.

"The location of the tomb," he said, "is here, according to the hieroglyphics. It says, halfway down the path of the woman-king's place—meaning Hatshepsut's temple. There used to be a straight road leading all the way from the temple to the Nile, though the river in those days was much wider. I've put the approximate halfway point on the road here. Then the directions state, roughly 1,300 yards south from that point, or to here—" He pointed to the map. "This area is now sugarcane fields. From here, east 2,200 yards, to this point, in the foothills. Then 1,100 yards north, into the cliffs. And there's where our tomb will be."

Conway bent over the map. "Five hundred feet up," he said.

"I'm afraid so."

"How accurate are the directions?"

"Fairly accurate. Allowing for conversion factors from the Egyptian units and shifts in terrain, I wouldn't think it's off by more than one hundred feet in any direction."

"That gives us a cliff surface of one thousand square feet," Conway said. "Can't you do better than that?"

Barnaby shook his head.

Nikos shrugged. "Then we search a thousand square feet."

"When the watchdog leaves," Pierce reminded them.

"Drink, anyone?" Lord Grover asked.

Conway walked over and looked Grover up and down. "Are you Holland?" he said.

The camp fell into a routine quickly. Breakfast at five—about which nobody complained, because it was cool—followed by work until ten, when lunch was served. Then, sleep until four, and another work session until seven, and dinner. For the first three days, everyone was too tired to stay up later; soon afterwards, the parties began. Hamid Iskander was carefully uninvited.

Their work consisted of minute examination of the Tombs of the Nobles and photographing of the hieroglyphics and friezes. Pierce marveled at the freshness of the paint, the vividness of the colors—they might have been painted last week, instead of three thousand years ago.

"Desert heat," Barnaby explained. "Best preservative in the world. At Karnak, there are beams and pillars that have been exposed to the elements, and still the paint remains."

The scenes they photographed were stylized but depicted everyday moments in the lives of the people—the rich people, a sort of three thousand-year-old *Vogue,* as Lisa put it.

Scenes of banquets, dancing girls, musicians; hunting expeditions, boating trips along the Nile; overseers directing the sowing and harvesting of the grain, the slaughtering of bulls for a feast, the crushing of grapes, and the tending of gardens. Soon, Pierce began to ignore the stiffness of the figures, the profiles and endless processions. The people came alive for him, a culture complete, vibrant, wealthy, and powerful.

Each night, he returned to his tent tired but thoughtful, turning over in his mind the things he had seen.

A week after they arrived, Pierce walked into Conway's tent and found him cleaning a gun. He stopped and stared.

Conway looked up mildly. "Something wrong?"

"Yes. Where did you get that?"

"I brought it with me."

"Why? Do you know what Iskander would do if—"

"He would congratulate me on my good sense."

Pierce frowned.

"You are confused. I can see by your face that you are confused. My good man, this—" he waved the gun "—this is a cobra pistol."

"Watch where you point it."

"Not loaded." He pointed the barrel at his skull and squeezed the trigger six times.

"Why?" Pierce said.

"Death wish."

"No. Why did you bring it?"

"For cobras, man."

"There are no cobras around here."

"Well, uh, you keep thinking that when the cobra bites

you. It's good for your morale in the last twenty minutes of your life."

"Nobody said anything to me about cobras," Pierce growled, and left the tent.

"I didn't want to frighten you," Barnaby said, "but it's all true. There are cobras around here, and whole expeditions have been canceled because of them. Carter and Carnarvon were digging at Sakha before the First World War, and work had to stop for a season because of an invasion of cobras."

Pierce reached for a cigarette and sat down on Barnaby's cot.

"The Egyptians used to worship them," Barnaby continued. "The goddess Wadjet, an ancient deity. The cobra was a royal creature and a symbol of royalty since the 1st Dynasty. Cleopatra probably killed herself with a cobra. In this region, around Thebes, there was a local snake goddess, and there is a cave on the road to the Valley of Queens which was the local center of worship. So you see, it's quite a real thing."

"Nice of you to tell me."

"I would have," Barnaby said, "eventually."

At the end of the first week, Pierce had a backlog of exposed color film, which he gave to Hamid Iskander to forward to Cairo. He developed the black-and-white film at night, and it kept him busy. Sometimes, when he had a lot to do, Lisa helped him, working in the reddish glow of the safelight. He was increasingly amazed at her—she knew a lot about photography, she was a good cook, and she never complained about the hardship of camp living.

In contrast, the other girls complained continually and spent most of their time drinking in their tent. Pierce did not think they would last long; Lord Grover himself seemed restless.

Pierce and Lisa did not talk much in the darkroom. When they did it was about the tombs, or the developing time, or the temperature of the stop bath. Often, he wanted to shift the conversation to something else, but he was not sure how to do it. She could make him feel extraordinarily clumsy and inept when she wanted to. He decided to let her make the first move.

The following Friday, they took the day off and visited the Valley of the Kings, Biban el-Moluk. Barnaby conducted them through the tombs, which were often quite simple, just a long corridor cut through the rock, opening into a central room where the sarcophagus had lain.

But the walls were covered with hieroglyphics, scenes of the pharaoh's great deeds, and pictures of deities. Though the air in the tombs was stale and dusty, coating the tongue, Pierce did not notice it.

Other tombs, from a later period, were more elaborate. False passages and empty chambers had been cut to confuse graverobbers, and the tombs were frequently buried deep in the rock. The work which had gone into them must have been monumental.

"I don't like it," Lisa said. "It's eerie—all this fixation on the dead."

Pierce knew what she meant. Thebes had been a necropolis, a city of the dead. It had been called "The Horizon," the interface between the worlds of the living and the departed. It was strange to see such efforts lavished upon a cemetery.

"You mustn't get the wrong idea," Barnaby said. "The Egyptians were happy and fun-loving and not preoccupied with death. Actually, they led lives much like the Greeks or Romans, who also had societies built on slave labor. Their parties were lavish, and everyone got drank and ate too much; their lives were pleasant, and they enjoyed themselves.

"The emphasis on tombs and religions comes only from the religion, which centered on the journey into the underworld and the need for a safe resting-place for the deceased to ensure the afterlife. The pharaoh had to be equipped with everything he might need in the hereafter, and so he was buried in splendor. It's not such an uncommon idea, culturally. Catholics need their last rites; the Norsemen wanted to die holding a sword; the Greeks needed to be buried with a coin in their mouths to pay Charon, the boatman on the river Styx."

"Blasphemy," Conway said.

"For an Egyptian, going on to the afterlife was a difficult thing, with lots of pitfalls—but it wasn't unhappy, and I don't think people regretted dying as much as they do now in an agnostic world."

"Is that an editorial?" Lisa asked.

Barnaby smiled. "I guess so. Shall we look at the other tombs?"

As they left the valley, Conway said, "Every time I see all those gods, I get confused. I'd never make a good Egyptian —I'd always mix them up. I'd get down and start praying to Horus or Hathor, and I'd really want Anubis, you see. It's like asking for something when you have the wrong guy on the telephone. You never get anywhere."

"All religions are confusing," Nikos said. "That's how the priests stay in business."

The days merged into weeks, and soon they found they were not counting anymore. Each day was the same—the weather unchanging, cloudless, hot—and it did not matter whether it was Tuesday or Thursday, October or January. Once in a while, Pierce would take out a calendar to keep track.

They grew hardened to life in the camp. They learned to go without a bath for a week, then ten days. They learned to accept each other's idiosyncrasies, to ignore them. Most of all, they learned to live with the sand.

Sand in your boots, in your underwear, in your collar; sand in your cameras, in your batteries, in your food; sand in your water, in your drinks, in your bed; sand in your eyes, your ears, your hair, your mouth.

Sand mixed with sweat, making clothes gritty, abrasive. Sweat stinging your eyes, and sand in your handkerchief when you wiped it away. Drinking liquids almost continuously. Salt tablets. Antibiotics for dysentery. Days when the supplies did not come from Luxor. Three days when the refrigerator went on the blink, and there was no ice and great fear that the film would spoil. One agonizing six-hour period spent repairing the Land Rover, which had gotten sand in the carburetor.

And the flies.

Every morning, Conway would get up, yawn, and smile: "Isn't it great? Life in the country."

Hamid was with them constantly. Often, he would burst in upon their work, asking where one member of the expedition was; he kept track of everybody during the hours of daylight. At night, Pierce suspected, he was also alert, sitting in his tent listening.

If so, all he would hear was the sound of a party. Every night, they had some sort of party The tensions of the work, the close living conditions of camp life, which robbed them all of privacy, were relieved by periodic drunks that went long into the night. At these times, Grover's two girls would revive, wandering gaily among the group, laughing and kissing everyone. Nikos became quite attached to the Malaysian, but Grover did not seem to mind. He presided over the parties like a huge, drunken Buddha, dispensing drinks, advice, and dirty jokes with tremendous energy and gusto. One of the girls had brought a portable phonograph and a stack of records, so they had music. Occasionally, someone would try to dance, though the sand made it difficult. But with rock-and-roll blaring, and a whiskey in your hand, it was almost possible to forget where you were—and that was the object of it all.

Hamid left them after six weeks. He came up to Pierce one morning and asked if he had films to be taken to Cairo. Pierce said he did. Hamid replied gravely that he must return to Luxor for "business and governments"; he would be gone some time, though he would come back periodically to see how work was progressing.

Pierce said they were grateful for his help getting started. Hamid said if they needed anything, just let him know. Pierce promised they would.

The following day, the search began.

5. The Search

The first step was logical enough: a survey to pinpoint the location of the tomb. Pierce and Nikos set out in the morning, down the road leading from Hatshepsut's temple, and fixed the midway point. From there, they proceeded to determine the north parallel line and drove out into the desert in the jeep. They used different coordinates, since it was not possible to go into the cane fields. By noon, they had established the third point, to the south, and had fixed on the rock cliff at the proposed location of the tomb. They noted it carefully and returned to the camp.

Meanwhile, routine work continued. This was necessary, for Cairo would be suspicious if color plates did not continue to arrive from the expedition. Barnaby still worked on his translations; Lisa had taken over the photography from Pierce. It was going more slowly, but not seriously so.

The next morning, Pierce and Nikos went out and repeated their survey. It was slow, hot work, but when they finished, they found their results agreed within a few yards. Now they could begin.

After dark, Pierce, Nikos, and Conway put on heavy sweaters and set out. They drove south through the little village of Qurna and parked in the foothills. The first-quarter moon shed little light as they began to climb.

Pierce had never climbed in the dark. He tripped constantly, scraping his knees and stubbing his toes. Of the three, Nikos was most adroit—he moved silently forward and seemed to see perfectly. When Pierce asked him about it, he said "Eat carrots" and laughed.

The first eight hundred yards were not bad, but then the land sloped upward steeply, and they found themselves at the base of a sheer cliff. Nikos eyed it critically and checked his watch. It was almost 2:00 A.M.

"Not tonight," he decided. "Each night, we will have more light from the moon. Let us return now."

Going back was easier; Pierce found he remembered the way surprisingly well. When they got back to camp, everyone was awake except the two girls. "Nothing yet," Nikos growled. "Get some sleep."

The second night, they penetrated farther and climbed a third of the way up the cliff. They had found a reasonable path but were eventually stumped by a rockslide. At three in the morning, they turned back. This time, nobody in camp was awake, though strange noises and giggles were coming from Grover's tent.

It took them a week to reach the proposed level of the tomb. They stood there—five hundred feet up the cliff face, standing on a narrow ledge perhaps twelve feet wide and running several dozen yards along the cliff.

Somewhere on this ledge was the entrance to the tomb, but it would take years to dig it all. With flashlights, they searched the area thoroughly, looking for clues of previous digging. They found nothing. Wind, sand, and the centuries had erased any trace.

"It's a bitch, isn't it?" Conway said.

At three-thirty in the morning, they stopped to talk it over and have a cigarette. Pierce dangled his legs over the ledge and looked out at the valley—the green cane fields black in the moonlight, the mortuary temples barely visible, the Nile hidden somewhere to the southwest. They could see the light of the big hotels in Luxor, but that was the only clear landmark.

"What do we do now?" Pierce asked, looking down the length of the ledge. "We can't dig all this—it would take all winter."

"I think," Conway said, "that we better get ourselves an archaeologist."

"I thought you were an archaeologist," Nikos said.

"I am, I am. It's just…"

"Yes?"

"I'm afraid of the dark."

Barnaby came with them the next evening. When they arrived at the ledge, he stopped, rubbed his hands together, and said, "Well now."

He looked down the ledge, a chalky white strip in the moonlight. It seemed to go on forever.

"Let's have some light and see what we can make of this."

They started at one end, four abreast, each playing their flashlight on the ledge so that a whole strip was illuminated. They moved slowly, while Barnaby watched the ground. Several times he called for a halt and marked the place with a rock. Sometimes he would stop, bend over, and peer at the ground intently, then stand and go on without a word. It took them two hours to cover the distance, and when they had finished, Barnaby had placed four rocks at different places.

"Start with those first," he said. They turned off their flashlights, which were now weak yellow, and stared at each other in the moonlight. "They're most likely, I think."

They began digging. First one spot, then the next, and so on down the line. They looked for signs of previous work— a rubble heap, a bit of artificially cut stone—anything that would signal the making of a tomb. They spent twelve days working in all four places—and covering up the evidence of their digging.

They found nothing.

In the camp, morale was running low. They were no longer a cohesive unit; Pierce, Nikos, and Conway spent most of the day sleeping, and the others felt isolated, forced to do mechanical and mundane tasks without the excitement of the search to sustain them.

The morning after they had dug the fourth hole, Lord Grover announced he was leaving. The girls were going with him; he would be back, though he was not sure when. Although Pierce knew this was logical and necessary—a rich man on a legitimate project would soon grow bored—he felt let down, deserted, and he said some nasty things to Grover, who simply smiled.

Lisa took him into the supply tent to avoid a fight. When they were alone, she said, "You're tired."

"I know it." He rubbed his eyes with his knuckles.

She went to the refrigerator and mixed him a drink. It was seven in the morning. "Did you expect it to be easy?"

"No," he admitted.

"You've got to relax," she said. "You'll tear yourself apart if you go on this way. Why don't you take a few days off and work with us on the nobles' tombs?"

"I don't want to."

She smiled. "You're being stubborn, Robert."

It was the first time she had used his name. Almost without thinking, he reached out and kissed her. For a moment, she relaxed in his arms, then pulled back.

"I'm glad you're still human," she said.

Not exactly a rebuff, but almost.

He looked at her—her face and arms were tanned a deep mahogany. Her hair had lightened to a soft auburn color, and her eyes remained as blue as the ocean. She smiled and said, "You should see how *you* look."

"I must be a mess."

"A shave would help," she said, rubbing her cheek.

He felt angry again, without reason. He stormed out of the tent, into the sun, and she followed him.

"Robert."

He turned.

She stood on her tiptoes and kissed his cheek. "Don't mind me," she said. Her eyes looked directly into his, and he thought for a moment she was going to say something else. But she didn't.

The next night, they returned with Barnaby to the ledge. They examined it again and placed three more stones. "It has to be here someplace," Barnaby said. "It *has* to be."

There was nothing to do but keep looking.

Lord Grover made preparations to go. Three days later, he emerged from his tent wearing his sport coat and ascot and found Pierce.

"Well, I'm off," he said, extending his hand.

"Have a good trip."

"We'll be in touch," Grover said, "I'll be in Beirut for the next month."

"All right."

"Don't get discouraged," Grover said. "And don't hesitate to order anything you might need."

Pierce nodded.

Grover lit a cigar and shifted his stance. He seemed suddenly uncomfortable. "Robert, there's something I've wanted to talk to you about."

"Yes."

"Well, I can't help noticing that you've taken an interest in my secretary. I should appreciate it if you would be kind to her."

The surprise must have shown on Pierce's face.

"I'm just asking you as a friend," Grover said, holding up his hand. "You do what you want. But I'm very fond of her, that's all I mean. All right?"

"All right," Pierce said.

That night, they resumed digging. It was slow, exhausting work, under a waning moon in the shivering cold. They dug beneath the first marker rock and found nothing. The second was particularly rough going, requiring more than ten days of concentrated effort. They found nothing.

Pierce and Conway celebrated a gloomy Thanksgiving with a half-starved chicken and a bottle of Scotch. Another week passed, then another.

"Three thousand years," Barnaby would remind them. "You can't expect miracles after that much time."

Christmas was now approaching. They had spent more than two months in the desert and had absolutely nothing to show for it. Not a clue, not a hint, not the slightest reason to hope they were on the right track. An informal meeting was held in the camp; charts were reviewed, steps were retraced. Pierce and Conway decided to survey the area once again, in the morning. Then, Lisa and Barnaby went to work on the tombs, while the others slept. Word had come back from Cairo that the pictures thus far were superb, by far the finest ever taken.

The surveying was completed by noon the next day. Pierce found what he had expected—that the original survey had been correct. According to the directions in the hieroglyphics, the tomb was up on that ledge. That meant that somehow they had missed it in the seven trenches they had dug so far.

But to dig the entire ledge—that was impossible. There had to be another approach, another answer, another way to attack the problem. He was irritable at lunch, lost in his own discouraging thoughts. Perhaps there had been a landslide that had changed the face of the terrain, burying the tomb beneath tons of rubble. Perhaps it was not on the ledge, but above it, cut into sheer rock. Perhaps, perhaps...

Lisa came up to him as he was finishing coffee.

"Unhappy?"

"I'm not overjoyed."

"Would you take me for a walk?"

He looked up at the midday sun, beating down on them fiercely. "Isn't it a little hot?"

"Yes," she said, "but I don't mind."

They walked north from the camp, toward Hatshepsut's temple. Neither said much, until finally Pierce said, "You're looking out for me, aren't you? Not letting me get depressed, keeping me out of fights."

"Not really." She was watching her feet, kicking up little puffs of sand.

"Why?" he asked, ignoring her answer.

"To tell the truth, I don't really know."

They came to the temple, huge and empty in the sun, and walked under the colonnades to get out of the heat. There were hieroglyphics everywhere, depicting scenes in the life of Hatshepsut. She had been a strong, domineering queen, one of the most famous women in Egyptian history—perhaps the most famous after Cleopatra and Nefertiti. The daughter of Thutmose I and Ahmes, she had married her half-brother, Thutmose II, in order to be queen. Then, when her husband named a boy as his successor, she seized power and ascended the throne. She often wore a false beard while acting as pharaoh.

Later, the boy she replaced became Thutmose III and proceeded to destroy all her monuments. Only two remained: the obelisk in Karnak, the tallest in Egypt, and the mortuary temple in Thebes.

"Tell me," Lisa said. "Why are you so interested in the tomb?"

Pierce shrugged. It was a good question, one he had never been able to answer for himself.

"Do you need the money?"

"No."

"Then what is it? The challenge? You're not like Lord Grover. It isn't a game for you, a way to kill time. I've watched you; you're serious about this, more serious than anyone else."

"Maybe it is the challenge," Pierce said. "A chance to prove something, to do something concrete."

"And dangerous?"

"I suppose."

They stopped at a pillar, and she leaned back against it. She looked at him and said, "I would like to be kissed."

He kissed her, pressing her against the warm stone, feeling her breasts against the rough cloth of his shirt. She did not draw back, but held him tight. When he stopped for breath, she said, "You've gotten much stronger since this started." She ran her hand over his forearm.

"It's all the clean living. No women, lots of exercise. I've spent most of my life sitting in front of a typewriter, you know."

"Were you happy as a writer?"

The question surprised him—he hadn't really stopped to think that he was no longer a writer. What was he now? He could not analyze it; he smelled her perfume and bit her ear.

"What kind of perfume is that?"

"It's called 'Desert Flower'."

"No kidding."

He kissed her again, and then she reached for his hand, and they began walking again.

"You know, I think you're much nicer than you act," she said.

"Oh, I'm mean and tough."

"I wonder," she said.

Later, when they had explored the temple, she said, "I've been thinking about the tomb. What if it isn't there on that ledge?"

"That's been worrying me, too."

"No, I mean, what if the directions were wrong?"

Pierce shook his head. "The directions are precise and unambiguous. Barnaby thinks they're accurate, and we have to take his word. They—"

Something occurred to him. Something so clear, so beautifully simple, that he was surprised he had not thought of it earlier.

"Come on," he said. "Let's go back to camp."

They parked the Land Rover in the foothills, looking up at the cliff and the ledge. As soon as they stopped, the heat settled around them; it was two-thirty, the hottest part of the day, and the air was like a palpable thing, a stifling, dense blanket

"Is that where you climb?" Lisa asked, looking up at the cliff. "Way up there?"

Pierce nodded, recalling all the evenings they had spent negotiating their way in the dark.

"It looks dangerous," she said. "Why have we come out here?"

"I have an idea," he said. "Look at this translation of the passage. The directions are explicit, but all the fixed points are dependent on one particularly crucial point."

He took out the map and sketched briefly.

"We've assumed, as a starting point, that the halfway mark of the road to Hatshepsut's temple is here." He pointed. "But the Nile has shrunk, as Barnaby said. We don't know exactly how much, though we have a fair idea from ruins which presumably were once docks and landings. But if our estimate was wrong, even by a little bit, the location of the tomb could shift radically." He sketched the variations on the cliff face.

"Now," he said, "back to the record. '…to the high cleft where the birds fly, for they draw near to [heaven] even as my majesty…' Let's look for a high cleft and forget about the ledge. Do you have the binoculars?"

With a puzzled look, she handed them to him. He got out of the jeep and scanned the cliff. A cleft, that was what they needed—a chink in the rock, a fault, a gash. He swept the rock face and saw nothing. It was difficult to distinguish details. The sunlight was so bright it washed out shadows.

"You can see better late in the afternoon," Lisa said.

"You may be right."

He swept again, slowly, looking hard. Nothing to the right of the ledge, then the ledge, then left, along the face… Wait… He stopped, went back. There was something there. A cleft, a true cleft though it was fifty yards south of the ledge and apparently inaccessible. How would they reach it?

It seemed awfully small. At the bottom of the niche, perhaps one hundred feet below the top of the cliff, there would hardly be room for a man to stand. Could a tomb actually be there, in so small a working space?

There was only one way to find out.

✽

"Possibly," Barnaby said, tapping the map with his pencil. "Quite possibly. How are you going to get to it?"

"We've got to ignore all our past work. The path to the ledge leads nowhere. We need to find a new route that takes us all the way to the top. We'll look for it tonight."

They searched that night, and the next, and the next each time without success. The third night Pierce could not sleep. He lay on his cot, staring at the tent cloth. Alongside him, Nikos slept soundly. Pierce envied the Greek's ability to relax in tense situations—Pierce was wound tighter than a spring, a bundle of nervous frustration.

He got out of bed and went outside, shivering in the cold air. A drink would relax him. He trudged across the sand to the supply tent and pulled aside the flap.

Lisa was there, eating a sandwich. "Can't sleep?"

"No. What's around to drink?"

"Some gin left."

He poured himself three fingers. "Cheers."

Lisa watched him; he was aware of her eyes on him. "Something the matter?"

She shook her head. "You fascinate me, that's all."

"Well, I don't understand you, either. How did you become Lord Grover's secretary?"

"It's a dull story."

"Maybe it'll help put me to sleep."

"Well," she said, "I've known Lord Grover for a long time, ever since the war. He was a good friend of my father. My father and mother both died in the London Fire. So later, he came back and looked after me, sending me to Girton College and seeing that I got all the proper things. It was quite a change, because Daddy had been a bank clerk." She pronounced it "clark."

"I had a super debut, and a year on the Continent, and schooling in Switzerland. Of course, I was grateful; I decided I wanted to repay him, but he wouldn't hear of it. Finally we compromised, and here I am. He takes me with him wherever he goes. Sometimes I think he looks upon me as a daughter. It's odd."

"I think he does, you know."

"What about you? Were you always a writer?"

"No." Pierce sipped his drink. "I was a student until Korea. After the war, there didn't seem much point in going back to that; I sniffed around for a year or two, working on newspapers and trying to write a book about Korea. I never did, but I had a chance to go to Brussels in 1958 to do a piece on the fair. It turned out well, and I never went back to the States. I don't really like America."

"Everyone in England wants to go there."

"Well, they're welcome to it. It's a vulgar country."

"Nobody is ever satisfied," Lisa said, almost to herself.

Pierce smiled. "It's too late to get philosophical."

"Yes," she said, "perhaps it is."

Pierce was awakened the next morning by the sound of a gunshot. He rolled quickly out of bed, pulled on his boots, and stepped outside.

Conway was standing there, holding the gun in his hand.

"What happened?"

"Son of a bitch gets hot," he said, looking at the gun. "Did you know they got hot?"

"What's going on?"

"I believe," Conway said, blowing smoke from the barrel, "that at one time you expressed an interest in the flora and fauna of the region."

Pierce said nothing.

"If you look behind my tent, you will see a superb example of local color."

He walked around the tent and saw the snake—curled, still writhing, the hood drawn back. It was large, nearly five feet long, and as thick as a man's wrist.

"Any others?" Pierce said.

"Come one, come all," Conway said.

"Christ," Pierce said, and went back to bed.

In the afternoon, he helped Lisa and Barnaby with the photographs. They were working in the tomb of Nakht, the Scribe of the Granaries for Thutmose V; the walls displayed scenes of reaping and harvest. One wall was particularly well preserved. It showed the scribe overseeing the winnowing, reaping, and pressing of the grain into net baskets.

Another wall, partially ruined, was famous for its scene of feasting: a blind harpist and dancing girls entertained seated guests. Nakht and his wife could be seen to one side, sitting at a table. At their feet, a cat devoured a fish.

"We'll get this whole wall," Barnaby said, moving the lights into position. The tombs did not have electric lighting, as did the Valley of Kings; traditionally, visitors saw the paintings with the help of a mirror which the guide held, reflecting the sunlight which came through the door onto the walls. "Then a close-up of the dancers and the family and cat."

Pierce adjusted the tripod and focused on the ground glass. All their color work was being done on 4 x 5 plates.

As he worked, Barnaby said, "It's going to be slow, Robert. Remember, Carter spent six years looking for Tutankhamen."

"We don't have six years."

"It isn't the worst thing in the world if we don't find the tomb."

Pierce looked quickly at him—it did not sound like the

Barnaby he had met in Cairo, quivering with excitement at the prospect of gold. The archaeologist had changed, and casting his mind back over the past two months, Pierce recalled the symptoms of change, which he had ignored at the time.

When the expedition began, Barnaby had talked feverishly of the tomb each night, his eyes glowing. In succeeding weeks, he had spoken of it less often; the pretense of complete absorption in his translating and photographing—begun for Hamid Iskander's benefit—had become reality. Barnaby was no longer so interested in the tomb. His daily work satisfied him.

Pierce felt a mixture of jealousy, frustration, and anger. "Perhaps we should stop looking."

"Not at all," Barnaby said quickly. "Don't misunderstand me. I just wanted you to relax a little and realize that impatience will get us nowhere."

"All right," Pierce said. "I'll relax."

That night, they found a path to the top of the cliff.

It was arduous and nerve-wracking, but it could be done. Standing on the top, the three men paused to catch their breath and smoke a cigarette. Pierce looked south, trying to see the cleft, but it was hidden somewhere in the dark. It was very quiet and cold—each night was colder now—and they could see their breath hiss out in the moonlight.

He sighed and tossed away his cigarette. On these night forays, they always brought Egyptian cigarettes, so that anyone who came upon the butts would not be suspicious. "Ready to go?"

They set off in a line, three shadows in the dark. Pierce led the way, picking a path among the boulders and sandy rubble. It took them half an hour to reach the cleft.

From above, it was not much to look at—just a jagged,

V-shaped notch in the face of the cliff that cut back into the hillside about nine or ten feet. They could not see down to the bottom, which was pitch black.

Pierce shined his light down. The beam dimly illuminated a small sandy area at the bottom, perhaps four feet square. "Only room for one," Nikos said.

Pierce moved the light up the side of the cleft, looking for footholds. The walls were sheer. "You'll have to lower me down," he said.

"Maybe it would be better if I go," Conway said.

"No, I'll do it."

Nikos began uncoiling his rope. It was good Dacron line, three-quarters of an inch thick. "Be careful," he said. "There is no room for error down there."

Pierce shined the light to the bottom again, one hundred fifty feet from where they stood. It was literally the size of a card table, and if he slipped, he would tumble down the rest of the cliff face, perhaps another five hundred feet.

"I'll be careful."

He took the line and knotted it around his waist, then tied a loop for a handhold. He was nervous, his breathing rapid and shallow. He clipped the flashlight to his belt and waited while Conway and Nikos took a firm grip on the line. Then, he swung himself over the lip and began his descent.

6. The Cleft

It was completely black. He could not use his light because both hands were working the rope. They lowered him slowly, and he held himself away from the rock surface with his feet but it was a slow, tense business. Occasionally, he would begin to twist on the end of the rope, and he would reach out with his hand to grip the rock; it was sharp, and he cut himself.

"Wait a minute," he called. His voice sounded odd, muffled. He felt himself stop.

How far down was he? It was impossible to tell—he was suspended in a void, a perfect blackness. He took out his flashlight and clicked it on. It showed the bottom, forty feet below. The rock wall was very near his face.

He needed the light, he needed to see. Something like a miner's cap was called for. He hesitated, then stuck the flashlight in his mouth. It was heavy, but he could hold it with his teeth. He tugged at the rope, and the descent continued.

The bottom came up toward him, slowly, slowly...

His feet touched the sand, and he stood cautiously. He removed the flashlight from his mouth and said, "Okay. I'm here."

From above, a light beamed down, and Nikos said, "How does it look?"

Pierce bent to examine the ground. He kept the rope around his waist—it would be good protection if he slipped. The surface was sandy, but not the thin film of eroded sand you expected to find in such crevices. It was yielding, thick, like a beach. He clawed at it with his fingers, and soon came to a lower layer that was harder packed, but still not rock. He broke a fingernail scraping. "Shovel," he called.

A few minutes later, he saw the shovel being lowered on another rope. It was a weird scene from his vantage point, standing at the bottom of two sloping rock walls illuminated by his own light and the light from above. The shovel came down, slowly spiraling on the rope, and it caught the light, scattering it on the walls. He did not look out of the cleft at the sheer drop of the cliff below. As it was, there was barely room to stand. Shoveling would be difficult.

He put his foot to the blade and pressed gently, careful to maintain his balance. He scooped up sand and flung it down the cliff. Another scoop, then another. He gained confidence and began to work quickly. The hard-packed layer was thick; he went down a foot, and it showed no sign of ending. An hour passed. He dug a hole two and a half feet deep, and found he could not go on; his muscles ached from working in such an awkward position, his back pressed to the rock, unable to really bend over.

"It's getting late," Nikos called down.

"All right. Pull me up."

He felt the rope tighten around his waist, and then his feet were lifted off the ground, and he was in the air again.

The following night was better. They had fashioned makeshift miner's hats from sun helmets and baling wire; the flashlights were held firmly in place, and it was easier to work.

They dug in shifts, each man working for half an hour at a time in rotation. The hole widened and grew deeper. By 2:00 A.M., they had gone down nearly six feet. It was very difficult now: space was even more restricted, and the sand had to be pitched up out of the hole.

As he dug, Pierce remembered Barnaby's words when they had reported the first night's findings.

"It's promising, I think. Maybe you're digging through the accumulated erosion of the centuries, but I wonder. There isn't any reason for sand to collect in a niche like that, and even less reason for it to be firmly packed—the climate is too dry. You may be on to something."

He dug.

He tried to keep a rhythm. It helped him forget the protests of his muscles. He hummed "Dixie" to himself, until Conway leaned down from above and shouted, "Cut that out!" and laughed. He switched to "Waltzing Matilda."

His light began to fail. He rapped it sharply, and it flickered more brightly. He continued to dig, hearing only the soft *hish* as the blade bit into the sand.

"Half an hour," Nikos called down.

Pierce looked at his watch. This was his last chance for the evening to dig, and he felt he still had something left. "Five more minutes."

He resumed digging. As he worked, he began to feel a strange sense of foreboding, something he could not define, but it was an anticipation, as if an extra sense were telling him something was about to happen.

The shovel cut into the sand, alternating with his grunts as he flung the earth out of the pit.

Clunk!

He stopped cold, then pressed down again on the shovel.

Clunk!

"That's five minutes," Nikos said.

"I've hit something."

From above, two lights shone down immediately. There was a moment when Pierce looked up, trying to see behind the two hot circles of light.

Nikos said, "What is it?"

"I don't know. Something hard. I'm down about seven feet."

"Well," Conway said, "what're you waiting for?"

Pierce bent and scraped the bottom with his shovel. The harsh grating sound was loud in his ears. He worked patiently, exposing a flat surface of rock—too flat to be natural. His heart began to pound in his chest. He brushed the rock with his bruised, aching fingers, whisking away the sand.

A bare, smooth surface. He could see faint chisel marks on it.

He began to dig again, frantically now, not caring if the sand came back down on him, working like a madman, uncovering the limits of the stone slab. It did not take long.

It was rectangular and narrow. He started to dig around it, exposing a distinct lip, a perpendicular surface, and then another flat slab.

Steps.

"What is it?" Nikos called.

"A staircase," Pierce said softly.

"What?"

He felt suddenly exhausted, drained of every ounce of energy. "Bring me up," he said. He was lifted, and it seemed to him he was being transported into a dreamworld, a fantastic existence that he could not dare imagine.

PART III: The Last Tomb

"…and the idols of Egypt shall be moved…."
ISAIAH 19:1

1. The Steps

"Remarkable!" Barnaby said the next morning. "I must see it—tonight, I will go with you. Remarkable! Absolutely remarkable!"

"I'd rather not be left alone," Lisa said. Although the camp was jubilant, Pierce noticed that she seemed more quiet than usual.

"Something wrong?" he asked.

"No, I just don't want to be alone in the camp."

That wasn't what Pierce had meant, and she knew it. "Alan will stay with you tonight."

"You must tell me all about it!" Barnaby said. "Everything, from the beginning. How do the steps lie?"

"Like this," Pierce said, sketching quickly on a sheet of paper. "The cleft runs down vertically to this short platform. We dug through seven feet of sand before we struck the first step; Alan and Nikos uncovered five more. They seem to be about six inches high."

"How are they oriented?" Barnaby asked, not taking his eyes from the drawing.

"Sideways," Nikos said. He drew them in running at an angle to the cliff face.

"They're directed north, then," Barnaby said. "That's good —very, very good. Oh, I must see it."

"So well excuse me," said a voice.

Everyone turned.

It was Hamid Iskander, standing at the entrance to the tent.

"Are you disturbed?" he asked, bowing slightly. "I am hoping no?"

Pierce worked to keep the surprise off his face, to control his features, but he was powerless to speak. How long had that man been out there? What had he heard?

Fortunately for them all, Nikos reacted smoothly. "You are just in time," he said. "We are playing with an interesting puzzle. Perhaps you would like to try. Normally, it is done with toothpicks, but we have only Miss Barrett's hairpins." Pierce looked over and saw that there were a half dozen hairpins on the table. He had not noticed them before.

Iskander smiled at Lisa. "Very beautiful."

"Now watch carefully," Nikos said. He took the sheet of paper, turned it over, and drew a spot. Then, he arranged four hairpins around it. "The object is to move only two hairpins to surround the spot. Do you wish to try?"

"I try, yes." Iskander grinned and bent over the paper. He fiddled with the pins for a moment, then began to frown. Finally, he did it, and straightened.

"Ah," Nikos said, wagging a finger at him. "But you moved three pins. Only two pins are allowed."

"Yes? Two?"

Hamid tried again. They all watched him, and Pierce felt his own shock draining away. The Arab did not suspect anything; he had accepted Nikos' puzzle.

"I am not possible," he said, finally.

Nikos quickly showed him how it was done. Hamid laughed when he saw and clapped his hands delightedly.

"Well, back to work," Barnaby said. They all went outside into the sun. "Any news from Cairo?"

"Yes," Iskander said. "News."

He said nothing more.

"What news?"

"The pictures are nice. Cairo says yes."

"Good, good," Barnaby said. "Anything else?"

"Yes? The translations are nice." He stuck his hands in his pockets and walked with Barnaby.

"That's good. How have you been since we saw you last?"

"Nice." He smiled. "And the peoples here?"

"Can't complain. There was a touch of dysentery a few days ago, but that's all cleared up. We're getting tired, though. I think we may take a few days off and go into Luxor to relax and sleep in a hotel for a while."

"But the Lord Grover comes."

"Really? I haven't received any word."

"Cairo says yes."

"Well then, we will wait for him. Let me show you where we're working at the moment. It's the tomb of Puimre, the priest, and we've discovered some quite interesting things."

"How long is *he* going to be here?" Nikos growled.

"As long as he wants," Pierce said. "There's nothing we can do about it."

"If he snoops around any more, I will break his nose."

"Why his nose?"

"As a service. In this country, a man who cannot smell is blessed." He laughed, but the tension behind the threat remained.

Pierce found Lisa in her tent, reading. He sat down next to her cot and said, "What's the matter?"

"Nothing."

"You don't seem pleased."

"Should I be?"

"I think so. We're on the point of a marvelous discovery."

She shook her head. "You're on the point of beginning a life where you must look constantly over your shoulder, afraid and worried."

"Not me," Pierce said, laughing.

"How long do you think Hamid will stay?" She seemed almost hopeful; it irritated him.

"Not long. He says Grover is coming back."

"I shouldn't be surprised," she said, putting her book aside. "He'll be getting curious about us soon." She looked at him steadily for some moments, then said, "Do you really want to go through with this? Rob the tomb?"

"Yes."

"Are you sure?"

"Yes."

She picked up her book again and read, as if to dismiss him.

"Listen," he said, "this thing is foolproof. There isn't the slightest chance we can be caught or that—"

"Robert, please."

"All right," he said, getting up. "All right."

He walked out of the tent and felt the sun burning his face. He put on his sunglasses and looked around the camp —at the Land Rover beneath its awning, the supply tent, the other tents ranged around the base of the reddish cliffs. Off to the right Barnaby and Hamid were walking down from the tombs in the hills; Barnaby was talking animatedly, hands moving, and Iskander nodded his head.

Pierce turned away and began walking. He left the camp and struck out for a small cluster of native houses a quarter of a mile away. It was miserably hot, and he moved slowly; the outlines of the mud huts shimmered before his eyes. He saw nobody around—it might have been deserted. He climbed to a rise where he could look down on the houses, which were built roughly square, each with a small courtyard or enclosure behind. Here the animals were kept—the chickens, the donkeys, an occasional dog with a taut-ribbed belly. The camels were kept outside. They were too large for the enclosure.

Near one hut was a baby camel sitting on the sand next to its mother. The baby imitated the parent, raising its head in a slow, dignified way to look over at Pierce and then away. Soon after, the baby got up on spindly, unsteady legs and wobbled over to a pile of dried straw, then sat down again.

It was very quiet where Pierce stood, overlooking the village. Once a young boy walked out into one enclosure, then returned to the house, pushing aside the dirty striped rag that served as a door. Once a dog barked, and the chickens clucked in reply. Otherwise, it was silent.

On the far hill, Pierce saw a figure approaching. It was several minutes before he could discern the shape of a woman in black balancing a water jug on her head. She walked smoothly, the natural undulating movements of her body exaggerated and distorted by the heat. He watched as she neared the village, conscious of the silence around him, the unnatural stillness. She was like a black ghost drifting forward, coming from nowhere with no past, no connection to reality.

The woman entered a house and left the jug outside the door. Pierce waited a long time for her to come out and retrieve it, but she did not reappear.

"God damn it, Robert! Good to see you!" Lord Grover extended a beefy hand. "I understand you've made marvelous progress."

"I hope so."

"Indeed, indeed. Though I confess I don't see how you've stood it. These flies—Christ, they're awful. Never leave you alone. The buzzing is enough to drive a man mad." Lord Grover whisked his face impatiently.

A girl came out of Grover's tent, a startling thing with

flame-red hair that glowed in the sun. She wore tight khaki trousers and a leopardskin blouse. She had high black leather boots.

"Ah, Sylvia," Grover said. "Do come over and say hello."

He grinned at Pierce: "I met Sylvia in Beirut. She was formerly attached to the German consulate there—or rather, to the vice-consul. She's a firm attacher, Sylvia. Beautifully tight."

The girl sauntered over, swinging her hips.

"Sylvia, meet Robert Pierce. He's the photographer of the expedition."

"How nice." She breathed deeply, throwing forward her chest. Pierce thought he saw her eyes flick downward to make sure they were properly displayed.

"Will you be with us long?" Pierce asked. He knew she would not. Once her makeup began to melt, she'd leave.

"I am not sure," Sylvia said. She put one hand on her hip and looked at Lord Grover. "I thought it would be jungle."

"What?"

"Jungle. I expected jungle. This is desert."

"That's right. We decided that it was better for the health."

"I expected jungle."

Grover smiled pleasantly. "You must be tired from the journey. Why don't you rest now?"

"Yes," she said. She turned and strutted back to the tent.

"Not my type," Pierce said, watching her go.

"Sorry about that," Grover said, "but I assure you she's mine. A little change of pace—just what I need for my heart condition."

"How is your heart these days?"

"The doctors tell me there is nothing wrong with it. Fortunately, I know better. In its old age, it is like a finely tuned engine, requiring expensive, exotic, high-octane fuel. Improves the compression ratio," he added, watching Sylvia bend to enter the tent. "Now what about the tomb?"

"Later," Pierce said, looking around. "Hamid is in camp."

"Was. He left half an hour ago. Apparently he is not planning to rejoin us. Now tell me about the tomb."

"I'll do better than that," Pierce said. "I'll show you."

They stood around the cleft. Pierce shined his flashlight down, lighting the pit. The steps appeared as parallel white bars.

"That's it," Pierce said. He looked around at the other faces in the darkness, saw their white breath. Barnaby and Grover were still panting from the climb up the cliff. Conway had remained back in the camp with the girls.

"How did you ever dig down there?" Barnaby asked, amazed.

"How did you ever *get* down there?" Grover asked.

"The hard way," Nikos said. He took the rope and knotted it around Barnaby's waist.

"You must be joking," Barnaby said, looking down the cleft.

Pierce shook his head and handed Barnaby the hat with the clip for the flashlight.

"I had no idea, really—"

"Don't worry," Nikos said. "You push off the wall with your feet. There is nothing to it."

"Well—"

Then he groaned, the sound of a trapped animal. He stepped to the edge and lowered himself over. Holding on to the lip with his hands, he looked up at them. "You're sure?"

"Piece of cake," Grover said.

Barnaby went down. He was clumsy at first, banging

against the rock with his shoulder and hip, grunting and swearing. Then he began to catch on and stiffened his legs, holding himself away from the wall. As he gained confidence, they lowered him more rapidly.

On the bottom, he began to untie the rope.

Pierce leaned over and said, "Leave it on."

Barnaby looked up uncertainly, then bent to the steps. There was a peculiarly professional quality about the way he did it; the way a doctor bends over an X-ray or a lawyer to examine a piece of evidence—the whole body reflected the interest and absorption.

Above, they waited tensely for his conclusion.

"Do you think this is really it?" Grover asked Pierce.

"I'd put money on it."

"His own money," Nikos said, laughing.

"Tools," Barnaby called. There was a strange tightness in his voice.

They clipped a small basket of tools onto a rope and lowered it over the side—a small shovel, a trowel, a whisk broom. Barnaby took the tools and worked several minutes in silence.

Grover took out a cigarette and was about to light it, when Pierce stopped his arm: "What kind of cigarette is that?"

"Benson and Hedges, of course."

"Not here. Have one of these." He held out a crumpled pack with Arabic writing.

"What are these?" Grover said, sniffing the pack.

"'Cairo' cigarettes, of course."

"Worried about stubs?"

"Just careful," Nikos said.

"I like that," Grover said. He shook out a cigarette and lit it, blowing a thoughtful stream of smoke upward. He shuddered. "Delightful."

"It grows on you," Pierce said.

"Bring me up," Barnaby called. Pierce and Nikos hauled on the rope.

"If this is really the tomb," Grover said, "how do you suppose the buggers ever built it in the first place?"

"Probably the same way we're uncovering it," Pierce said.

"But there's only room for one man down there. The translation mentions fifty slaves."

"I was worried about that, too," Pierce said. "But once the tomb was begun it would take many more people to cut through the rock and hollow out the large chambers."

"Ah."

Barnaby appeared out of the cleft. He stood silent for several minutes, then lit a cigarette with trembling fingers.

"Well?" Grover demanded.

"That's it. It must be. It has to be. I dug around the steps and determined that there is a passage into the rock, cut artificially. It won't be a very large passage—just big enough for a man to scramble down, hunched over—but that isn't uncommon in the outer entrances to some of these tombs. It will enlarge later."

He frowned. "There's only one problem, as I see it, and that's excavating in those narrow quarters. Maybe we could get two people down there and form a bucket brigade for the dirt."

"Sounds all right," Pierce said, "but we'll need every man we can get." He turned to Grover. "How long will you be staying?"

"Well, my darling Sylvia is not, I think, the type to flower in the desert. No more than five or six days."

In the darkness, the men looked at each other.

"If you stay in camp, we'll have four men free for that period of time. We'd better get moving."

Pierce and Nikos went down and began to work in tandem

—Nikos digging and filling the basket with earth, which Pierce carried up out of the pit and dumped over the side. It was slow, tedious work, but within an hour they had cleared the seventh step. The outline of a sloping tunnel into the rock was now better defined; they traded jobs and reached the level of the eighth step. Then they went up, and Barnaby descended with Grover, who insisted on going, wouldn't hear of anything else. He laughed delightedly all the way down, but soon was coughing in the dusty air of the pit.

Barnaby, as a trained archaeologist, worked more slowly, giving extra care to the details which Pierce and the others did not bother with. He seemed to have an instinctive feeling for where to dig, exposing outlines, limiting boundaries, bringing the passage out of the sand. Lord Grover, whose bulk restricted movement in the pit considerably, would often climb to the lip and stare down at the sheer drop of the cliff, shaking his head and saying "Wonderful" over and over. He was as cheerful as a child in a sandbox.

Barnaby cleared away the ninth step, and the beginnings of the tenth. When they came up, Lord Grover said he'd better be getting back to Sylvia. They returned to the Land Rover, happy and laughing, delighted with their success, and their secret.

Work stopped at the camp the next day. The four men slept until midafternoon; Conway and Lisa went up to the nobles' tombs, just to put in an appearance, but didn't actually accomplish anything. At dinner, the conversation was quiet, striking light subjects for the benefit of Sylvia, who wore bell-bottomed trousers and a knit top of lewdly clinging fabric. She seemed in an ill mood and sulked, making occasional complaints to her martini.

✿

They were back at the cleft by ten. Working in forty-minute shifts, changing jobs at the twenty-minute mark, they finished the tenth, eleventh, and twelfth step. By now, the passage extended seven feet into solid rock; the person digging had to use a hand shovel and work crouched over in an uncomfortable position.

They quit for the night at the thirteenth step.

Grover came into Pierce's tent in the morning. "How'd it go last night?"

Bleary-eyed, his body still aching, Pierce said, "We got to step thirteen."

Grover seemed unhappy.

"What's the matter? I thought we made good progress."

"I was talking to Barnaby. He says it is impossible to predict how many steps there will be—perhaps as many as thirty."

"Well?"

"It's Sylvia."

Pierce groaned and rolled over in his cot.

"She's very unhappy here."

Pierce sighed.

"She's being dreadfully obnoxious."

"How long can you stall?"

"Tonight's our last night. I've promised her."

Pierce looked disgusted. "All right," he said. "Then tonight is the last night. Now let me get some sleep."

"Sorry," Grover said.

"Don't mention it." He rolled away and put the pillow over his head.

They left early that evening, dangerously early. As the Land Rover rumbled out of the camp, Sylvia watched the lights, visible dimly through the cloth of the tent.

"Why does the truck leave each night?"

"They're going for supplies," Grover said.

"Every night?"

"Of course. It's standard procedure."

"How many people go?"

"Just one, usually."

"Good," Sylvia said. "Let's have a party."

"You're not dressed for it, my dear," Lord Grover said, shifting his position and sitting on her clothes.

"I'm not dressed for anything, right now."

He smiled. "That's not exactly true."

She sat in his lap and put her arms around him. "Wouldn't you like to have a party?"

"No," he said, running a finger down her spine. "I'm not in the mood."

"What are you in the mood for?"

"I'll show you."

In the cleft, Barnaby and Pierce worked silently, saving their breath and energy. This was the last evening they could use four men in two shifts; once Grover left, one of them would have to stay back in camp, and work would slow considerably.

The fourteenth step was uncovered, then the fifteenth. The air, illuminated by their flashlights, was yellow with suspended dust. They had reached the sixteenth step and were working on the seventeenth when the shift changed. The passage now descended twelve feet into the rock.

Up on top, Pierce lit a cigarette, then threw it away. His mouth was already too dry and caked from working in the tunnel. He said, "Sometimes I think it will go on forever."

"The steps? It might, you know. There were only sixteen for Tutankhamen's tomb—but thirty-four for Seti I. We could dig for weeks."

"What do we find at the end? A room?"

Barnaby shook his head. "I doubt it. Probably a door."

"Sealed?"

"Undoubtedly."

The time passed quickly. In what seemed like a few minutes, they were hauling Nikos and Conway up and preparing to go down themselves. Pierce felt stiff from the exertion and the dried sweat on his body.

They dug furiously at the bottom. Barnaby had by now caught the fever and was working as fast as the others; the twenty-second step was cleared away by midnight. Pierce was exhausted when they came up. Barnaby opened a thermos of coffee, and they poured themselves cups that steamed in the dark air. Below, they could hear the muffled sounds of the other two working.

Pierce went down for his last shift at 4:00 A.M. Never before had they worked so hard or so long into the morning. He was an aching bundle of fatigue; every muscle protested as he moved. His eyes were tired, stinging from the sweat and dust.

They began at the twenty-eighth step. It was painfully slow going, now; he marched up and down the passage with buckets of debris as Barnaby worked. He no longer thought, no longer reflected—his actions were mechanical, liberated from consciousness. It was easier that way.

Twenty-nine steps.

"It can't go on much farther," Pierce said.

Barnaby just looked at him, with dead eyes.

They dug.

Thirty steps.

"It's getting late," Nikos called down. "Shall we quit?"

"Tell him soon," Barnaby said.

"Soon," Pierce called.

At the top of the pit, he could see the sky lighten, the black turning to deep blue, then azure.

He descended into the tunnel. As he came down, he realized that Barnaby had stopped digging.

"What's the matter?" Pierce said. Barnaby was sitting silent, looking at his hands, a stupid expression on his face.

Then Pierce saw: The steps had ended. They were facing a square door. On the door was a seal, and imprinted on the seal was a hieroglyphic. The seal had not been broken.

"It says," Barnaby said, "It says 'Meketenre'. It's his tomb."

"Never heard of him," Pierce said.

"Well, this is it. This is the last tomb."

He gave a long sigh.

2. The Door

Lord Grover left at noon the following day, in time to catch the plane from Luxor to Cairo. Sylvia went with him, and Pierce was relieved.

"Let me know," Grover said, "if anything serious comes up."

"Right," Pierce said.

Grover turned to Lisa, who was the only other person awake in the camp. "Take care of yourself, my dear."

"I will."

"We'll miss the plane," Sylvia said.

"I'll be in London for two weeks, and then back at Capri," Lord Grover said. "I may go to Tangier for a few days—a wedding of a dear friend—but I'll let you know."

"Right," Pierce said. He felt like hell. His eyes were blood-shot, and he had a miserable headache.

"Doesn't he ever say anything else?" Sylvia said, looking with open distaste at Pierce.

Lisa seemed about to reply, then closed her mouth abruptly. In contrast to Sylvia, who wore a tight-fitting polka-dot dress, Lisa was dressed in dirty khakis. She looked better, too, Pierce thought.

"I don't know when I'll be back," Lord Grover said. "If I got a telegram—" He broke off and shrugged. "Say, a cable requesting seven thousand, five hundred."

"All right," Pierce said. That would be the signal: a telegram requesting seventy-five hundred dollars. "Have a good trip."

"I hope so."

"Anything would be—" Sylvia began.

Lord Grover patted her shoulder. "Now, now, my dear. Let's not get excited."

She frowned, then bent her neck, and kissed his hand.

When they were alone, Pierce said, "Do you want to come with us tonight?"

She shook her head. "No," she said. "Not yet."

He accepted that, without knowing why.

"Was it very difficult?" she asked, taking his hand and running her fingers over the calluses.

"Pretty awful." Now that the digging was finished, he could look back and see how nightmarish it had been. "But it's over now."

"I hope so." She lit a cigarette, cupping her hand against the hot breeze. She did it competently, like a man. "What are you going to do with your money?"

"We haven't got it yet. We may open that door and find that the inside passages are full of rubble—boulders, heavy stones, that sort of thing." Barnaby had mentioned the possibility, which nobody wanted to think about.

"But if you do succeed, what will you do with the money?"

He shrugged. "I haven't really thought about it."

"You're going to have millions."

"I'll go somewhere—South America, maybe. I think I'd like to live in Rio."

"And do what?"

"I don't know. Just live."

"You'll go mad from boredom," she said.

Conway stayed behind that evening. Nikos, Barnaby, and Pierce returned to the cleft. Pierce and Barnaby went down together to work on the door.

Barnaby worked carefully, absorbed, feeling the mortar and seal, touching as delicately as a safecracker.

"Give me the chisel and the mallet—not the wooden one, the rubber one."

Barnaby began to chip away at the upper border of the door, which was perhaps four feet square. As he hammered, he talked to himself: "Superb masonry...definitely 19th Dynasty craftsmanship...uniform mortar...nothing to waste...easy, now, easy...that's a boy...all right, steady here...just a little more here, and there..."

He stopped, having cut away all four edges. Only the seal remained.

"I hate to do this," Barnaby said. "That seal is unbroken. This is the only tomb in all Egypt which has ever been found intact, never subjected to robbers."

"Then it's fitting we found it," Pierce said.

Barnaby smiled, then smashed the seal with a single blow of the mallet.

"Crowbar."

Pierce handed it to him and watched while he inserted it into the groove the seal had covered.

"Normally, the seal is opposite the hinge, but sometimes they try to fool you." Barnaby tugged on the bar. The door did not budge. "Then again—" He strained, but still could not move the door.

"Let me try," Pierce said. He changed positions with Barnaby, who lit a candle.

"What's that for?"

"Gas."

"What?"

"Poison gas. It's a very distinct possibility. Not done purposely, of course—but the decomposition of any organic materials inside may produce carbon monoxide, methane, and other harmful gases."

"I thought you said you didn't have any more secrets," Pierce said.

"It's only a possibility."

Pierce tugged at the crowbar, experimentally at first, then harder. He shifted it, trying for better leverage, but got nowhere. He was pulling as hard as he could, without response —no creaking, no cracking, nothing.

"I don't understand it," Barnaby said. "The seal is very good, perhaps even airtight, but it can't be that good."

"Let's see if Nikos can do anything."

Barnaby went up, and Nikos came down.

"What's the problem?"

"Can't open the door."

Nikos spit on his palms and rubbed them together. "You have come to the right man. I can open anything."

He took the crowbar and pulled.

Nothing.

He strained, the muscles in his neck and arms standing out in the pale light of the lamp.

Nothing.

He grunted, tried rhythmic pulling.

Nothing.

He stepped back in disgust and kicked the door. "Harder to open than a virgin's legs," he said, then stopped. "Wait a minute."

He leaned against the wall of the passage, bracing himself, then planted both feet on the bar, and pushed away. The response was immediate—using his powerful leg muscles, the door began to give way with a rumble and crack. As it opened, there was a loud hissing sound.

"What's that?"

"Better step back," Pierce said. "Barnaby said something about gas."

He took out his handkerchief, put it over his nose and mouth, and carried the lighted candle toward the tomb. As he brought it past the door, the flame flickered and went out.

"Back!"

They both scrambled up the pit.

From above, Barnaby had been watching. "Give it a few minutes to air out," he said.

Nikos looked up. "We need an expert down here," he said. "The strong-man stuff is over."

Barnaby hauled him up, and the archaeologist was lowered in his place.

"The candle went out?" he asked.

"Yes."

"Probably just carbon dioxide. Let's go back. It's been bothering me," he said. "I couldn't understand why the door was so hard to open. And I think I know..."

They went back, and Barnaby shined his flashlight into the tomb. There was a large room, perhaps twelve feet square, cut out of the rock. It was bare, roughhewn, and empty, except for dozens of candles on the floor.

"Tricky devils," Barnaby said. "Look at that."

"I don't understand."

"They lighted candles, then sealed up the tomb."

"Is that part of the religion?"

"No, no—they created a vacuum behind the airtight door."

"No wonder!"

Barnaby nodded and stepped into the room. He shined his light onto the four walls and the ceiling. It was a rather depressing room, Pierce thought, nothing like his dreams. So bare...

"This is only an antechamber," Barnaby said. His voice echoed off the rock walls. "There may be several more. But somewhere in here, there is a door leading on." He kicked the candles on the ground, and Pierce saw with surprise that they disintegrated into waxy dust, shattered on the spot.

"Three thousand years," Barnaby said, almost to himself. "That's a hell of a long time. Now let's find that door. Bring our light over."

With their two flashlights, they checked the surface of the walls, beginning low, then higher up. Barnaby was using his fingers as much as his eyes, running his hands gently over the surface, occasionally halting to probe with a dental pick. He grunted periodically. After an hour, they still had not located the door.

"They were good masons, we've already seen that. They would be careful to hide their work. Somewhere in this rough surface is a clue—perhaps just a thin line filled with dust."

He continued the search. Another fruitless half hour passed.

"What about the ceiling?" Pierce asked.

"Doubt it," Barnaby said. He flicked his light over the roof, which was low and unfinished like the walls. "On the other hand, the floor—"

He concentrated on the floor. It was more smoothly chiseled and covered with dust and the remains of candles that fragmented at the gentlest touch. Barnaby used the edge of his shoe to scrape away the debris, exposing the bare rock surface.

It took only a few minutes to locate the door.

"Very good," he said. He bent to examine the stone door and check the edges. This one, unlike the first door, was not scaled.

He checked his watch. "This is it, I think. We'll begin here tomorrow night."

"Oh, we are making excellent progress. The project is working out extremely well, and we are all very optimistic," Pierce said.

"Yes?" Hamid Iskander said. He had arrived without warning that morning, his ferrety eyes darting around the camp.

"Is anything wrong?" Pierce asked.

"I wish to ask. The governments worry for you, because the pictures…" he shrugged "…are not so often. You understand?"

"Well," Pierce said, "I'll tell you. We've been out here three months now, and I think we all need a rest. Except for Dr. Barnaby and Mr. Conway, none of us are really experienced archaeologists, you know."

"You know."

"Yes." Pierce was being cautious. He had arisen at ten. Lisa and Barnaby were not in the camp—presumably they were up at the Tombs of the Nobles, working. Had Iskander seen them? Had they already given him a story? It would not do to conflict with an earlier explanation.

"Where is the Dr. Barnaby?" he asked.

Pierce gave a sigh of relief.

"Up at the tombs, I imagine. He's been rather sick. That's one reason we need a vacation."

"I do not hear. I am sorry for his healthy."

"Much improved now. Just a touch of dysentery."

"Ah yes. He is terrible."

Whatever that means, Pierce thought.

"About the requests," Iskander said. "Always, you say flash-light batteries. Why, yes?"

So this is it, Pierce thought. He had wondered if Hamid would notice their requisition of so many batteries and so much gas for the Land Rover.

"Well, it's just the way things worked out. While Dr. Barnaby was sick, I went ahead, to examine other tombs we plan to study. Whenever I worked in the afternoon, I needed a flashlight, since the sun does not enter the tombs at that time of day."

He could not be sure Iskander had understood that, but it seemed to satisfy him.

"And the others are how? Mrs. Barrett?"

"Fine, just fine."

"I would see them."

Pierce began to think fast, trying to figure out a way to tell the others his story before they cooked up one of their own. He could take Hamid up and say, "I've just been telling Mr. Iskander about your dysentery." That would work.

"But," Hamid continued, "I cannot be. I am back to Luxor. Please, my fond regards."

"Certainly."

"And to the Mrs. Barrett?"

"With pleasure."

"Beautiful," Hamid said.

"Very beautiful."

"Very."

"Thank you," Pierce said.

"She is nice," Hamid said.

"Yes."

"Yes, I think so." He sighed. "Well, I go now. If you will need, please."

"Of course."

Hamid Iskander left. Pierce frowned as he watched the Antiquities Service Land Rover bounce over the sand. He did not think Hamid was a fool, though he acted it. A wise man could play the fool, when it suited him. Why should it suit him?

That night, they did something they should have thought of earlier: they set up a rope ladder at the cleft so all three could go down together. Nikos sniffed as he entered the antechamber and kicked at one of the candles; he jumped back as it collapsed in a heap of dust.

"The door is over here," Barnaby said, leading the way to the spot they had cleared. "Notice that no mortar was used —we have only to pry it up."

"What do you think is down there?" Pierce asked.

Barnaby shrugged. "Another passage, another room, or perhaps even the tomb itself. I rather doubt that; we will have to go much deeper into the rock before we meet Meketenre himself."

He wedged the crowbar into the crack and began to press against it.

"Let me," Nikos said, and Barnaby stepped aside. The Greek struggled for a moment and then the heavy stone began to lift. When it was half raised, Pierce slipped a rope around it and pulled as Nikos pushed.

With a heavy thud, the stone crashed down, raising a cloud of dust. They coughed, their flashlights cutting narrow beams in the air. Then, they stepped to the hole and looked down.

It was a narrow room piled high with bodies. The figures

were thrown into awkward attitudes of death, the eyes closed, the skin darkened and pinched. They were all men, skinny and naked except for rotted loincloths.

The smell was dry, stale, and dreadful.

"The slaves," Barnaby said.

3. The Passage

Pierce stepped back in horror. Somehow, it all became real to him—the room, the tomb that lay beyond, the passage through the rock. All this had been done by men, the physical power of slaves, who had received death as their sole reward. He looked down again, noticing the emaciated bodies, the ribs visible through the leathery skin. They had been glad to die.

"What do we do now?" Nikos said. He was frowning in disgust.

Barnaby walked over to a wall and leaned against it. "We have to go down there. They may be guarding the entrance to the tomb itself. Or, they may have been buried with the plans. Don't forget, the architect was murdered as well."

There was a long silence in the room. Pierce lit a cigarette and paced up and down, feeling his legs move, testing his muscles. It was as if he wanted to reassure himself that he was alive.

"I'll go down," Nikos said.

"You don't have to," Barnaby said.

Nikos spat. "You think a few bodies worry me? Give me a light."

Pierce handed Nikos the light, and the Greek jumped down through the opening into the room below.

He winced at the smell. It was stronger in the little chamber than it was above. He shone the light onto the bodies, looking at the faces, eyes closed, mouths open. The teeth were very white. He walked over to one. "How did they die?" Barnaby was leaning over the hole. "Probably strangled… You can see the marks at the throat."

Nikos looked and saw the thin lines. A few bodies still had ropes knotted around their necks. He reached forward to touch one.

"Careful!"

It was too late. The body disintegrated before their eyes, the skin flaking off, the innards falling to the floor as dust, the bones crumbling.

"Don't touch anything," Barnaby said. "They haven't been mummified and in this dry air are imperfectly preserved."

"I've noticed." Nikos coughed in the cloud of human dust.

Pierce was astonished. It really is true, he thought—you return to ashes and dust. He shuddered.

"Look for a man better dressed than the others," Barnaby said. "He will be the architect."

Nikos moved among the heaps of bodies, picking his way carefully. At length, he found an aristocratic-looking man stiffly propped against one wall, with dark hair, a long nose, and a narrow face. He was dressed elegantly in loose white robes coming to the knees, belted with a gold clasp. In death, the man wore a sad expression, as if disappointed.

"I think I found him."

"Wait a minute," Barnaby said, "I'm coming." He climbed down and went over to Nikos. For a moment, he stood silently examining the man.

"That's him, all right. Now let's find the plans." He flicked his beam around and saw a half-burned papyrus. Very little remained, just a corner of the roll. He looked at it closely.

"Don't touch," Barnaby warned. "This is it—the architect's drawing. You can see there the passage leading in from the cleft and here the antechamber directly above us. From that room, another passage runs off—" He stopped. They had reached the point where fire had devoured the papyrus. Barnaby straightened.

"Well, at least we know that much: The main passage runs from the room upstairs, not here. Let's go back."

In the antechamber, Pierce was looking very pale and green.

"Not feeling good, Robbie?" Nikos said, smiling.

"Screw," Pierce said.

Barnaby walked to the far wall. Now that he knew what to look for, it took only a few minutes.

"Here it is," he said.

They broke away the door and saw a long passage ending in blackness. Pierce shined his light down it and saw smooth stone at the far end. The passage was perhaps four feet high and one hundred feet long.

"Shall we?" Barnaby said.

"I'll lead," Nikos said, "in case the door at the far end is difficult."

"No," Barnaby said, "I'll lead."

Nikos shrugged.

Barnaby led. Nikos followed, and Pierce came third. Bent over, they walked along, panting softly. The walls here were smooth, carefully finished. Pierce marveled at the competence of the stonemasons. It was very dark, the only light coming from the flashlights.

They reached the far door.

Barnaby pushed at it with his open hand, and it gave way easily.

"Well, what do you know?" he said.

He stepped forward and suddenly screamed, a high-pitched wail that trailed off into cold silence.

4. The Second Chamber

In the passage, Pierce felt Nikos freeze at the sound. For a moment, they stood motionless, listening, trying to understand what had happened.

"Barnaby?" Nikos called. "Barnaby!"

No answer.

"Try your light," Pierce said. "Careful."

Nikos flashed his light forward and gave a low whistle.

"What is it?"

"Get me a rope," he said.

Pierce backed out to the anteroom and found the rope they had brought with the other tools. He carried it back to Nikos.

"What's going on?"

"Hold this end of the rope while I go down. It's a sunken room."

Pierce sat down and braced himself against the walls of the passage. Nikos threw the free end of the rope out, and soon Pierce felt the weight tugging as he held the rope in his hands. In a moment, Nikos called, "All right."

Pierce crawled forward to look through the opening.

It was a second room, empty but larger than the first, and finished smoothly. The walls were adorned with colorful hieroglyphics in long rows that reached from floor to ceiling. The passage they had crawled through entered this room, but not at floor level—instead, it broke through the wall near the ceiling. Barnaby had stepped through and fallen twenty feet to the bottom.

He lay sprawled on the ground, his flashlight alongside him. Nikos was examining him.

"How is he?"

"All right, I think. He's breathing. He may have broken some bones. I'm not sure. We must wait until he comes around. Did we bring anything to drink?"

"No."

Nikos reached over and rubbed Barnaby's hands, then shook him gently. He worked in silence for several minutes, and then Barnaby stirred. He groaned, the sound amplified by the room.

"Barnaby," Nikos said. "How are you?"

Barnaby rolled his head back and forth and groaned again. He opened his eyes.

"How do you feel?"

"Nikos," he said, in an astonished voice. And then, abruptly, he vomited, retching violently all over his clothes. Nikos helped him up on one elbow.

"My God," Pierce whispered.

"Doesn't matter," Nikos said, glancing up at Pierce. "It happens often when a man is unconscious."

Barnaby vomited again, a dry, ugly sound. Nothing came.

"I wish we had something to give him," Pierce said.

Barnaby looked up, glassy-eyed. "Hello, Robert," he said. He wiped his mouth with his sleeve, then groaned.

"What's the matter?"

"I got it up my nose," Barnaby said. "It's awful."

"Just sit there," Nikos said, "while we figure out how to get you out. How do you feel? Anything broken?"

"I don't think so. My ankle hurts, and I banged my knee when I fell. And my head feels like a watermelon. Otherwise, I'm okay."

"Just sit," Nikos repeated. He looked up at Pierce.

"Can you haul him up if I put the rope around him?"

"I think so."

Barnaby started to get up, but Nikos pushed him back. "Relax. There is no hurry."

Barnaby sat, and his eyes began to look around the walls. He was scanning the hieroglyphics rapidly, running down the columns. Color returned to his face, and Nikos offered him a cigarette.

Barnaby took it absently.

"What does it say?" Pierce asked. Barnaby shook his head slowly.

Nikos stood: "Where do we go from here?"

Barnaby said nothing. He merely sat, reading. He was mesmerized.

Up in the passage, Pierce leaned back and lit a cigarette. He was feeling strange—the three men in this brilliantly colored room were, to him, the entire world. Objectively, he knew that they were deep in the rock of the cliff, in a tomb hollowed out thousands of years ago. He knew that he had only to retrace his steps and he would find himself outside, in the air, looking at the stars and the Nile Valley. He knew that if he traveled a short distance, he would come to the Land Rover and the camp.

He knew all this, but somehow it was unimportant.

"Incredible," Barnaby said softly.

"What's that?"

"This room. It relates the deeds of the Pharaoh Meketenre, including his war expedition against the Hyksos. He was apparently a brutal and vicious man."

"He certainly screwed you," Nikos said, and laughed. Barnaby seemed to return to the present, a slow process in which his eyes grew alive, focused.

"It's going to be difficult from here on," he said. "If this tomb is like some of the others with sunken chambers, the passage will continue up there." He pointed up to the wall, near the ceiling.

"Nice," Pierce said. "How do we find it?"

"It won't be easy. The whole room has been plastered over. You can do it—but it takes time."

"Speaking of time, we had better leave," Nikos said. "Can you get up now?"

"I think so." Nikos helped him up. He let out a squeal of pain as he stepped down on his bad foot; the ankle was swollen and discolored, but nothing else seemed seriously damaged.

Lisa wiped his brow with a damp cloth. "It's all so unnecessary," she said. Barnaby lay on his back, his face flushed, his clothes soaked with sweat. He shivered despite the heavy blankets covering him. His mouth, worked, but no words came out.

"We couldn't avoid it," Pierce said.

"You could have given up this wild scheme before you ever started."

"Damnit, it was his own fault!" Pierce exploded. "He walked right out of that passage without checking first. There was nothing any of us could do to stop him."

Lisa gripped Barnaby's jaw tightly and slipped a thermometer under his tongue. She held it so he would not chomp down deliriously. "Well," she said, "what now?"

"Do you think he needs a doctor?"

"Yes, I think he needs a doctor."

"I was just asking, for Christ's sake."

She gave him a cold stare, and for a moment Pierce thought she was going to hit him. Then, she looked away and removed the thermometer. She held it up to the light. "One hundred and four."

"I'll get the Land Rover," Pierce said.

A vacationing German doctor in Luxor pronounced the ankle broken—and insisted that Barnaby be flown to Cairo for X-rays and hospital treatment. Lisa and Pierce drove him to the airport and saw him safely onto the little plane. They watched as it climbed into the clear sky and was lost in the sun.

"I hope he's all right," she said softly.

"Oh, I think so."

"I believe," Lisa said, "that I could learn to loathe you."

"It's been done before."

"You're frustrating."

"Sorry."

They walked back from the runway to the taxi they had hired in town.

"Please give it up, Robert. Quit now."

"No."

"But I don't understand—"

"It's out of the question. I can't stop now."

She looked at him, shook her head, and sighed.

In the evening, they received a telegram forwarded through the American embassy. It was reassuring: Barnaby's fracture was minor and would require hospitalization for only a week. Pierce felt immense relief, but Lisa, who had been gloomy and irritable all day, did not improve.

"I just think something awful is going to happen," she said. "This is only the beginning."

After a week, they had managed to fix a rope ladder from the passageway leading into the sunken chamber and to sling a hammock on the far wall, permitting them to search for the continuation into the depths of the tomb.

In Barnaby's absence, Conway took over; he worked cheerfully in the hot, chalky air, whistling and talking. He told Pierce about his youth in Cincinnati, about the digs he had worked on, about his family, and about Parisian girls. They seemed to be his favorite topic. He kept returning to them.

"The greatest chick I ever knew," he said, "was four and a half feet tall. And tough. So tough, you wouldn't believe it. She never wore shoes, even in the middle of the winter. And she used to grind out cigarettes in her bare feet."

Another time: "You ever had a scratcher? I mean a real claw-you-to-death scratcher? I used to know one. Named Michelle. A nice name; you'd never have guessed it. Michelle ate all sorts of things to make her fingernails strong, and when she got through with you, you had to whip over to the hospital for a transfusion, honest to God."

And still another time: "Did I ever tell you about the lady weight lifter? She was a mean one. I picked her up on the rebound—she had accidentally broken her boyfriend's wrist, and he left her. Well, uh, this girl used to sit around all the time, you know, in parties and places like that, and flex. She squeezed rubber balls. She lifted dumbbells. All the time…"

His supply of anecdotes seemed endless.

One night, as he chipped away at the plaster, looking for the next door, he said, "What's going on with you and the girl?"

"What girl?" Pierce was sitting on the floor, smoking. The hammock could support only one person at a time.

"What girl?" Conway imitated him. "What girl do you think?"

"Lisa?"

"The man has a lightning-fast mind. He strikes to the very

heart of the problem with the swift speed of a cougar. Yes, my man. Lisa."

"I don't know. I haven't really thought about it."

"Well, uh, you should. You know what we talked about, those nights when I was in the camp and you were out digging?"

Pierce waited.

"You, that's who. Hour after hour, sitting and drinking and talking—" he chipped at the rock "—about—you."

"So what?"

"She's crazy about you, that's what."

"You want me to bleed all over the floor?"

"I'm just telling you, is all."

"Well, what am I supposed to do about it?"

"That's not my problem. But the chick is crazy for you."

"And?"

"And you're just sitting there like a dumb American."

"You want me to punch you in the nose?"

"I'm glad you like her," Conway said, smiling happily. "I was worried you might not."

"It's nice of you to look out for her."

"Are you kidding? Listen, I just want to set things up so she'll change the topic of conversation. It gets boring, listening to her talk about you all night."

Against his will, Pierce said, "What does she say?"

Conway laughed.

"Come on, damnit. You started this—what does she say?"

"She talks about the way you look. She likes your ugly face. She talks about how healthy you look. Then, some days she decided you look tired, and she worries like she was your mother. Then she tells me what you said to her that day—just reels it off, verbatim, a tape recording."

"If you're so interested," Pierce said, "why don't you get her interested in you?"

Conway shook his head: "I'm not the marrying kind."

"Well, neither am I."

"Ha ha."

"What does that mean?"

"That means, ha ha. An expression of amusement."

"Christ." Pierce stubbed out his cigarette. "You want to let me work for a while?"

"No, I like it up here."

Pierce shrugged and lit another cigarette. "Confidentially," Conway said, "I make an excellent best man. The best man is responsible for throwing the stag party the night before, and I can arrange a lulu. Particularly if you have it in Paris. I can throw you a stag party that you'll never forget."

"Let's talk about something else," Pierce said.

"Also, I never forget the ring. I'm very good about that."

"You must be getting tired. Why don't you let me work for a while?"

"All I ask is a chance to kiss the bride before you whiz off for the honeymoon. Now, what's a good place for the honeymoon? Did you think of that?"

"Lord Grover's villa on Capri," Pierce said, irritated at the way Conway was prolonging the conversation.

"That's the boy! That's a great idea!" He frowned. "But what will you do afterward? You can't keep bumming around Europe, and—"

"I don't bum around Europe."

"Get off my ass. You know who you're talking to? You're talking to an experienced bum-spotter."

"I bum around Europe," Pierce said dutifully.

"Right. Now, what are you going to do instead? This girl

needs to settle down, have a home, some nice kids—don't you think she'd look good pregnant? All radiant, and—"

"You must be out of your mind," Pierce said.

Conway laughed and chipped away at the wall.

"Think about it," he said.

Two weeks passed. They managed to do the upper rim of the whole far wall and discovered nothing. Pierce felt a sagging sense of discontent fall over him again. January had passed, and they were into February. Each day, he x-ed out another day on the calendar.

Soon, they would have to quit for the summer. It was already growing warmer; by the end of March, it would be unbearable.

Nikos had caught a case of dysentery—they all had it, sporadically—so Conway and Pierce worked alone on the tomb each night. He rarely saw Lisa except at meals. Conway no longer kidded him about her, and Pierce found this disturbing. He wondered if Lisa had said anything further to him. She seemed much more friendly and open with the other two men. He had trouble speaking to her, and he avoided her eyes.

One night, they received word that Barnaby would be back in three days' time. Nikos was feeling better, and he had a drink with Pierce in their tent.

His first words alone were, "If you don't do something about that girl, I'll kill you."

Pierce was startled. "What's the matter?"

"She's okay," Nikos said. "She's a good girl. Just do something about her, will you?"

Pierce shrugged helplessly.

"Put the poor girl out of her misery. Do something for her, or stomp on her." He paused, and looked down at his glass. "Alan and I will work on the tomb tonight. You stay here."

"All right."

"And do something, will you?"

Pierce helped them load the Land Rover in the evening and watched it drive away across the desert. He turned and walked back to the camp.

Lisa sat by the fire, poking the embers with a stick. Sparks rose in the air and were extinguished among the stars. It occurred to him as he looked at her that this was the first night they had been alone together since the expedition had begun.

He sat down and said, "Want a drink?" Very classy of you, he thought. What suave Continental charm. But she disarmed him, that was the trouble. She saw right through him.

"No thanks."

"You seem unhappy."

"Not really."

"Anything I can do?"

She looked up at him and seemed about to speak, then shook her head.

He went to the supply tent and mixed himself a gin and tonic. When he came back, she was still at the fire.

"Nice night," he said.

"Do I embarrass you?"

He looked at her face in the firelight, at the dark tan and the glossy hair curving around her cheeks.

"You're beautiful."

"You sound like Iskander."

"A thousand heartfelt apologies."

He bowed elaborately and lit a cigarette. A painful silence fell between them.

"I suppose there must be pictures to develop," he said. As

soon as he said it, he felt foolish, like a tongue-tied ado-
lescent.

"Not enough to worry about."

Another long silence. She stopped poking with the stick
and sat there, very calmly, her hands in her lap.

"We're really at odds about this, aren't we?" he said.

"Yes," she said. "We are."

"Why?"

"Because I don't like it. I don't think it's right."

"Why take it out on me?"

She shook her head, and looked at the fire. "I don't know.
I guess I can't help it."

"Now you sound like me."

"Maybe that's the problem," she said.

For a moment her face grew tender, and he wanted to kiss
her and hold her in his arms. Then he felt a wave of irritation.

"You don't bitch around the others."

She frowned. "I don't bitch around you."

"Yes, you do. You're needling me, all the time."

Her voice rose. "You know it's wrong, that's all. Deep down,
you *know.* It's wrong."

She sighed. "Why are we fighting?"

"Who's fighting?"

"You are. You're trying to pick a fight with me. You have
been for—"

"All right," he said. "Forget it."

They sat in silence.

"I was looking forward to tonight," she said. "I didn't expect
it to be like this."

"It has to be."

"Just because that's the way you want it." She caught herself
then and asked him for a cigarette. He recognized it as a
trick to bring him nearer to her. He threw the pack over to

her. She picked it out of the sand and lit a cigarette with a burning ember.

"Look," he said. "You're asking something that I just can't give you. I'm going through with this project, and that's all there is to it. You can't stop me. Nothing can stop me. I'm going to rob that tomb."

"You sound like a maniac."

"Maybe I am."

"You're not."

"All right, I'm not, then. But I am going through with it."

"But why? Why is it so important?"

"Don't ask me. It is."

"Robbing an Egyptian tomb. That's...that's childish, it's infantile, unreal, divorced from everything in the world. It has no relation to anything. And this elaborate plan, with all the moves and countermoves—it's like little boys playing commando or something."

"I'm still going through with it. And you have no right—"

"I have every right. I care about you."

"Why pick on me? Why don't you lecture the others? Why don't you tell them about your schoolgirl morality, your—"

"Because I care about you." She said it quietly.

"Listen," he said, "from the very first day we met, from that first breakfast in Cairo, you've had a chip on your shoulder—"

"*I've* had a chip on my shoulder?"

"Yes. I don't know what it is about me that you've hit on, but—"

"That's not true."

"You know it's true. Now you're trying to order me around, when we hardly know each other."

"I've known you for months."

"You don't know me at all. We haven't even—"

Her voice was sardonic: "Slept together?"

He looked down at the fire. "Well, yes, if you want to put it that way."

"That makes a difference to you, does it?"

"Of course it does."

"Suppose I told you I was lousy in bed. Then what would you think?"

"Stop it. You're being ridiculous."

"You brought it up."

"All right, I apologize."

She sighed, closed her eyes, and flicked her cigarette into the fire. She stood up. "I'm tired," she said. "You'll have to excuse me."

He suddenly felt the night around him and the isolation, the vast space stretching for miles.

"Don't go."

"We're not getting anywhere," she said. "We just seem to make things worse."

"Let's talk about something else."

She shook her head and walked off to her tent.

5. The Second Passage

The next night, in the sunken chamber, Conway chipped away in silence for an hour while Pierce sat smoking. Finally, Conway said, "How'd it go?"

"I made as much progress as you did."

"We didn't get anywhere," Conway said.

"Welcome to the club."

They were both, silent. The only sound was the biting chisel and the thump of the wooden mallet. The plaster flaked away and fell, shattering on the floor.

"God damn it, why'd you have to fight?" Conway said.

"Who said we fought?"

"You did."

"I did not."

"Well, did you fight, or didn't you?"

"Yes," Pierce admitted, "we fought."

"You see? What did I tell you?"

"Someday," Pierce said, "I really am going to punch you in the nose."

"My grandpappy used to say that people who loved each other fought in order to avoid intimacy."

"I thought your grandpappy was a Sioux Indian."

"This is the other side of the family. This is my grandpappy the psychiatrist."

"All right. You've made your point."

"But you don't listen to me, that's the trouble. Here I am, giving you all this good advice, and you sit there without hearing—"

He stopped.

"What's the matter? Got a cramp in your tongue?"

Silence. Then Conway said, "No, no. It's just that I've come upon this little crack, you see, and it looks as if it might be another door."

Pierce was on his feet immediately, looking up where Conway was working in the hammock. The edge of a smoothly cut stone block was clearly visible.

"Keep going," Pierce said.

Conway worked furiously. In less than five minutes, he had found the outline of a rectangle four feet square.

"That must be it," Pierce said.

Conway jumped down from the hammock. "I think so, too."

The block was located near the ceiling and near a corner. "Tricky devils," Conway said. "I've never heard of a connecting passage being cut in a place like that."

"Do you suppose it opens out or in?"

"I'll give you money it opens out, but let's try to push it in first."

Pierce clambered up into the hammock and pushed with both arms. Then, he took the crowbar and tried to wedge it forward. Little flakes of loose plaster and limestone came free, but that was all.

"Try to bring it out," Conway said.

Pierce applied reverse pressure to the crowbar. Almost immediately, he felt the big stone move.

"Easy there. It must weigh more than a Buick. It'll fall right into your hammock and take you with it."

It required half an hour to drive a new spike into the rock and sling the hammock so that the rock would miss it when it fell. Working from the new position was difficult; Pierce had trouble maintaining his balance and gaining leverage. But he made progress—the block moved out farther, then farther. Soon, he could see it in cross section.

"It's thin. No more than four inches thick."

"What're you complaining about?"

"Stand back," Pierce said. When Conway had crossed to the other side of the room, he gave a final heave with the crowbar.

With a crunching sound, the rock came free and fell. It struck the floor with a heavy crash and shattered into a thousand fragments, almost a powder. The air was opaque with dust, and both men were coughing.

"Now look what you've done," Conway said.

They rearranged the hammock, swinging it back to its old position. Pierce climbed up and shined a flashlight down the corridor. It was long and smoothly finished but lacked the colorful hieroglyphics of the other chamber.

"What do you see?" Conway said.

"It goes about fifty feet and then ends in a blank wall. But it's smooth, so it must be another door. I'll go have a look."

"I'm right behind you."

Pierce scrambled up and entered the passageway. Crouching, he walked down, feeling his backbone scrape the rock. Behind him, Conway grunted as he hauled himself up into the hammock; rear light was momentarily blocked— Conway must be entering the passage.

"Wait for me," he said. "What're you trying to do, hog all the glory for yourself? Remember who found this tunnel in the first place. Yours truly. Keep that in mind, fella."

Pierce reached the door at the far end—and it was a door; he could see the mortar around the edges.

"Better get the chisel and crowbar," he said.

"Okay," Conway said, "but don't try anything foolish while I'm gone."

He backed down. Pierce waited by the door. He rapped it with his knuckles and was surprised to hear a hollow sound.

It couldn't be very thick. It sounded like a garden slate, no more than an inch thick.

Tentatively, he pushed on it with his palm.

It moved.

"What do you know?" he said aloud.

"What's that?" Conway called.

"I think we can do without the tools," Pierce said.

"Okay, man."

Pierce pushed again. The door gave way farther. Conway was back in the tunnel, moving toward him.

"Be careful there."

"I will."

Conway was still thirty feet back. He gave a hard push, and the door fell away, slapping down on the rock floor of the next room.

"Made it!"

He stepped into the next chamber.

And then he heard a sound behind him—a grinding, grating sound, like heavy sandpaper scraping.

The light coming through the corridor dimmed.

With a heavy *thunk*, the corridor was sealed off. Surprised, he dropped his flashlight, which clattered on the floor and went out.

"Hey!"

It was pitch dark. The room smelled dead.

6. Darkness

He knelt down and felt the wall. He could feel the opening of the tunnel and then the walls of the tunnel itself for a distance of about three inches. Then a new stone, completely closing off the corridor.

It must have been actuated by the original door, he thought. When I opened it, I released another stone which came down and resealed the passageway.

Nasty.

He tapped the stone. This one, unlike the door, was solid.

"Can you hear me?" he called.

Silence.

"Alan!"

Nothing.

And then a horrible thought occurred to him. Suppose the stone had crushed Conway when it descended?

He did not have long to wonder. In a few moments, very faintly, he heard a tapping. He tapped back, waited, and heard an answer.

Listening, he realized that Conway was signaling to him in Morse code.

"God damn it, I don't know Morse code," he shouted.

The words echoed.

Must be a fair-sized room.

After a while, the tapping stopped. Pierce tapped, but there was no reply. Probably gone for help.

"God knows I need it."

He listened to his own voice and tried to judge the size of

the room, its dimensions. Impossible. Maybe a blind person could do it.

"Got to figure something out," he said. He realized that he was talking because he was afraid. He was trapped in a space of unknown dimensions, unknown contents, deep in the earth. It was a terrifying idea.

"Keep busy. Don't think about it."

He bent over and ran his fingers across the floor, searching for his flashlight. He found it and touched the smashed glass face. He pressed the button, but there was no light. He dropped it again.

"Matches?"

He felt his shirt pocket and discovered that he had brought his cigarettes. It occurred to him that he should not light a match, since it would consume oxygen, but he had to see what was around him, at least for a few moments.

Anything was better than not knowing.

He patted his pockets: no matches. Cigarettes, but no matches. He must have left them on the floor in the other room.

"Damn."

At least, they would come back for him. Conway was probably already scrambling out of the cleft, going for the Land Rover to get help. He wondered what reaction would be in the camp. How long would it take them to get back? Would they come immediately or wait until night? What if Iskander showed up and wanted to know where he was?

In the darkness, he looked at his wrist. The dial glowed faintly, the only light in the room. It was three-fifteen in the morning.

If Conway returned to the camp and came directly back, it would be at least three hours. It was impossible to say how long it would take them to move the block and reopen the passage.

Suppose it took days? Suppose the block weighed several tons?

He coughed and breathed stale, dry air. Was this place airtight? How much air was in the room?

How long could he last?

He shook his head and sat on the floor. Better stay calm, breathe slowly. Conserve everything. Try to form a plan of action.

They might take days.

Horrible thought.

If he did not suffocate, what would be next? Not starvation: you could go quite a long time without food. Water: that was the problem. Somewhere, he had read how long a man could go without water. It was not very long. Two days—something like that.

As he thought, he felt himself begin to sweat. Don't sweat, you're wasting water. He felt ridiculous. His heart pounded in his chest. He breathed deeply and forced himself to be calm.

He tried to remember an article he had once read about two Germans lost on the desert. They had survived weeks, drinking their own urine.

He leaned back against the wall and sighed. He was being morbid and needed something else to think about. They'd probably have him out of here in four hours.

He looked at his watch. Three-nineteen.

"Give them time."

He turned around and ran his fingers over the wall. He felt a thin vertical groove. Moving his hand laterally, he felt another groove about seven inches away. In between, shapes had been shallowly cut into the rock.

Rows of hieroglyphics.

So this room, like the sunken chamber, was covered with painted figures in long vertical rows from floor to ceiling.

This might even be the burial chamber itself.

The thought was disquieting.

Whatever the room was, he was the first person to set foot inside it for three thousand years. All around him were sights no man had witnessed for all those centuries.

In a way, it was fitting that he could not see them either. "Explore."

But he had no idea how large the room was, and he had a vision of himself stepping away from the wall, losing it forever. Lost in a world of blackness.

Did he have any string?

Again, he patted his pockets: no.

A knife? No.

Then he had an idea. He stripped off his shirt, found the tail in the darkness, and ripped it with his teeth. The fabric was surprisingly strong, but he finally managed to tear several long strips from the back up to the collar. He knotted them all together to make a single long strip, like a kite tail.

Using the flashlight and a small rock that he found, he anchored one end of the improvised ribbon to the wall near the entranceway and took the other in his hand. He moved down the wall, feeling it with his hands, counting his steps.

Fifteen feet, and he reached a corner. He was about to follow the next wall, when he felt the ribbon tighten. He went back and started the other way. This one ran nine feet before reaching a corner.

So one wall was twenty-four feet long. At least he knew something.

He returned to the passage and sat down to think. He was

tempted to step out and explore the central portion of the room, but at the same time he was hesitant.

Finally, curiosity overcame him, and he crawled forward on his hands and knees, holding one hand out in front of him.

After a few moments, his fingers touched something.

He felt and gripped the object.

It was an upright, muscular human calf.

7. Help

He pulled his hand back as if scalded. He listened tensely in the darkness. No sound, no breathing.

Tentatively, he reached forward again, lower.

A foot. Five toes encased in a sandal. He ran his hand up the leg. Hairless, cold, smooth.

Mummies were always wrapped in cloth, weren't they?

Emboldened by this thought, he reached up to the knee, then felt the folds of a stiff tunic.

He rapped it with his fingers: wood.

It was a statue. He sighed and relaxed.

"A goddamned statue."

He stood and measured himself against it. It was big, nearly seven feet tall. With his hands, he felt the outlines, forming an image of the pose in his mind. It was a classic Egyptian stance—erect, one foot forward, one hand down, fist clenched, the other arm bent at the elbow, holding a staff.

Several minutes passed before he realized the significance of his discovery.

"A statue!"

They had found it. This must be it. This must be the tomb itself.

"Christ."

They had found it.

He looked at his watch. Three-forty. Wouldn't they ever come? He was practically choking with excitement. The last tomb. It was right here; he was in it.

A sobering thought came to him—it might be his tomb, too.

He decided to explore further. A few moments of groping brought him to a second statue, apparently identical to the first. They were standing on both sides of the passageway through which Pierce had entered.

He felt like a child with a new Christmas present. It had all come true, all his hopes, his desires. They had done it.

They had done it.

Later, he crawled back to the wall and leaned against it. The excitement, the exertion of the evening, and his own fear combined to make him utterly exhausted. He fell asleep.

When he awoke, he found he was breathing rapidly. He forced himself to slow down, but in a few moments found his breathing was again fast.

What would McKernan have said?

Pierce had interviewed him eighteen months ago; he was a physiologist working for NASA. He allowed his mind to wander back through the conversation. They had talked about problems astronauts faced. Acceleration, where the forces made a man's blood as thick as liquid mercury; vibration, which could flap your kidneys against your backbone until they were a bleeding pulp; heat and cold; air.

McKiernan had talked about air. What had he said? Something about carbon dioxide.

He could not remember. The time was eight-twelve.

He fell asleep again, and when he awoke, he remembered. Too much carbon dioxide stimulated respiration—it made you breathe faster.

That meant Pierce was running out of air.

He winced in the darkness.

"The last goddamned tomb."

For any man, his first tomb was his last.

He looked at his watch. It was eight-twelve. It must have stopped. Hours ago—or minutes ago.

Where were they, anyhow?

The next time he checked his watch, he could no longer read the luminous dial; so obviously, time had passed. He was weak now, unable to do more than lie against the wall, breathing shallowly.

He tried to count his breaths. It gave him something to do. He quit at 1,791.

Then he heard scratching.

At first, he could not be sure, it was so faint. Then there was a tapping sound. He turned to the passage and tapped back.

Next, a metallic ringing. There were tapping to him with the crowbar.

They were out there.

Thank God.

He sank back against the wall. The tapping stopped. It was silent, then a crunching sound, and the stone moved slightly. A moment later, it fell back into place.

Then silence.

They were having trouble.

He felt dizzy, unable to think clearly. He waited passively.

More crunching.

Silence.

"The problem is air," Barnaby said. He had come back from Cairo just as the other three were about to leave in the Land Rover. Conway and Nikos had been grim; Lisa was obviously upset, struggling to control herself.

Now they stood hunched in the passage, looking at the stone that blocked their way.

"Air," Barnaby said. "These people knew the secret of airtight construction. We've already seen that. We must get air to him."

He turned to Conway. "How long was the original length of the passage?"

"Are you kidding? We didn't stop to measure, man."

"It would have helped if you had," Barnaby said. "Then we could measure the new length, and determine how big this block is. It could be four feet long and weigh several tons."

"Talk, talk," Nikos said irritably. "Get away from there."

The others stepped back. He wedged in the crowbar and pushed.

A crunching sound, and the rock moved slightly. "It doesn't weigh several tons," he said. "Five hundred pounds at most."

"That still doesn't help much," Barnaby said.

"Try to look on the bright side, will you?" Conway said.

From the sunken chamber, Lisa called: "Can I do anything?"

"No," Barnaby said.

"Yes," Nikos said. He turned to leave.

"Where are you going?"

"Use your head," Nikos snapped. "We have to move a heavy object. What have we got to work with?"

Barnaby shook his head.

"The jack from the Land Rover," Nikos said. He hurried down the tunnel, and they heard him say to Lisa, "Come on."

Barnaby and Conway looked at each other.

"The man is forgetting something," Conway said. "That

jack requires several inches of space to wedge itself in. This rock sits flush with the ground."

"What do we do?"

"Look, man, you're the one who's supposed to be all rested up and fresh. I'm tired." He was; he had not slept since he and Pierce had gone out the night before.

"I don't know."

Conway bit his lip. "Remember Easter Island?"

"What about it?"

"Do you remember," Conway said patiently, "the big stone heads?"

"Yes." Barnaby did not see the point. Easter Island was an isolated place in the South Pacific where had been erected huge stone heads in the earth.

"You remember how they managed to raise those heads?"

"Sure," Barnaby said. "With little rocks…"

"That's right," Conway said. "The man is right. Now will you get me some rocks?"

"Where?"

"Well, there's a whole mess of them in the other room. That door fell out and shattered on the floor, remember?"

"What are you going to do?"

"I'm going to wedge this mother up with the crowbar while you slip the rocks under. Then Nikos can fit the jack in when he comes back. Right?"

That was what they did.

A grinding sound, different from the crunching he had heard for the last half hour. This sound was smooth, continuous. Pierce blinked as pale light spilled into the room. Cool air rushed in; he breathed deeply and relaxed. Dimly, he heard voices.

"There he is."

"Give me your light."

"Just a minute, just a minute. Stand back. Give the fella air." Somebody was shaking him. "Robbie, you okay, man? You still got the old pizzaz?"

Something soft and warm. Hair in his face. Perfume.

"Oh, Robert, Robert. I was so worried."

Tears.

"Now look at that. Here the poor fella has been suffocating, and the first thing she does, she smothers him."

Kisses. He felt her lips and opened his eyes.

"Oh, Robert."

He put his arms around her.

"He has the old pizzaz, after all."

He began to feel better. He looked up at the three flash-lights glaring down at him.

"Hey," he said, "can't a guy have any privacy?"

They laughed, blowing out their relief.

She kissed him.

The flashlights turned away. Then Conway said, "Son of a bitch!"

They all looked over.

In the flashlight, they saw a huge statue of a man, stiffly erect. His clothes were gold.

The beam moved. It caught the glint of a second statue. Then around the room, heaped with articles of all sorts—chests, weapons, clothes, urns of alabaster and brightly painted clay, canes, miniature statues of the gods, golden stools, oars, a full-sized gold chariot.

"Welcome to the tomb," Pierce said.

"It's not much," Conway said, "but he calls it home."

On one wall was a monumental frieze showing the Pharaoh being embraced by Horus, the god with the head of a hawk. The colors were still vivid—reds, blues, purples. On another wall was a large rendering of the scarab beetle, a sacred animal to the Egyptians; above it was a depiction of the sacred procession carrying the king's mummy to its final resting place.

Across the ceiling stretched a long line of gods, each dressed like the pharaoh: Anubis, the jackal-god, Sebek, the crocodile, Hathor, the cow, Thoth, the ibis, Horus, the hawk.

Men's bodies with the heads of animals. Barnaby ticked off the names, then stopped. Nobody said anything for a long time.

8. The Burial Chamber

In his dusty work clothes, Pierce felt out of place in the lobby of the Winter Palace. The clerk looked at him in suspicion. "You wish to send a telegram to Tangier?"

"That's right."

"Please fill out the form. Are you a guest in the hotel?"

"No."

"That will be five pounds."

Highway robbery, Pierce thought, as he paid and filled out the form.

> *REQUEST ADDITIONAL 7500 DOLLARS*
> *IMMEDIATELY*
> > *PIERCE*

Four days later, Lord Grover sat with them around the evening fire.

"What have you done so far?"

"Nothing," Conway said. "We haven't touched a thing." He nodded toward Barnaby. "He's playing archaeologist."

"We must proceed slowly," Barnaby said. "We must learn all we can."

"Have you found the coffin?"

"Sarcophagus," Barnaby corrected automatically. "No, not yet. The room we have discovered seems to be an antechamber or storage room. It communicates through a plaster door to another room, which we suspect may be the actual burial chamber. But we have not yet opened that door."

"I want to see the mummy," Grover said, rubbing his hands.

"In good time," Barnaby said. "We must go about this in an orderly fashion."

"You shouldn't have called me," Grover said, "until you had the mummy. I was all set for the mummy."

"You ought to be able to amuse yourself until then," Conway said. Grover had brought along a new pair of girls: a silently beautiful girl from Hong Kong and a robust, hugely proportioned German. They made an absurd pair, but he seemed to relish variety.

Pierce sat by the fire, holding Lisa's hand. They had been inseparable for the last week. The tension between them had snapped abruptly, after the accident.

"In Cairo, I tried to buy some marijuana," Grover continued. "And you know what they told me? That it was illegal. *Illegal*. Bloody wogs." He turned to Pierce. "I understand you had a bit of trouble," he said. "Feeling better now?"

"He feels fine," Lisa said.

Grover blinked but said nothing. He shot Pierce a quick glance, then turned to Conway.

"How's the weather been?"

"Nice. Real nice. A little unpredictable, but that makes it interesting."

Barnaby said, "How long will you be here?"

"Long enough," Grover said, "to see the mummy. I just want to see the mummy. Then I can die a happy man."

"Nobody dies a happy man," Nikos said.

Barnaby bent over the alabaster vase. It was delicately shaped like a lotus bud. They had moved floodlights into the antechamber to give them working light.

Barnaby read the inscription on the vase: "May your *ka*

live eternally; may you pass millions of tranquil years, you who loved Thebes, seated with your face turned to the north wind and your eyes contemplating happiness!"

"Very nice," Nikos said. "Who's *ka*?"

"The *ka* is the soul," Barnaby said, turning the vase in his hands. "And a north wind is the prevailing direction of wind on the Nile. It was then and still is."

"That's nice. When do we open the door?"

"You mean to the next room? Soon."

Lord Grover walked gingerly among the objects in the antechamber. This was his first chance to see it all, and he said very little. He walked up to the twin statues and peered into the faces, which stared solemnly forward.

He looked down at the base of one statue. "What's this?"

"Don't touch!" Barnaby said.

"I wasn't going to touch," Grover said, withdrawing.

"They're offerings. Olive and persea."

Grover peered down at the branches and leaves. "Three thousand years old," he said. "Remarkable." He looked over to Nikos. "Do you suppose they used hashish? I wouldn't be adverse to a little three-thousand-year-old hashish."

Nikos shrugged: "It's all the same."

"Yes, I suppose so. Perhaps that's the point, isn't it?"

He walked over to the gilded chariot and ran his hand over the golden rim of one wheel, which was inscribed with hieroglyphics. "What does this say?"

"Don't touch!"

"All right, all right."

"That's a chariot," Nikos said.

"For the use of the soul in the afterlife," Barnaby said. He was busy deciphering an inscription on a small wooden chest. Inside the chest was clothing, carefully packed in linen—

sandals, necklaces, robes. The cloth had rotted in places, but it was still easily identifiable.

"Thought of everything, didn't they?" Grover said.

"Don't touch!"

"God Almighty," Grover said, sticking his hands in his pockets. "The man's gone berserk."

Later, Grover spoke to Pierce alone. "What's the matter with Barnaby? He wasn't like this before."

"It's the tomb," Pierce said. "He's been officious ever since we found it. Believe it or not, in the last few days, he's improved considerably."

"I should never have suspected."

"Well," Pierce said, "in a way, I can see his point."

Grover's eyes narrowed. "What do you mean?"

"Just that, considering what's in there—what it's like and what it must have been like—we can't really barge through and plunder it, can we?"

Lord Grover thought to himself, I am a good judge of character after all. He said, "No, I suppose not."

"You're new here," Pierce said. "Barnaby will relax in a day or so, and I'll show you some of the things we've found. They're really quite interesting."

Pierce showed him everything.

A clasp, tooled in red gold, depicting the pharaoh in his chariot, returning with prisoners from a triumphal war.

A scabbard of gold, ornamented with prancing horses, which held a gold knife and a jeweled hilt.

A fly whisk made of thin pounded gold, fan-shaped. It showed the king hunting ostriches on one side, waterfowl on the other.

An unguent box shaped like an oval cartouche and inlaid

with lapis lazuli. It was empty; Barnaby thought it was probably used for rituals only.

A footrest of blue glass and another of wood, on which was carved the images of the pharaoh's enemies—Assyrians and Nubians, Libyans and Sudanese. A small box with a secret catch, containing a piece of soft wood and a hand drill for starting fires.

Gloves of soft skin.

Boomerangs, constructed in all shapes and sizes, for killing the wild birds that lived in the marshes along the riverbanks.

Small jeweled statues of the cobra and vulture, royal symbols of Upper and Lower Egypt.

A square box inlaid with ivory; inside was a round wooden knob at the end of a stick. Barnaby thought it was a box for storing the king's wigs.

A remarkable collapsing bed that unfolded to three times its stored length. Probably for the pharaoh's use on the battlefield.

Dried food: meat and grains, as well as various kinds of seeds. Large jars of wine.

Alabaster lamps elaborately carved in decorative motifs—the lotus and papyrus and other flowers. One lamp was carved in the shape of a crocodile.

Lord Grover watched Pierce carefully as the objects in the room were shown to him. He found Pierce's own attitude toward the objects unusual. There was pride in his voice as he explained them, but it was not simply pride in the quality of the work or pride in his own discovery of the tomb. It was neither, or both. Grover could not be sure.

At the end of the evening, Conway came up and said to Grover, "How do you like it?"

"Fabulous," Grover said.

"Well, I've been thinking. This was a rich fella, all right, but he had a few extra things going for him."

"Like what?"

"No income tax," Conway said, and laughed.

Several days later, they broke down the plaster door. First, they cut open a small hole, a foot in diameter, and shined a flashlight through. Barnaby peered in.

"What do you see?"

"Gold." He sucked in his breath. "A solid wall of gold."

They continued work, widening the hole. It was soon clear that the room was almost entirely filled by a huge gold box, intricately chiseled. There was barely room for a man to slip around it, so completely did it fill the room. When the door was cleared away, Barnaby entered the next chamber and examined the carvings and inscriptions and tapped the box.

"Gilded wood," he said. "A gilded wood shrine." He looked at it, estimating the dimensions. "Say ten feet by sixteen. It must contain the sarcophagus."

He edged his way around the box. The others followed.

"Careful," he said. "There are things on the floor." He stooped to pick up a necklace of semiprecious stones.

"This room is oriented on a north–south axis," he said. "The door should be over...ah, yes. Here it is."

"Door?" Lord Grover said. "Wait a bit. I must see this." He was having difficulty squeezing his bulk through the narrow space between the shrine and the walls.

At one end was a set of hinged doors.

"I thought it opened upward," Grover said.

"No. This is just the shrine. The sarcophagus itself will open upward."

Grover nodded. The others clustered around.

"Well, go ahead man, go ahead."

Carefully, Barnaby freed the latch and swung the doors open.

Another shrine sat inside, covered with a yellow veil and sprinkled with tiny daisies of solid gold. The veil was held in place by a wooden frame. Barnaby pushed it aside and opened the next set of doors.

Still another shrine was revealed.

"My God," Grover said. Outside the shrine were stacks of weapons and linen bandages neatly rolled in small bundles.

Barnaby broke the seals on the third shrine and found a fourth. Like nesting boxes, each fitted with close precision inside the next larger.

"Bring the light closer," Barnaby said. His voice was tense; a rivulet of sweat ran down his forehead to his neck. "This one is different." He examined the door, which showed Isis, arms raised, protecting the contents of the shrine.

"I think this may be the last one."

He broke the seals. The doors creaked open, with the dust of centuries fluttering down from the hinges.

A glimpse of red stone. The doors opened wider. The sarcophagus.

There was still room within the fourth shrine for a man to walk inside. Barnaby stepped in and circled around the sarcophagus, which was square and smoothly finished.

"Red sandstone," he said. "A very nice job."

"The mummy's in there?" Grover said.

"Yes. There will be several nesting coffins, just as there are several shrines. The first coffin is probably gilt wood. The second may be an alloy. The final coffin may be solid gold."

"Hey," Nikos called from another part of the room. "Look at this."

The others came around the shrine to where he was standing.

A low opening led from the burial chamber to another room. The entrance was guarded by an immense statue of a black crouching dog, ears pointed, nostrils flaring.

"Anubis," Barnaby said. "The black jackal. He opens the roads to the other world for the dead and supervises embalmings. They called him the usher of Osiris."

The statue glared fiercely at them.

"Wouldn't like to tangle with that," Conway said. He patted the forepaw. "Nice doggie."

"Let's see what's in the room he's guarding," Barnaby said, ducking through the opening. "You see, Anubis was responsible for seeing that the gifts given to the deceased by mourners actually—"

"What's the matter?"

"Come inside and look."

Nikos entered and whistled softly.

"Yes," Barnaby said, "I was right. This is the treasury." Gently, he lifted one of the many chests and boxes stacked around the room.

It was filled with jewels.

"Merry Christmas," Conway said. He opened another chest and found stacks of gold weapons and canes. Solid gold.

Grover went over to a small gilded box, inside which rested an urn draped in linen. He plucked away the linen, and started to lift the lid. "What do you suppose is in here?" Urns in the antechamber had contained rare spices and oils, frankincense, and myrrh.

"Probably," Barnaby said, "the guts of the king."

"Oh." He stepped away from the urn without opening it.

"How do you know?" Pierce said.

"I don't. But you'll notice there are three other urns, set around the room in a rough square. Probably all four are canopic jars containing the pharaoh's viscera, which were removed at the time of embalmment." He went to one urn, picked it up and pointed to the figure painted onto it.

"Hapi, the dog-headed ape, guardian of the lungs."

"I'll take your word for it," Grover said. "Show me some of those jewels."

The next chest they opened was a beautifully inlaid piece containing a scribe's complete equipment—an ivory pallet, a small alabaster bowl, three cakes of ink, and a reed pen.

Behind the chests were stacks of furniture, carelessly jumbled, for the king's use in the afterlife. Then several *ankhs*, the staff of life, in gilded wood and numerous small statues.

Finally, they came upon a miniature coffin shaped like a human body but only six inches long. It was made of copper inlaid with colored glass. Conway opened it and handed the lid to Barnaby.

"A royal cartouche," he said, puzzling over the inscription. "But a woman's name. Probably the queen."

Conway found only a small object wrapped in linen. It turned out to be another sarcophagus. Within this, wrapped in more linen, was a curl of auburn hair.

"What do you know," he said.

"The soul of a romantic," Grover said.

"It was probably his mistress," Nikos said.

Pierce had wandered back to the shrine and the sarcophagus. He was curious to know how heavy it was and whether they could remove the lid. A few moments of inspection convinced him that it would be quite difficult; the lid was a single slab of stone, six feet by three and nearly a foot thick.

Nikos came back, and together they examined the problem. They decided it would be necessary to dismantle the four shrines and then to jack up the lid. That would take several days.

"Of course," Nikos said, "we already have enough without breaking into the sarcophagus. It's not necessary."

"Yes," Pierce said. "It is necessary."

"Barnaby says that there are probably several more interlocking coffins inside, but not much easily transportable—"

"We have to do it," Pierce insisted.

"Why?"

"Because I want to have a look at him."

A week later, grunting and straining, they removed the lid. Lying inside the stone sarcophagus was a coffin of gilt wood. The Pharaoh lay on his back, arms folded across his chest, each hand gripping a scepter. He wore the headdress of the vulture and cobra, twin symbols of Upper and Lower Egypt, and his beard was carefully braided. His lips were set in a firm line, and his eyes stared upward at the ceiling.

The expression was peaceful but expectant, as if the king were awaiting the gods who would carry him through the twelve chambers of the underworld, down the eternal Nile in the sky.

Pierce looked at the face and said nothing for a long time.

"Meketenre," he said at last. "He's lucky. If we didn't discover him, nobody would ever remember him. But he's going to be famous. We're doing him a favor."

"You'll have to pardon him," Conway said, "if the man doesn't say thank you."

The next day, Nikos left for Aswan.

9. Aswan

The tourist train, A special air-conditioned express that made the trip to Aswan once daily, covered the distance in four hours. But the tourist train did not carry natives; Nikos rode the afternoon train along with the other fellahin. The windows were thrown wide, admitting dust and hot air. The seats were rude wooden slats, worn smooth by thousands of sitters. It was packed with men in *galabas* and women in black *malaayas*, veiled. Some wore ornaments of gold through their noses, and one or two young girls of marriageable age had bright red shawls.

Nikos sat at the far end of one car, leaning over and looking out the window. He was unshaven; his face was smeared with dirt and grime. At his feet was a crate of clucking chickens. If anyone asked him, he would have explained that he owed them to his brother in Darawa, outside Aswan.

But nobody asked him. He was allowed to sit in peace, staring out at the monotonous countryside. The train passed down the east bank of the Nile, stopping at each small village along the way. The villages were all the same—mud huts, dusty streets, and date-palm trees, stately camels and barking, hungry dogs. The people were animated and talkative; riding the train was obviously an event in their lives.

Abdul Badia, born in Alexandria, 1919. Lived in Luxor since 1938, fought with the British during the war. Occupation: shipbuilder. Not a very profitable occupation these days, since wood was so scarce.

He repeated these facts over to himself, again and again.

For the next two weeks, he was Abdul Badia. The man at the Luxor train station had not blinked when he had purchased a ticket to Aswan, but sooner or later he was bound to be stopped. When that happened, he would need this information at his fingertips.

Abdul Badia.

Nikos had made up the biography himself; it had the virtue of being partially true. He had been born in Alexandria in 1919, the son of a Greek merchant sailor and an Egyptian whore. His father had apparently been quite taken with the woman; he spent eight years in Alexandria with her, until she died of influenza. Then, he returned to his home in Patras, taking young Nikos with him.

Giorgio Karagannis was the acknowledged black sheep of his family and was never quite accepted on his return to Greece. Nikos, the illegitimate son by a foreign woman his father never married, was not accepted at all. In fact, he was totally disregarded. His father returned to the sea, leaving him in the hands of unwilling relatives for months at a time. For nearly a year, at the age of eight, he spoke little Greek. It was a difficult time. Finally, when he was twelve, he ran away from Patras. He had never returned.

Like his father, he became a sailor, and he soon learned to supplement his meager pay by smuggling goods from the ship to sell ashore. He became familiar with all the countries of the Middle East and learned all the languages. When the war broke out, he was nineteen and in Alexandria. The British Army badly needed interpreters, and he was hired immediately. For reasons which he dimly understood, he never fought, never held a rifle in his hands. The last thing he did before leaving Egypt in 1948 was visit the cemetery at El Alamein, where the tombstones stretched for acres across the desert.

Madness.

He sighed and watched as the train pulled into the next town. He was bored, that was why he was thinking this way. Before he had left Luxor, he had picked up a book, intending to read it on the way up. Pierce had, fortunately, stopped him.

The fellahin did not read. He would have stood out like a sore thumb on this train.

He looked at his fellow passengers. A woman feeding her baby, staring off into space; two men engaged in animated conversation, laughing; an old man, his face a wrinkled prune, his ankles spindly beneath his robes, looking disconsolately at the floor. A young boy with eye disease, turning one eye milky white and outward. (The gift of the Nile—what did they call it? Trachoma.) An infant, sitting quietly in its mother's lap, while the flies crawled around its nose and mouth.

It was hot on the train. He pressed his legs firmly against the chickens so that no one would steal them. And through his robes, he felt the slight bulge of the scarab. It was a small thing he had picked up from the floor of the tomb, a personal memento of no consequence. It was a habit of his: he always kept a souvenir from each of his jobs. He still had a hubcap from the Aga Khan's car.

And the scarab, though pretty, was a minor thing. It was cut from pale amethyst and nicely done, but there were thousands of scarab beetles in Egypt, and tens of thousands of fakes.

A small thing.

Still, one never knew…

He touched the bulge absently and drifted off to sleep.

Aswan.

Once, it had been the limit of the Lower Kingdom, the farthest outpost of civilization, the frontier town. From Aswan, the endless desert began, and only a few daring caravans set out across it, into Nubia, the "Land of Gold." Savages lived to the south, the wild tribes of Wawat, Arthet, and Iam, often attacking Egypt in hope of conquest, never succeeding.

In those days, it had been two towns, like Luxor: one for the living and one for the dead. Souanou, on the east bank, was the marketplace of the twin city; Elephantine, an island, had been the spiritual center.

In more recent history, Aswan had been a minor town en route to Khartoum, which was then the center of commerce, exploration, and slave trade. Aswan never lost importance, however, for the First Cataract of the Nile was here, marking the first major obstacle to navigation for a boat traveling south.

The Nile at this point was broad but shallow, with bare rock outcroppings and two large islands in midstream, Elephantine Island and Kitchener's Island. The first was massive, formed from black granite in odd, smooth shapes that, seen from a distance, resembled a herd of elephants in the water. Kitchener's Island contained the home and tropical gardens of Lord Kitchener, the English general who conquered and rebuilt Khartoum after the Mahdi's whirling dervishes had destroyed it in 1885.

Aswan was situated in an area of excellent granite, and the Egyptians cut Aswan granite for all their important monuments and buildings. The stones were floated downstream for use in the major temples; one large obelisk could still be seen in the quarries outside town. Had it been fully removed, it would have been the largest single block of stone ever used by the Egyptians; it was estimated to weigh one thousand tons. Three sides of the column had been cut free before a flaw was discovered in the granite, rendering it useless.

Nikos had not visited Aswan since the war, and he was astonished to see the changes now. White and shining, the New Cataract Hotel stood out on Elephantine; other modern hotels stood on the east bank. The town had a new, prosperous look. From conversations he heard in the street, he learned that two new universities were located there.

But the real source of wealth was unmistakable: the dam. Aswan was a boomtown, thriving on the money brought in by the workers on the High Dam, seven miles south. Begun in 1960 the dam now employed thirty-three thousand laborers in three round-the-clock shifts. As summer approached, most of the work was done at night under floodlights.

He walked along the river's edge, carrying the chickens on his head. It was cooler here than in Luxor, and a strong breeze kept the flies away. He looked out at the *feluccas*, the sailboats with triangular sails, moored at the shore. They had been built in all shapes and sizes and stood in various degrees of disrepair.

Tonight, he thought. Tonight is the time.

As night fell, the bazaar came to life, and he sold his chickens without difficulty. He ate a dinner of *ful*, the national dish of beans in oil, and hoped he would not be sick.

The bazaar had a strangely cosmopolitan look. Wandering through it, he felt he was standing in the Egypt of the future, a new country, more politically aware, more prosperous and proud. He noticed little things—a barbershop with newspaper pictures of Nasser on the walls; a stall where books and magazines in foreign languages were sold; students passionately arguing philosophy; foreign women shopping, particularly heavyset, red-faced women with net shopping bags.

He wondered about them, until he heard the language they spoke. They were Russians, the wives of engineers flown in to work on the dam. Aswan was a Russian colony with five thousand technicians in residence, a carpet-seller explained to him.

Egypt is changing, he thought.

Around ten, he returned to the Nile's banks and walked down past the rows of *feluccas*. A few sailors sat by their boats, smoking and talking quietly; otherwise, the area was deserted. He picked out a likely boat, one unusually large and sturdy-looking. Then, he lay down on the ground and pretended to sleep.

"I say," Lord Grover said, as they sat around the evening fire. "I heard a rather remarkable story when I was in Tangier."

The others looked over.

"I happened to meet a relative of Lord Carnarvon, and he described two incidents that occurred when Carnarvon died. Apparently, he died of an insect bite here in Egypt."

"A mosquito," Barnaby said. "He was taken to Cairo and died there."

Grover nodded. "There was a great fuss at the time, about the curse of the pharaohs."

"Surely you don't—"

"Oh, certainly not. But the stories are interesting. He seemed to be recovering from his bite, when he developed pneumonia and died in April. Supposedly, at the precise moment that he died, all the lights in the city of Cairo went out and did not come back on for several hours. Allenby was High Commissioner in those days, and he investigated the power failure. He found no reasonable explanation."

Pierce shrugged.

"You've not heard it all. In England, Carnarvon's dog howled pitifully and died at the exact moment his master died in Egypt."

He sat back and folded his hands and waited.

"Worried?" Conway said.

"Of course not," Grover said. "Just interested."

"You have a dog?"

"No."

"Then you're safe," Conway said.

Grover sipped his gin.

"Tell me," Conway said. "Does the curse only work on the rich people, or does it hit the poor ones, too?"

Grover snorted and lit a cigar.

"There's no basis for all this," Barnaby said. "There is no 'curse of the pharaohs' inscribed in any tomb. On religious monuments, there are a few vague warnings against the living who violate the peace of the dead, but they are hardly blood-curdling curses. When Carnarvon died in 1923, the newspapers leaped onto the story and interpreted it as reporters will."

"I resent that," Pierce said.

"When the tomb was discovered," Barnaby said, "the publicity was immense. It was the first major archaeological find in the days of mass communication, radio and newspapers. Reporters swarmed over the site—and so did visitors, at the rate of four thousand a month. Carter received fifteen crank letters a day; he once joked about a letter he was sent asking if information from the tomb would shed light on the fighting in the Belgian Congo."

"When was this?" Pierce asked.

"1923."

"Nothing changes," Lisa said.

"Certain things are preserved in those tombs, of course," Barnaby said. "Wheat, for example. You've heard of mummy wheat? Two and three thousand years later, you can plant it, and it will grow."

Grover snorted again.

"But I wouldn't worry about the curse," Barnaby said. "There's nothing to it. Of course," he added, "twenty people connected with the Tutankhamen tomb have died under mysterious circumstances. But other than that—"

"What? What?"

"Twenty people, the man said twenty people," Conway said.

"*Twenty,*" Lord Grover repeated.

"Better enjoy life while you can."

Lord Grover stood. "I believe you are right."

He returned to his tent. Soon after, they heard giggles.

Pierce turned to Barnaby. "You remember those urns which you said contained the king's viscera? Why did they do that?"

Barnaby smiled, obviously pleased with the question. "It is all involved with the process of embalmment. The word 'mummy,' for instance, is derived from an Arabic word, *mummiyah,* meaning bitumen, or 'Jew's pitch.' In certain places, this pitch used to ooze out of rocks. There's a Mummy Mountain in Persia. The Egyptians had access to natural supplies, since they drew resources from a very large area. They used to mine gold and copper in Palestine five thousand years ago, remember.

"To us, of course, mummy means a preserved body. Natural conditions can preserve them on occasion."

"Sure," Conway said. "There was a fella in Denmark who was strangled and thrown in a peat bog. The bog tanned his skin and clothes and preserved it all for a thousand years."

"In Egypt," Barnaby said, "with a dry, hot climate, bodies could literally be buried in the sand, without artificial treatment, and be well preserved. This happened with many peasants, who could not afford costly embalmment and were maintained by the climate. In fact, it is now generally agreed that the chemical treatment of mummies had little preservative effect.

"In the case of a pharaoh, the mummification process took nearly three months and was very expensive. First, the brain was pulled through the nose with a metal hook. Then, the stomach was cut open with a stone knife and the viscera removed. Sometimes, they were dragged out through the anal aperture, but—"

Lisa got up and walked off.

"Anyway, the viscera were placed in four urns, the so-called canopic jars. The heart went into one, the lungs in another, the liver in a third, the stomach in the fourth. In the cadaver, the heart was replaced by a stone scarab beetle. Sometimes, the actual heart was returned, since the Egyptians felt the heart was the seat of the soul, not the brain.

"Finally, the remains were washed and soaked in salt water for a month. Then the cadaver was dried out for a two-month period. By now, it was thoroughly pickled. The body openings were plugged with linen or resin to prevent the entrance of bacteria, and then the pharaoh was wrapped in linen and pitch poured over the linen.

"Hapi, the baboon-god, and Anubis presided over embalmments. In some pictures, you can see Anubis watching as the embalmers weigh the Pharaoh's heart on a gold balance. Needless to say, each step of the embalmment was accompanied by rituals and rites. It was a very complex process."

"Seems like a hell of a lot of trouble," Conway said, "just to keep the worms away."

✿

The boats were not left unguarded for the night. A young boy of fifteen or sixteen was assigned to watch them; the sailors went home when he arrived about eleven-thirty.

Nikos sighed and hoped the boy would fall asleep. That would be the simplest way. If there were trouble, he could be hurt—and he was, after all, just a boy.

Nikos lay on the ground, feigning sleep.

An hour later, the boy came around to check the moorings. He did it leisurely, going from one boat to the next. When he came to Nikos, he bent over and shook him.

"Hey," he said, "you can't sleep here."

Nikos shook his head, as if trying to clear it. "What?"

"You can't sleep here."

"Why not?"

"The police will—"

Nikos swung. The punch was low, striking the boy in the chest. He coughed and fell backward. Nikos was up instantly, moving toward him.

Something glistened in the moonlight. A knife.

"Careful," Nikos said. "You can hurt yourself."

The boy laughed tensely. He got to his feet and held the knife in his left hand. He glanced up the hill at the road.

In a few moments, Nikos knew, he would call for help.

He lunged.

The boy was frightened, too scared to use the knife. Nikos caught his hand, kicked him in the groin, and punched him viciously in the face. He felt something snap, probably the jaw.

The boy crumpled without a sound.

"Sorry, little one," Nikos said. "It is unfair, eh?"

He shook the boy. He was unconscious, but breathing.

Nikos scooped up the knife and headed for the boats. He began to cut one free, when he felt something smooth and cold in his back.

"Very slowly, my friend," said a voice. "Take one step forward, and drop the knife. Very, very slowly."

10. A Fair Trade

Nikos moved forward and let the knife fall to the ground. It clattered, glittering in the moonlight.

"All right. Now turn, slowly."

Nikos turned.

The man he faced was tall and lean, wearing a striped robe and cowl that hid his features. In his hands was an old rifle, pointed directly at Nikos.

"That one there," said the man, nodding toward the boy. "My brother. You are very strong with children."

"He was in the way."

"That was his job," the man said softly.

There was a pause. The boats along the shore rocked and creaked in the gentle breeze.

"You came for a boat?"

Nikos shrugged, said nothing.

"Last month, another came for a boat. We also caught him. The police never knew. This man stole for the wood. Would you like to know how he died?"

Nikos waited.

"They cut off his arm," said the man, "at the shoulder. The knife was not very sharp…And then, we watched while he bled to death. It took an hour."

Nikos hesitated. "I have money."

The man shook his head. "A man with money does not steal."

"I have something better than money." Nikos looked at

the gun, measuring the distance, judging the accuracy, the man's reflexes.

"My brother will be in the hospital for weeks."

"I have something very valuable," Nikos insisted.

The man paused, but did not lower the gun. "Gold?"

"Something better. A jewel. Very old, very valuable."

"What kind of jewel?"

"A scarab beetle."

The man laughed and shook his head. "The others will arrive soon. They will decide the manner of your death."

"This one is real," Nikos said.

"They are all real," said the man, with another laugh.

"No, I swear it. This is real, pure lapis lazuli, from Luxor."

Still laughing: "Where could you get a real scarab?"

"I...I killed a man."

The man with the gun became quiet. He nodded slowly. "Let me see it."

"It is here, in my pocket."

"Bring it out. Carefully. Very carefully."

Nikos reached into his robe and withdrew the stone. He held it forward in the palm of his hand. Even in the moonlight, the superior quality of the gem and the masterful workmanship were evident.

The man looked and reached.

Nikos sprang. His hands closed on the rifle barrel, swinging upward. He raised the gun and brought the stock down hard on the man's neck. He gave a heavy grunt and lost his balance, falling to his knees.

Nikos raised the gun and brought it down again. The wood struck bone. The man groaned and lay still. He dropped the gun.

Now where was that scarab?

It had fallen in the scramble. Nikos got down on his hands and knees, searching for it. He could not find it anywhere. Nearby, the man groaned. Nikos searched frantically. He had to get it back. He *had* to.

Above, on the road, he heard shouts.

No time.

He picked up his knife and ran, leaping into the first boat, cutting it free, pushing it away from shore. He saw a half-dozen men scrambling down the hillside toward him. He picked up a paddle and used it to push farther out into deeper water. The men were shouting and waving their hands. When he was twenty yards into the river, drifting with the current, he began to raise the sail.

The shots began. The first bullet ripped through the sail; the second struck the wood of the mast. Others splattered into the water. He ducked down, allowing the ship to drift. The shooting continued. He wondered how soon they would attract the police and whether the police had a motorboat. As the boat moved farther from the shore, he crawled up again and finished hoisting the sail. The wind caught, and he took the tiller. He gathered speed.

The boat passed between Aswan and Elephantine. There were no more shots; the night was deathly silent. A fish jumped in the water, and he heard the creaking of the rigging. Otherwise, nothing.

All around him were rocks awash; he was kept busy for the next fifteen minutes. He struck one, but it was so smooth the boat slid off. Luck, he thought, wiping his forehead. Plain, simple luck.

Soon he passed around the slow bend approaching the town of Kattara. The river broadened and became deeper. He passed a paddle steamer tied up on the east bank, brightly lit as tourists drank and sang long into the night.

He waited to hear the sound of a motorboat in pursuit, but the sound never came. He was alone on the wide, placid river, slipping quietly past the reddish mountains with desert on both sides. It was a scene of eerie beauty.

He rummaged through the sack of plain food he had purchased in Aswan for the trip, found an orange, and peeled away the skin with his teeth. He dropped a piece of skin overboard and timed it as it drifted past the stern.

He figured the speed in his head; he was making roughly five kilometers; it was about 225 kilometers to Luxor. That meant forty-five hours sailing, if the wind held. It was from the northeast now, perfect for him, but if it shifted due north, he would have to let the current carry him. In any event, it was at least three days to Luxor. They should be pleasant enough if the police did not catch up with him.

And, he thought grimly, if the scarab were not found.

"You shouldn't have left so early," Pierce said. "We found out some interesting things."

Lisa wrinkled her nose.

"Did you know, for instance, that the Egyptians worshiped the Nile as a young god who took physical possession of his mistress, the land, each spring when it flooded?"

She raised an eyebrow.

"I just thought I'd tell you," he said.

Dawn. In a cloudless, dry sky, the sun rose abruptly, without preamble. One moment it was gray, and the next, pale light flooded the sky, casting deep shadows. Nikos was slumped over in his boat, relaxed, half asleep, drifting downstream. Soon he would pass Komombo; if he were lucky, he would reach Edfu by night.

He looked out at the shore. This is the way to see Egypt,

he thought. The real Egypt, the country totally dependent on the Nile, the strip-civilization where life could not be sustained more than a mile from its banks. He was not surprised that the ancient Egyptians had revered the Nile; even to a modern man, it was a source of wonder.

The Nile: the longest, most varied, most powerful river in the world. It covered a distance of more than four thousand miles, greater than one-tenth the world's circumference. Its basin, the broad valley, was a third the size of the United States, more than a million square miles. Forty million people in Egypt, the Sudan, and Uganda depended upon it for their livelihood.

Yes, the Nile could be worshiped. He understood it and felt the mystery of it. A map, statistics, facts and figures could dispel the mystery.

From the damp, rainy mountains of Ethiopia, the river came, past smoky volcanoes, descending through swamps so vast they were almost beyond human comprehension. Past the highlands of the Sudd, where Nilotic tribes lived in conical mud huts. Past crocodiles, herds of elephants, zebras, and cranes. Past herders and farmers, warriors and tribesmen, until it reached the flat desert—two streams, the Blue and White Nile, uniting in Khartoum and flowing straight to the Mediterranean.

A marvel. A source of mystery. And the great provider, the Mother Nile, which spawned one of the first great civilizations in the history of man.

Lisa screamed.

Then the sound of a gun once, twice, and a third time. Pierce had been refilling the Land Rover's gas tank. He ran over to the supply tent.

Smoke billowed out. Lisa was standing there, rigid with fright, and Conway held the gun.

"Man," he said, "you'd better be glad I brought this thing."

Writhing on the floor were two cobras.

"You must be a good shot," Pierce said. Lisa buried her head in his shirt, and began to shake uncontrollably.

"I must be," he said.

"How did they get in here?" she asked. "I pushed open the flap, and came inside, and…"

"Who was the last person in the tent last night?" Pierce asked.

"I was," Conway said.

They watched the cobras twist and coil upon themselves.

"You zip it shut when you left?"

"Of course. I always do."

"It was open this morning," Lisa said, "when I came in. I was going to make breakfast." She shuddered again.

Pierce frowned: "Who left it open?"

"Maybe Grover," Conway said.

"Didn't stir all night," Lord Grover said, coming up in his pyjamas. He looked at the snakes. "Nasty buggers, I must say."

"What about Barnaby?" Pierce asked.

"He was with me," Conway said. "He slept like a log. In fact, I got up to make myself a drink because I couldn't sleep. He snores."

"Then who left the tent open?"

The question hung in the air. They all shook their heads.

The German girl with Lord Grover came running up in her nightgown. She took one look at the cobras and fainted on the spot, never uttering a word.

✿

"And how is the Mr. Nikos?" Iskander asked.

"Well, thank you," Barnaby said.

"I see him?"

"He is working now. Up in the tombs."

"Yes?"

"Yes."

Hamid Iskander had arrived at noon in the black Land Rover. As usual, he displayed his own peculiar variety of polite suspicion. Barnaby had tried to divert him, showing him the two dead cobras.

"They did not taste you?" Iskander asked, his face grave.

"No."

"Very nice."

He hesitated then, and seemed embarrassed. Finally, he said, "I will take."

"The cobras?" Barnaby was surprised.

"Yes please."

"Be my guest. But why do you want them?"

Again, Iskander hesitated. "Some peoples will like them."

"But who?"

"In the bazaar."

"I don't understand."

"They are…some things."

Curiosity overcame Barnaby. Although he knew Iskander was proud of his English, he said, "Explain in Arabic."

Iskander, looking both hurt and relieved, explained that apothecaries ground up certain parts of the cobra, particularly the fangs and the eyes, and sold them. They supposedly cured infertility and impotence.

"Makes you strong," he said, indicating graphically. "You can last all night, and all day, and all night. Ten women, twenty women, it does not matter."

"Remarkable."

Hamid Iskander now looked rather embarrassed. *"Mafeesh keteer fuloos,"* he explained. He did not have much money.

"You cannot pay," Barnaby said, bowing slightly. "It is our gift to you."

"Mutta shakker."

"It is our pleasure."

"My humble thanks."

Barnaby had thought that the gift of cobras would put Iskander off his guard, but he was wrong. The Arab made a complete inspection of the camp and noticed that Nikos was not there.

"He comes back soon, for the lunch?"

"Probably," Barnaby said.

"Yes."

At that moment, Lisa came up and dutifully extended her hand for his sloppy kiss.

"Excuse me," he said. "Are you very beautiful on today?"

Lisa looked startled. "Yes."

"Yes. Thank you. I too am pleased."

He stood smiling, hopping back and forth, doing a private nervous dance. "It is to see you so well again."

"Thank you."

"Yes?"

Oh my God, Lisa thought.

The most remarkable thing about the countryside was its monotony. It never changed. Each village was like the last; each water wheel, driven by a patient buffalo, was like every other. The colors, the dusty brown and green and pale reds of the cliffs, never changed. And the sunlight was overpowering.

Nikos kept a hood over his head and tried to sit in the shadow of the sail. The sun was merciless. He had passed

Komombo at midday, a silent town, the people huddled away from the heat. There were few boats on the river at this time of day; heat shimmered up from the surface of the water, distorting the image of the single white sail farther downstream.

For him, this was a dangerous time. The Nile shifted its course almost daily. The only way to avoid sandbars was to follow the local traffic, which knew where the water was shallow. Now, virtually alone on the river, with nobody to go forward and check depths with a dipstick, he felt vulnerable. Often, he felt the boat scrape bottom, but thus far, he had never run aground. He was very lucky.

Earlier in the day, along the water's edge, he saw women in black coming down to draw water and carry it back in balanced jugs to their villages. Skinny donkeys, ribs protruding, also carried jugs. They were driven by shouting young boys. An occasional camel was brought to the shore to drink.

But now, everybody was home, resting, waiting for the sun to begin to drop.

He listened as the bow rippled through the water.

In another day, he would arrive in Luxor. He reached into his pocket and felt the small blue square he would pin to the sail and raise when he came within sight of the Theban hills. That way, people in the camp would know he had made the trip safely.

A very Greek signal, he thought.

"Hey," Pierce said. "Watch your hands."

Lisa was looking through the Polaroid pictures they had taken of the tomb. Several rolls had been shot, in color and black-and-white.

"Why?"

"You shouldn't touch those without gloves."

"Oh."

He took a cloth and wiped the prints she had handled. "Hate to see you in jail," he said.

"Why, Robert, that's the nicest thing you've said to me all day."

She was smiling. He kissed her nose. "Nice nose," he said. "Nice eyes, nice mouth."

Giggling: "Robert."

He stepped back and reached into his pocket. "Okay, I'll buy you. Good teeth? Let's see."

She opened her mouth but shut it quickly, teasing him.

"Not bad. Good housekeeper, strong. How much do you cost?"

"I'm very reasonable."

"Oh, I know that. But how much do you cost?"

"Ten million dollars."

He frowned. His share of the money. "I thought we weren't going to talk about that."

"All right, let's not. When is Nikos coming?"

"Probably tomorrow, if all goes well."

Iskander left that afternoon, dragging his cobras after him. They worked hard in the tomb during the night. The chests of jewels and solid gold artifacts were packed carefully in cardboard boxes and loaded into the Land Rover. They chose well. "Probably five million dollars of stuff right here," Pierce said.

"More," Barnaby said. "Much, much more."

Pierce was irritated. "Sorry you decided to get involved?"

"No," Barnaby said, "of course not. It's just—"

"You can think about your reluctance," Pierce said, "when you're sitting by the pool of your new home, in the mountains somewhere, in some country, surrounded by adoring women.

You can think it all over then. You'll have time, because you'll be rich."

"All right," Barnaby said.

Pierce picked up a gilt wood cane. The handle was carved in the shape of a man, an Assyrian, to judge from the features and the squared-off beard. He looked at it and tried to imagine the power of the king, the strength of his armies, the wealth of his treasures—the tomb could only be a sample.

He held the cane in his hand and leaned on it. After three hundred centuries, it held firmly.

And then, abruptly, it snapped.

11. Return to Cairo

A perfect night, dead silence under a pale quarter moon. With headlights doused, the Land Rover rumbled up to the muddy shore and ground to a halt. They got out and heard the water lapping quietly.

Nikos had beached the boat earlier in the evening. He was waiting for them now, smoking. Pierce got out and gave him a sandwich.

"Lisa thought you might want this," he said.

"She was right," he said, biting into it.

"*I* thought you might want *this*," Lord Grover said, passing him a bottle of brandy.

"God!" He gulped noisily, then set the bottle aside. "Metaxa! Where did you find it?"

"Athens. I picked it up on my way back."

Nikos drank again.

"How was your trip?" Pierce asked.

"Dull."

"Trouble finding a boat?"

Nikos thought of the boy, and the scarab. He shrugged. "No."

"Good. We'd better load up now, before somebody sees us."

There were seven large cardboard boxes, all heavy. It took them nearly half an hour to load them into the *felucca*, which creaked and groaned with each new weight. Pierce threw a ragged blanket over the lot and stood back from the shore.

"I guess that's it. Take it easy out there—those boxes are worth a lot of money."

Nikos nodded and passed the brandy back to Grover.

"Keep it. You'll need it."

Nikos waved: "See you in Cairo."

"Look," Grover said, "do you want a gun?"

"No. What would I do with it?"

"Shoot somebody," Grover said.

"Blood depresses me."

"How long to Cairo?" Pierce asked.

"Ten days, perhaps twelve."

"You remember the plan?"

"I remember."

"Good luck."

"Thanks."

They pushed the boat off the shore and watched as the sail was hoisted, a dead gray in the moonlight. Nikos waved a final time.

They returned to the Land Rover.

For Nikos, the days passed with quiet uniformity. Nothing happened, nothing changed. His *felucca* drifted gently down the river, past the large towns of Qus and Qena and the smaller villages, Khuzam, Shanhur, Danfiq, Abnud. He passed the desert, which began abruptly where the vegetation ended, and he passed the chanting workers in the fields. The harvest of sugarcane, cotton, barley, and wheat had begun, in anticipation of the June flooding. It was a time of intense activity, though he hardly noticed it. The landscape seemed to absorb the petty efforts of men without difficulty.

Farther downstream, river traffic increased. The boats were larger and broader of beam; the sailors called them *naggars*. Loaded down until the gunwales were mere inches above the water, they frequently ran aground, an event accompanied by wild arguments on board and much shouting.

At night, Nikos always stopped. He wanted to remain fresh

for his sailing in the day; it would never do to sink with all the treasure aboard. As the sun went down, he would watch the sailors, agile as apes, climb their masts and furl the sails in the twilight.

When he went to sleep, he propped his feet up on the boxes of gold. It gave him a good feeling. He forgot the scarab.

In camp, the five days preceding their return to Cairo were quiet ones. They spent their time packing and talking; Barnaby regaled them with stories of the pharaohs, anecdotes of love and war, honesty and greed. His supply seemed endless, his memory infallible.

"You know," he said one night, "there were graverobbers in antiquity, and they were caught."

"I don't want to hear about it," Conway said.

"It's actually very interesting."

"Were they hung?"

"No."

"Drawn and quartered?"

"No."

"Drowned? Burned at the stake?"

"No."

"Did they get away?"

"Yes, apparently."

"Tell me the whole story."

"Well," Barnaby said, "there was a man named Peser, the mayor of Eastern Thebes, who lived during the 20th Dynasty, during the reign of Ramses IX. He had a rival, Pewero, and he discovered that Pewero had been robbing tombs—ten royal tombs, to be exact. So Peser reported this to the governor of the region, and the governor sent a formal investigating committee across the river to the necropolis to look into the charges.

"It seems, however, that the committee was rigged. They decided that only one tomb had been robbed, not ten; a special protest demonstration against Peser's unfounded allegations was arranged. Pewero got off scot-free. Some think the governor himself had been getting a cut of the plunder."

"Sounds modern," Conway said. "Maybe there's hope for us yet."

"But that's not the end. Peser was so angry that he threatened to go directly to Ramses with his complaint. The governor got very upset at this—it was a breach of normal bureaucratic channels—and so he put Peser on trial. He was convicted of perjury, poor fellow."

"More and more modern," Conway said.

"Of course, not all tomb-robbers got away with it. A few years later, eight fellows were hauled up for stripping the mummies of a pharaoh and his wife."

"And what happened to them?" Pierce asked.

"They were poor men, you see," Barnaby said. "A stone-cutter, a slave, a peasant, a water-carrier."

"No influence, you mean," Conway said.

"Afraid so."

"Heads rolled?"

"Heads rolled."

Conway turned to Pierce: "How much influence have we got?"

"Not enough."

"That's what I thought you'd say. Always a kind and cheerful word."

"Tell me," Pierce said, "how were these tomb-robbers caught?"

Barnaby smiled.

"We don't know that. The story doesn't say."

✻

The night before they went to Cairo, they visited the tomb a final time. Barnaby chose an object suitable for the museum officials—a mirror with a solid gold handle inscribed with the name of the king, Meketenre.

As they were leaving the tomb, Conway stopped in the outermost chamber.

"Just a minute."

"What's the matter?"

"Uh, give me the crowbar, will you?"

"What for?" Pierce asked.

"Just give it to me, will you?"

Pierce handed it to him. Conway quickly pried up the trapdoor and looked down at the jumbled bodies of slaves in the chamber beneath.

"What're you doing?"

"I'm saying goodbye, that's what. Anything wrong with that?"

Pierce could not tell, for once, whether he was joking or not.

A moment later, Conway jumped down into the room. He walked around the shriveled corpses.

"Do you suppose they believed in all this?" he asked, glancing up at Barnaby. "This whole religious bit?"

"Probably," Barnaby said. "Some of the tomb-builders were very dedicated."

"I hope so." He looked at the bodies. "I hope you fellas were dedicated. If you were, it's okay. You're entitled to your beliefs. Maybe you thought you were doing a good thing out here, right?" He smiled. "And maybe you didn't."

He bent over and picked up the skull of a body that had completely decomposed, except for the skeleton. "Pardon me," he said, lifting the skull free of the backbone.

"Now you see, that didn't hurt a bit."

He looked up at Pierce and held the skull up in his hand.

The sockets were hollow, the nose a black opening, the toothy jaw leering.

"You want to know about the last tomb?" he asked Pierce. "I'll tell you."

He tapped the white cranium.

"That's the last tomb, man. Right there, and you're buried there all your life. You can't ever escape it."

There was silence in the room above. Barnaby and Pierce looked at each other uncomfortably.

Finally Barnaby laughed. "What's he talking about?"

"I don't know," Pierce said.

It was late when they returned to the camp. They decided to have a nightcap and walked over to the supply tent.

As they approached it, a figure darted out and ran across the desert in the moonlight. They could see his flapping robes.

"Hey!"

Conway took off after him.

"The pictures," Pierce said. "The pictures of the tomb are in the supply tent."

He was thinking furiously. If the man had seen the pictures, he would have to be killed. There was no other way.

Conway caught up to him and tackled him.

Pierce went into the supply tent and looked at the small strongbox they used for storage and for the pictures. It had not been tampered with—at least, it did not appear so.

He looked quickly around. Nothing else seemed disturbed. The liquor was all there.

He went back outside. Conway was leading him back. In the dark, they saw that he was an Arab, a thin man with a large moustache, gangly, quaking with fear. His eyes were wide, pleading.

"Here's the boy," Conway said. "I didn't have any trouble

catching up with him, because he was all burdened down with this." He threw two objects down onto the sand.

"What are they?"

"Have a look," Conway said.

Pierce looked: two cans of soup.

"That's all?"

"That's all," Conway said.

"Christ."

Pierce looked at Barnaby. "Talk to him. Tell him he'd better explain himself, or he'll be floating facedown in the Nile tomorrow morning. Scare the hell out of him."

Barnaby spoke rapidly in Arabic. The man said nothing. His tongue hung out, like a dog. Barnaby spoke sharply, and the man replied haltingly.

"He is from a village to the north, toward Quamula. He says he has heard it is easy to steal food here. Several others have done it, at night. He says he has never been here."

"If we were feeding the region, we'd have noticed it," Pierce said. "He's lying."

Barnaby spoke again, harshly. The man groaned, then answered.

Barnaby practically snarled at him. The man quavered and fell to his knees.

"What's going on?"

"He admits he is the only one. He admits he was here last week."

Then Pierce remembered: the cobras.

"What did he take then?"

A rapid question and a halting answer.

"Beans."

Pierce felt suddenly tired.

"Tell him to get up. Tell him we'll give him another can of soup if he'll get up and leave us alone."

The man got up cautiously, holding the two cans in his hinds. His eyes flicked around the three men.

He ran.

Pierce sighed.

Conway said, "He didn't see the pictures?"

"No. I checked."

"Uh, would you have killed him if he did see the pictures?"

Pierce shook his head. "I don't know."

The airplane carried them high over the Nile Valley. From here, it was no more than a muddy, twisting streak in the endless desert, a small rivulet surrounded by green, beyond which extended a trackless waste on which nothing survived.

"I can never quite get used to it," Lisa said, looking out the window.

Pierce nodded.

"You've been quiet lately. Are you always so moody?"

"Will we have a good time in Cairo?"

"We'll have a hell of a time in Cairo."

Barnaby stood frowning outside the door to the Department of Antiquities of the Cairo Museum. He had stopped by to see Varese, only to be told by the staff officer that Mr. Varese was away at the moment.

Where? Barnaby had asked.

The staff officer was rather surprised. Luxor, of course, he had said.

Barnaby did not know why this information bothered him, but it did. No doubt, Varese's reasons for going to Luxor were perfectly straightforward. It might have to do with tourist problems or the German concession within the Valley of Kings. Any number of things.

Still, it bothered him.

❖

"I was promised a room overlooking the river," Lord Grover told the man behind the desk. "I was *promised* it."

The man shrugged helplessly. "We have given you a very beautiful room overlooking Liberation Square. The light is excellent there, and—"

"I'm not interested in the light. I want a view of the Nile."

"I am sorry sir. We are nearly full up at the moment, and I am afraid—"

"Don't be afraid." Grover pushed ten Egyptian pounds across the desk. "I wouldn't want you to be afraid."

The man stared at the money, not moving. He licked his lips. Silently, Grover added another five pounds.

"I believe it can be arranged."

"Now?"

"Of course, sir." He deftly scooped up the money.

"Got it," Grover said as he entered Pierce's room. Pierce was standing by the window, looking out over the Nile through his binoculars. "No problem."

"Any bugs this time?"

"No. I am apparently considered trustworthy."

"Good," Pierce said. "That means we have three rooms facing the river—mine, yours, and Alan's. Somebody will be sure to see him."

"I should hope so." Grover looked down at Pierce's bed and picked up an earring. He looked at it and dropped it again. "You haven't got anything to drink, have you?"

"It's eleven in the morning."

"That's hardly an answer to a civil question."

"Scotch in the bathroom," Pierce said. Through his binoculars, he could see the sailors in the *feluccas* on the river.

"Scotch in the bathroom? *Scotch,* in the bathroom?"

"Yes," Pierce said. "Glasses, too."

"Whatever for?"

"To drink out of."

Grover shook his head. "Oh, Robert, Robert. I fear you'll never make a proper Englishman. In the bathroom—good God."

"Who said anything about being an Englishman?"

From the bathroom came a clink and the sound of pouring liquid. "Well, I just thought...."

There was an embarrassed silence. Grover came back into the bedroom. "Well, what I really mean to say..."

Another uncomfortable silence. Pierce continued to stare through the binoculars. He heard Grover walking around the room. "Well, I have a certain duty to discharge."

"You carry out that duty admirably, judging from appearances."

"The Americans," Grover said sadly, "are given to crude remarks. Frankly, I cannot imagine what she sees in you."

"Oh, so that's what we're talking about."

"Yes." Grover breathed deeply. "Now, will you please put those damned binoculars away and talk to me?"

Pierce put them down, poured himself a glass of Scotch, and sat on the bed. He saw the earring; it was Lisa's. He slipped it into his pocket.

"Robert, I'm afraid I must ask your intentions concerning my private secretary."

Pierce nearly choked on his drink. "What?"

"You heard me quite clearly," Grover said, standing stiffly.

"Don't you think that's a matter between myself and her?"

"Robert, that girl has almost been a daughter to me."

"She doesn't need you to look after her in this respect."

Grover sighed. "She is very dear to me. I never had any

children of my own, you know. When I married each of my three wives, I looked forward to the prospect anew, but the better I knew my wives, the less I wanted *anything* to come of the union. Horrible creatures, my wives. True harpies. Lili was different."

"Lili?"

"Lisa's mother. Lili Castellani."

The name was familiar. Lili Castellani was a French-Italian countess who had been the toast of prewar London; the most elegant woman, the most sophisticated hostess, the most desirable woman in the town.

"Oh," Pierce said. "Does she know?"

"Lisa? Certainly not. She thinks both her parents were killed in the London Fire. Her mother was, actually. Her mother was a beautiful woman."

"Who was the father?"

"A very close, very dear friend of mine. You will understand if I am no more specific than that." Grover shook his head sadly. "I wanted to marry her, you know, but she wouldn't hear of it. Terribly unconventional—she was the only woman who ever turned me down. After the war, I found out that the child had been sent to the country when the bombing started. I looked her up and arranged the records. I couldn't adopt her—I'm not regarded as a proper guardian, you see —but I did manage to see that she received everything she needed. I became a sort of uncle, but I am deeply attached to her, and I feel responsible."

He shrugged. "So there it is. But you still haven't answered my question."

"I don't have an answer."

"I've always approved of you, Robert."

"I still don't have an answer."

"So infernally *stubborn*," said Grover, walking to the window. "Americans are proud of it. National trait. I hope you are aware that when I die, she will be a very wealthy woman."

"I'm not for sale," Pierce said, suddenly angry.

Grover smiled.

"That's what I'd hoped you'd say."

"You should have known that's what I'd say."

"One can never be sure," Grover said. "The prospect of wealth does strange things to people."

12. An Unexpected Visit

Hamid Iskander, trembling with fear, stumbled to his feet. He looked at his visitor and managed to stammer in Arabic, "Sir, what a pleasant surprise."

"I am sure," Varese said. He stood straight and motioned to the servant to bring in a small cardboard box. The box was placed on Iskander's desk.

"Be seated," Varese said.

Both men sat down and stared at each other over the box. Finally, when he could stand it no longer, Iskander said, "What is in the box?"

"You are a fool," Varese said, shaking his head rather sadly.

"Yes, sir."

"You were appointed before I became Director of Antiquities. I have allowed you to continue your sluggish performance only because I had no clear evidence of bungling."

"Yes, sir."

"However, now I have evidence. Can you guess the nature of it?"

"Yes, sir," Iskander said, hanging his head.

Varese was genuinely surprised. "You can?"

"I know," said Iskander, "What the charges are against me. I know that I am guilty. But I beg you to leave her out of this. I am simply a man, and women…"

"What are you talking about?"

"My guilt," Iskander said. "Perhaps you have seen her. She is beautiful, and I cannot resist the temptation to spend some afternoons—not every afternoon, why not even *one* afternoon this week—at her side. I cannot resist it."

"Fool," said Varese irritably. "You think I care about your fat mistress?"

"She is not fat!"

"Fool!" Varese opened the box and removed a small piece of polished stone. He placed it in front of Iskander, who was sweating profusely.

"What do you make of this?" Varese smiled grimly. "I ask you in your capacity as regional representative of the Antiquities Service in Luxor. I ask for your professional opinion."

Hesitantly Iskander picked up the stone and turned it in his hand. He fingered the etched markings.

"It is a scarab beetle," he said.

"Brilliant."

Iskander shrugged. "They are for sale anywhere. On the streets of Luxor you can buy them of quartz which looks like lapis lazuli. Fifty piasters, or one hundred for a large one. They are manufactured in the home of Abdul—"

"May Allah preserve especially the fools," Varese said, sighing. "You think that is quartz?"

Iskander paused, squinted at the stone, and bit his lip. "You mean it is real lapis lazuli?"

"Yes, former employee. It is real lapis lazuli."

"Then this is a genuine and priceless artifact!"

"No." Varese shook his head. "Order tea."

"But if it is real—"

"Order tea," Varese commanded.

Iskander scrambled to his feet.

Later, Varese became calm. Iskander started to think of ways to ingratiate himself with his boss and keep his job. His only alternative was the Transport Ministry, where his cousin worked, and there, the pay was less and the hours longer— altogether unsatisfactory.

"The scarab," said Varese, "came into my hands last week. A wealthy visitor came to the museum and was so impressed he wished to make a donation. Naturally, I was amenable. At the conclusion of our meeting, he jokingly brought forth the scarab, which he had purchased that morning in the Cairo bazaar. He said he knew it was fake, but he wanted my opinion of it anyway. It is the kind of foolishness one puts up with for a donation."

"Only this time it was real."

"Silence," Varese said coldly. "Your stupidity will carry you to an early grave. I am trying to explain that the scarab is, indeed, a fake."

Iskander spread his hands. "Then where is the problem?"

"In the stone and the quality of the cutting. It was seen by Professor Hakim, and Professor Imman. Both agreed it was probably a copy, but neither could be certain. In any case, the stone itself was the genuine article and the workmanship excellent. We decided to investigate."

Iskander knew what was coming. The story of tracing antiquities was oft repeated in Egyptian history. Squads of police would set out to track down the route that a piece had taken from its source.

"It was a precaution," Varese said dryly. "A routine matter. The dealer was questioned. He explained he had purchased it from a Nubian traveler. The traveler was located. He explained that he had bought it in Aswan. We discovered that the dealer there was a Turk. He said he bought it from a sailor. The sailor was difficult to locate, but when we found him, he told an unusual story.

"It seems he got it from an unknown stranger, a man who stole a boat in Aswan. The stranger had offered it as a bribe and then beaten the sailor, but did not retrieve the scarab. A most unusual story."

"And you believed it?"

"Yes. When we were through with him, we believed him."

"It seems unlikely," Iskander ventured.

"It seems more likely all the time," Varese said. "The story of the boat was puzzling. We reexamined the scarab and still could not be certain it was a fake, though we suspected it. So we made still further, very subtle inquiries."

"Yes?"

"It may interest you to know," Varese said, "that I have been in Luxor for two weeks, and I am satisfied that I know the truth."

Iskander shifted again in his chair. A long silence fell. Finally, he said, "And what can I do to help?"

"Remove all personal belongings, and vacate this office by morning," Varese said. "Your replacement is already on his way from Cairo."

With that, he got up and left the room.

13. The Meeting

Conway sat in a chair in the Hilton, looking out at the river through the glass window. From the bathroom came the sound of a shower running; the little girl from Hong Kong. She had become quite attached to him.

On the Nile, several boats drifted up and down. There was a good breeze; the sails were puffed full.

He watched as one boat came downstream, passing beneath the Koubry el-Tahrir, the bridge connecting the east bank with the island of Zamalik. It was an old boat, riding low in the water, unremarkable except for the sail.

A blue patch.

He looked again, then picked up the binoculars. In the stern, slumped in the sun, was Nikos. He watched as Nikos brought the boat down past the Hilton, then around the northern point of the island.

A cool customer, Conway thought. He never once looked up at the windows of the hotel.

Conway met Pierce at dinner. "We have a visitor."

"Nikos?"

"Uh-huh. Came by right on time, at twelve-thirty."

"How'd he look?"

"Like anybody who had just spent two weeks on the Nile. Bored out of his mind."

"We have a busy night." Pierce said. "Where's Barnaby?"

"Probably in his hotel room."

"Go see him. Tell him to meet us in Liberation Square at ten tonight."

"Okay."

"Meet me in the lobby here at nine."

"What're we going to do?"

"Get a taxi."

"It won't take us an hour to—" He stopped. "Oh. I see. You mean you want to get a taxi."

"That's right," Pierce said.

They walked quietly through the eastern quarter of the city, down dark streets.

"I feel like a fool," Conway said. "When I was a kid, I used to wear pyjamas like this."

He was dressed in a *galaba* which they had bought new and made appropriately dirty by dropping in the street and stomping on.

"Don't worry," Pierce said. "You look fetching. Are you sure you know how to start up one of these cars?"

"A Fiat? You insult me."

After half an hour of searching, they found what they wanted. A Fiat taxi parked by itself. It stood alongside a café brightly lighted in red neon. The owner was probably inside, eating dinner.

"Risky," Pierce said.

"Naaa."

Conway wore a suit and tie beneath the *galaba*. If anything went wrong, he would run down the street, into an alley, and pull off the robe, emerging a new man. Nobody would challenge a Westerner. "It's my superman act," he explained.

They stopped at the end of the street.

"Okay man," Conway said. "Now you wait here, and if you see anything coming, you start coughing. Cough like hell. I'll hotfoot it out and meet you back at the hotel. Otherwise, wait here, and I'll pick you up. Right?"

"Right."

"Now, uh, give me the cutters and the knife."

Ho took them and walked quickly across the street. Pierce saw him stop at the taxi, bend over, and open the door. Conway shut the door silently and disappeared from view. He was working underneath the dashboard.

It seemed to take forever.

Pierce lit a cigarette and felt a sudden urge to cough. God, not now. He swallowed hard. The urge passed.

Nobody appeared on the street. Then, three blocks away, a policeman. Coming toward him.

What was Conway doing down there?

The policeman came nearer. Now he was only two blocks away. Pierce saw his uniform clearly in the streetlamp.

Conway sat up in the car and slipped behind the wheel. The taxi roared to life. He shoved it in gear and sped around the corner.

The policeman walked steadily forward. He had not noticed anything. Pierce stood on the corner and waited. He smoked the cigarette and tried to appear unconcerned.

A Fiat came around the corner, three blocks away. It sped by.

"Taxi!"

Red brake lights.

Pierce got into the back seat.

"Sahib?" Conway said.

"Let's get out of here."

Inevitably, they became lost. It was a natural consequence of the labyrinthine city and street signs in Arabic. Nearly half an hour later, they pulled into Midan el-Tahrir, Liberation Square. It was a scene of great activity, even at night. Trolleys and buses rumbled around the turnabout; pedestrians walked, talked, argued, or stood at the little stands that squeezed fresh fruit juice.

Pierce spotted Barnaby: "There he is."

"Where?"

"Pull over to the right."

Conway did. Pierce got out and waved Barnaby over.

"Listen," Barnaby said. "We can't trust a cab driver—"

Then he saw Conway.

"Oh."

"Whaddya mean, oh? Is that all you have to say for the fella who presented you with this marvelous machine? Oh?"

"Sorry," Barnaby said, slipping in. Pierce followed him and shut the door. They pulled out into traffic.

"Why a cab?"

"Because," Pierce said, "it's the least likely vehicle to be stopped at night. You're an archaeologist, I'm your friend. We want to see the pyramids by moonlight. How do we get there? By taxi, of course."

"Did you have trouble stealing it?"

"No," Conway said. "I'm an old joyrider from way back. Now where do I go?"

"Turn right," Barnaby said. "I'll direct you."

"Try to keep us on back streets," Pierce said.

The taxi sped off into the night.

Sixteen miles to the south, they passed the sleepy village of Badrshein, and continued on toward Masgun. The road was lined with date-palm trees; there was no traffic, except for a few donkey-carts returning to their villages for the night.

"Near Masgun, the road runs near the river," Barnaby said. "Slow now."

They passed a camel sitting by the roadside.

Barnaby was looking out at the river. It was a dark night. "Slower."

Suddenly, up ahead, they saw the boat moored at the shore. "There."

Conway pulled off the road onto the sand. Nikos was sitting in the boat.

"About time."

"We came as soon as we could," Pierce said.

"Who pinched the taxi?"

"I cannot tell a lie," Conway said.

"Nice job." He stood up. "A taxi. That was very clever."

"Let's unload the stuff," Barnaby said, glancing around nervously.

Half an hour later, the boxes were stacked in the trunk and back seat. Conway had removed his *galaba;* Nikos would drive, in case the police stopped them. He spoke Arabic.

"What do we do with the boat?" Barnaby asked.

"We leave it," Nikos said. "What else?"

He put the car in gear, and they turned west toward the desert.

14. Storage

Outside Dashur, the taxi headed north into the vast necropolis of Saqqara, the largest burial ground of ancient Egypt, an area five miles long and a quarter mile wide, running along the river. Here, in the desert, there were literally hundreds of pyramids and *mastabas*, the underground tombs of court officials.

Barnaby sat in the front seat, a large map on his knees. He shined a flashlight onto it and directed Nikos.

"That's the pyramid of Shepseskaf up ahead," he said. "Bear left around it."

They were no longer on a road. The Fiat ground through hard sand.

"Now right, toward the pyramid over there. That's Pepi II."

Pierce sat in the back seat, holding one of the boxes.

"Is this place guarded at night?"

"Yes," Barnaby said. "What time is it?"

"Nearly midnight."

"There's an armed patrol at midnight. They go around in a Land Rover," Barnaby said. "Better turn out your lights."

"I'll have to go slow."

"Use your parking lights," Pierce said.

The Fiat slowed.

"Almost there," Barnaby said. "Another few hundred yards." Shortly after, he said, "Pull behind that sand dune up there. We can stop now."

The engine was silent. They heard the wind.

Barnaby got out of the car and looked around. "It's over there," he said, pointing west.

"I don't see anything," Conway said, squinting.

"There isn't a lot to see. An old Coptic monastery was built here, on the desert edge of Saqqara, in the fifth century A.D. It's collapsed now."

"So?"

"The underground storerooms are still intact."

They collected the boxes and trudged forward across the desert. Until he was quite close, Pierce saw no evidence of ruins. Then, he distinguished the remains of a foundation, a bit of wall. It had originally been built of mud brick.

"Nobody comes here anymore," Barnaby said. "There are better monasteries around, and this one was very small and unimportant. Follow me."

He led the way through the rooms to a small passage, where sandy steps led down into the earth. He shined his flashlight down.

"We'd better go one at a time," he said. "The place could collapse at any time."

"I'll go," Conway said. "I'm fearless. It's well known."

"When you get down there, you'll find a large room. Put the boxes near the stairs and cover them with sand."

"Okay."

"And watch out for snakes."

"I'll charm them," Conway said. He took the flashlight and went down.

"Homey," he said. Then silence. A few minutes later he came back up, took Pierce's box, and carried it down. Pierce returned to the taxi to get the final box.

He opened the trunk and groped in the dark for the carton.

Then he saw the lights.

On the horizon, to the east. Bouncing, occasionally lifting to send twin beams stabbing into the night. He heard, faintly, the sound of an engine.

The police.

15. A Meeting of Minds

Quickly, he removed the box and hurried back to the others.

"What's the matter?"

"Cops." He gave the box to Conway, "Get this thing down there, and hurry. We've got to get out of here."

Nikos looked over at the lights. "They're coming this way."

Conway clambered down with the box. The others watched the lights.

"They'll see the taxi," Barnaby said. "What do we do then?"

"We can take care of them," Nikos said, clenching his fists. "There are probably only two or three."

"No," Pierce said. "If there's trouble here, the police will be back in the morning and search the area thoroughly. We have to get out of here without detection."

"But they'll see the taxi," Barnaby whined.

Conway came back up. "I hear the man despairing," he said. "But have no fear." He turned to Nikos. "You speak Egyptian, right? And I speak French. Here's what we do."

He whispered to Nikos, who nodded.

"It might work."

The lights came closer.

"What's going on?" Barnaby said.

"You two hide," Conway said. "We'll take care of everything."

Pierce and Barnaby ducked behind a dune several yards away. Nikos sauntered back to the taxi, took out the ashtray, and dumped the butts on the sand. Then, he lit a cigarette and leaned against the door. Conway ran off into the desert, away from the monastery, and disappeared in a ravine.

"What are they doing?" Barnaby whispered.

Pierce shook his head.

The car came closer. The lights were very bright now, and he could see the outline of the Land Rover. The headlamps fell on the taxi. The Rover ground to a halt.

A spotlight was turned on and swept the area. It came back to Nikos, leaning against the taxi.

From the Land Rover, a voice spoke rapidly in Egyptian.

Calmly, Nikos raised a finger to his lips and shook his head in warning.

Nikos had watched the lights approach and waited until the spotlight fixed on him. He was terrified, but he knew he must remain calm. He must excite their interest, and hold it so that they would not ask for his ID card. If they did, he was as good as jailed.

From the Rover, a voice called: "What are you doing here?"

He pressed his finger to his lips and waved them silent. He walked over to the car, shaking his head vigorously.

A man leaned out and said gruffly, "You know you can be shot, stupid one."

"It would bring scandal to our country," Nikos said solemnly.

There was a hesitation. He felt his heart leap—perhaps he had done it. In the dark, he tried to compose his face, showing smugness, a secret.

"What do you mean?"

"I beg you to keep your voice down," Nikos whispered. "It is vital. And turn out your lights."

"Explain yourself," the voice snapped. But it was quieter. Nikos peered into the Rover. Two others, both armed with rifles.

"Foreigners," Nikos said. "You would not believe it." He spat on the ground.

Then he leaned close, confidential.

"You will not tell?"

"I will decide that."

The lights on the Land Rover went out. Victory was almost sure, he thought.

"It is," Nikos said, "the French ambassador. His excellency and his excellency's mistress."

"Here?"

Nikos nodded. "They have been here for two hours." He sighed. "They make such sounds!"

"What are you talking about?"

"Twice each week, I drive the French ambassador and his mistress to this place. They stay most of the evening. She is very passionate."

"This is true?"

The voice was definitely interested now.

"Yes," Nikos said. "They are just beyond the hill. I have been listening."

"Despicable pig! If you are lying, it will go badly for you."

"You would like to hear?"

"No," the man whispered stiffly. "But it is my duty to verify such an unusual story. Show me the way."

He climbed out of the jeep, carrying the rifle.

Nikos led the way. "We must not go too close."

"Why do you suppose they do it out here?"

"Foreigners," Nikos said, as if that explained everything.

Conway stood in the ravine, sighing and groaning. *"Ma chère… mon petit chou…oh, c'est formidable!…incroyable…ma chère, ma chère…ooooh…c'est ca…"*

He kicked the sand with his feet, lay down, and rolled in it. He giggled and kicked and giggled again.

"*Encore...*"

"I do not understand what they are saying," the policeman whispered. He seemed disappointed.

"French."

"Yes. Do you understand it?"

"No," Nikos admitted.

The policeman listened to the groans. "Is she beautiful?"

"Ravishing. Such breasts."

The policeman edged closer.

"No, no," Nikos said. "It would do no good. There is only a quarter moon. But on other nights..."

The man licked his lips. "You come twice a week?"

"Yes."

"Always to this spot?"

"No. Usually to a pyramid. They like to be near a pyramid."

"Desecration of the proud monuments of our country," the policeman said, starting back toward the Land Rover. "He must pay you well."

Nikos shrugged.

"What he does is against the law, of course. He is immune, because he is a diplomat. But you—"

"Perhaps we can make an arrangement," Nikos said quickly.

"Perhaps. How much dues he pay?"

"Five hundred piasters."

"You are robbed!"

Nikos shrugged: "I am a poor man."

"You will require police cooperation. This will cost you 300 piasters."

"Impossible," Nikos said, "I must buy gasoline. The prices are high."

"Then charge him more," the policeman laughed. "Three hundred piasters is our fee."

"I can afford only two hundred."

"Let us agree on two hundred eighty."

Eventually, they settled on two hundred fifty. Nikos paid him, and the policeman climbed back into the Land Rover. A few moments later, it rumbled off across the desert.

Going back in the taxi, Conway chortled gleefully. "Am I," he said, "or am I not the world's greatest lover?"

"You are," Pierce said.

"I'm worth two of any other kind," Conway said. "A regular one-man band."

Nikos flicked a cigarette out the window. "You love yourself. There is nothing unusual in that."

"Oh, but I do it so well. Such finesse, such heights of passion, such technique…"

They reached Cairo at two in the morning.

In Grover's room, Pierce and Barnaby finished typing the ransom note and pronounced themselves satisfied. Pierce gave it to Grover, who would remain behind in Cairo while the others returned to Luxor.

"There it is," Pierce said.

Grover read it through quickly. "Day after tomorrow?"

"Yes. Wait until then. It'll give us a chance to get back to the site."

"All right. Day after tomorrow," Grover folded the letter and placed it alongside the pictures and the gold mirror. He sipped a Scotch and looked over the glass at Pierce.

"This is your last chance," he said, grinning. "Sure you don't want to pull out?"

"I'm sure," Pierce said.

"Well then, good luck to us all," Grover gulped back his Scotch.

Four hours later, tired and unshaven, Pierce caught the plane back to Luxor.

16. A Moral Dilemma

Lord Grover was practically beside himself. He spent the afternoon roaming through the Khan el-Khalili, the bazaar, questioning the Persians and Turks who owned it, hunting for hashish. For more than two hours, he had no success— but he heard stories of fines and imprisonment until he thought he would be ill. He did not care about the fines; he just wanted a little pot and a quiet place to smoke it.

Finally, he found a man whose brother or uncle or father ran a perfume shop. This man had access to pot. Grover bought five cigarettes and several bottles of perfume for good measure. The salesman favored Desert Flower. He thought Lisa would like it.

After that, he returned to his hotel and ordered three bottles of champagne, which he drank in solitude as he smoked the cigarettes.

This made him feel much better.

Lord Grover did not think of himself as an immoral man. He had personal idiosyncrasies, true, but nothing really reprehensible. Now he was faced with this robbery business. Clearly immoral, but what could he do? He had his friends to think of. Their hopes. Their dreams.

For a time, he considered paying them from his own resources, pretending that he had gotten the money from the Egyptians. But he brought himself up rather sternly—there were limits to friendship, after all, and fifty million was a lot of money. Besides, if the Cairo government were passively told about the tomb, they might get clever and decide to catch the thieves. That would never do.

Fright. Fright was the key. He had to scare Cairo and scare Barnaby's people.

He sweated champagne and tried to think of something.

He was not successful. Later, one of the girls showed up and diverted him; he was able to forget his troubles for an hour or so.

And afterward, when he was taking a shower and drinking the champagne that the girl so kindly held for him, the solution came to him in a flash.

All along, they had been making a mistake. They had been thinking that the Egyptians were fools and they were geniuses. Neither was true.

Faith in humanity was called for. Faith in human ingenuity and human foibles. Lord Grover believed firmly in the fallibility of the human spirit.

He had to.

Because he was sending the letter and the mirror the next morning, and the letter would demand fifty million dollars.

"We could all be roasted alive," he said aloud, chuckling.

The girl misunderstood him. She reached in and turned down the hot water. He yelped as the cold spray hit him and got quickly out

He would send the letter in the morning.

The more he thought about it, the better it seemed.

He was so pleased, he ordered another bottle of champagne and sent for his other girl.

The letter was mailed at nine; Grover spent the rest of the morning in his room, reading a mystery novel and privately rooting for the villains.

At noon, there was a knock at his door, and a man opened it without waiting. He was a uniformed guard with a gun on his hip. He saluted curtly.

"Lord Grover?"

"Yes?"

"Your presence is requested by Mr. Ali Varese of the Antiquities Service."

"Now? But I haven't breakfasted yet."

"Your presence is requested immediately," the guard said.
He touched the butt of his gun, not a threat—just the faintest
suggestion. "Immediately."

"Well then, if that's how it is…"

"Yes," the guard said.

17. The Face of Pharaoh

Pierce awoke early that morning, tense with expectation. To his surprise, everyone else was up. At nine, Pierce went over to Nikos, who was throwing his knife at a cardboard box he had set on the ground, retrieving it, stepping back, and throwing it again.

"Well, the letter's sent."

Nikos just grunted.

Barnaby and Conway sat around the dying fire and told each other stories. Lisa remained in her tent and refused to talk to him when he poked his head in.

He wandered around the camp until ten. Then, bored and restless, he decided to go to the tomb.

He drove the Land Rover out of camp, feeling the sun on his neck. He steered across the desert, past the mud villages, to the foot of the cliff.

Looking up, he saw the cleft.

He had never been there during the day.

He started to climb, and immediately felt a new ease, a sense of relaxation. He remembered how difficult it had been to climb at night; how his eyes ached from the strain; how he cut his fingers and scraped his knees. It was all so much easier in daylight. So much simpler and open.

He reached the top of the cliff and walked to the cleft. He saw the cigarette butts, remnants of the long nights they had worked here. Now they seemed almost artifacts themselves, signs of long-dead activity. He lowered a rope and climbed down into the cleft.

In the daylight the mystery was gone from the descent.

The sense of darkness, of swinging in space, had disappeared. It was all a mechanical, straightforward process. He reached the level of the steps and entered the tomb.

Then, he realized he had forgotten a flashlight.

He hesitated and checked to see if he had matches. He did. He struck one and in the flickering light moved down the passageway to the first chamber.

The match went out. He was surrounded by black. He lit another match and looked around the room. The candles on the floor. He remembered how difficult it had been to break down that first door.

He struck another match and passed on to the sunken chamber. He stared at the hieroglyphics that covered the walls. They meant nothing to him, yet Barnaby could read them. Barnaby was a lucky man.

The flame fluttered and died. He lit still another and continued down to the antechamber where the two huge statues guarded the entrance. He looked at the treasures piled in this room, the personal objects destined for the pharaoh's afterlife.

He had never used them. Or perhaps, now for the first time, he was using them. He was coming to life again, in the eyes of men thousands of years later. It was possible that he would soon be more famous than he had ever been during his reign.

Pierce moved on to the burial chamber. The great statue of Anubis frowned at him from the entrance to the treasury. His match went out; blackness closed in. Quickly, he lit another.

He faced the gilded shrine. Once more, its immensity astonished him. He squeezed around to the open doors and stepped inside the four shrines, moving next to the sarcophagus. The lid was still blocked up as they had left it. He stared down at the Pharaoh Meketenre.

The face was composed, neither relaxed nor deathly rigid. It had a peaceful, convinced look; the eyes looked forward, straight ahead, as if awaiting some predestined goal.

"I would give anything to know what you thought at the moment you died," Pierce said.

His voice echoed in the tomb.

The flame went out.

He returned to the camp at noon. As he came over a sandy rise, he looked down at the tents and could hardly believe what he saw.

Four black Land Rovers had pulled up, and a dozen armed guards were leaping out, encircling the camp.

He drove down and parked alongside the Antiquities Service cars. Conway came up, shaking his head.

"Bad news," he said. "We lose."

Pierce glanced around at the guards.

A thin man with a glowering, moody face came over to them. He approached gravely.

"Mr. Pierce?"

"Yes."

"I am Ali Champs," he said, bowing slightly. "Mr. Iskander's replacement."

"Replacement? Has something happened?"

"Yes," said Ali Champs. "Something has happened."

18. Bad News

Ali Varese stood as Lord Grover entered and waved him to a seat. The director's face was stern, but his manner seemed friendly enough. Of course, that meant nothing with Egyptians; they could smile sweetly as they ran you through.

"I am interested to meet you at last," Varese said carefully.

Lord Grover nodded and waited.

"The association between England and Egypt in archaeological work is a long and honorable one," Varese said.

Lord Grover lit a cigarette.

"It has been marked by honesty and fair dealing on both sides."

What the hell? Grover thought. He smiled and said, "I have always believed that the tradition should be upheld."

"Precisely."

Varese shifted papers on his desk.

"What I have to say does not concern you directly," Varese said. "But it concerns your associates. I must speak in the strictest confidence. No word of what I tell you may pass this room."

"You can count on me."

"Today, I received some remarkable news. It arrived, oddly enough, in an anonymous letter."

"Hmmm."

"You will be quite surprised to hear this," Varese said.

A boy came with tea.

"Sugar?" Varese asked.

"No, thank you," Grover said, patting his stomach, trying

to hide the fact that it was churning nervously. "I must watch calories."

"Yes," Varese said. "I must also. The curse of old age. Old men become cautious and timid in all respects, I fear."

Grover said nothing. He tried to relax, to loosen his taut muscles, to keep his face calm. He could not be sure what Varese knew, but clearly he knew something.

"However, I was telling you the news," Varese continued. "In a sense, it is bad news. In a sense, good news. It seems that a band of robbers have discovered a new pharaonic tomb in the region of the Valley of the Kings."

Grover sat upright. "No!"

"Indeed," Varese said mildly. His eyes were watchful. "I said you would be surprised. You will be more surprised when you hear the rest."

"I can...I can hardly believe it. Robbers? Astonishing."

"Frankly, I have difficulty myself. But Egypt is a land of surprises, particularly where the ancients are concerned."

"Yes."

"And we have corroborative evidence. You see, we know who the robbers are."

"Excellent! Well done!" As he spoke, Grover felt a twisting pain in his stomach.

"Thank you," Varese said, sipping the tea. "We move swiftly. In fact, justice has already been meted out."

"Oh?"

"Yes." He glanced at his watch. "Those who attempt to steal our national treasures will always receive harsh punishment. The robbers were executed by firing squad ten minutes ago."

Grover wanted to speak but found he could say nothing. Nothing at all.

19. Good News

Varese waited several minutes before continuing. He obviously relished this moment, and Grover hated him for it. Finally, he said, "It was a matter of small consequence. The thieves were pure riffraff, simple vagabonds. It's really quite remarkable that they managed to take the pictures of the tomb and compose in English the letter which was sent to us. The pictures and letter are quite expert. You'd think it had all been planned by a trained archaeologist."

Grover found his voice. "How curious."

"Naturally," Varese said, "this business represents a considerable embarrassment to the government. Neither the ransom note nor our efficient dealing with the criminals will be publicly announced. To announce that petty thieves have discovered a tomb is not in the interests of…shall I say, our national image? You understand, I am sure."

Grover frowned. He did not understand anything. "Why are you telling me all this?"

"Because I had hoped you might help."

"I shall do whatever I can."

"Your generosity is well known," Varese smiled. "We are most grateful. You see, the criminals died without revealing the hiding place of a cache of treasure. We know that the mastermind is still at large and have spread the word discreetly that if he reveals the hiding place to us by anonymous letter, we will not pursue him."

Varese chuckled. "I have no doubt that I shall receive such a letter shortly. The man must be quivering with panic at this very moment."

"I should think so," Grover said, rubbing his palms together nervously.

"However, that doesn't solve the problem of the tomb. The government today has few available funds for the exploration of new monuments. This new discovery presents a problem in financing."

"I see."

"What the government needs is an interested person of considerable private wealth and humanistic concern who is willing to underwrite the cost of an expedition to search for the tomb."

"Ah."

"Naturally, should great treasures he discovered, you would be fully reimbursed, as was Carnarvon."

"That is very kind."

"And, of course, there would be great fame for all involved…"

"I imagine so."

"But even with money, a final problem remains. We need a group of specialists to do the actual work. Our own position is rather difficult. We are informed of the existence of a tomb. Can we call in experts from throughout the world without arousing curiosity, embarrassing questions? How can we dispose of the fact that we know of this tomb before we start looking?"

"Quite a problem."

"Indeed," Varese said, nodding wisely. "Indeed,"

"You're in a terrible bind. What do you propose?"

"I was wondering about the group that you now support so generously—Professor Barnaby's expedition. Could they be diverted from their present project to search for the tomb?"

Lord Grover sighed. "I doubt it. Professor Barnaby and

his team are immensely dedicated, I don't think they would wish to abandon their present work in the midst of their heroic effort."

"You might perhaps persuade them."

"You overestimate my powers, sir."

"But think of it." Varese said. "They would be the acknowledged discoverers of a new Egyptian tomb! The world would applaud them. They would receive the highest praise. Surely, you can make it a tempting proposition?"

"Well, when you put it that way…"

"The ransom letter has been kept secret," Varese said. "The criminals have been executed. No one knows the true story, except us. Why don't you take these pictures with you and show them to Barnaby? I think they would excite him."

Grover took the envelope and slipped it into his breast pocket. "I will try, though I doubt I can change Professor Barnaby's mind. He is a specialist, and I am not; and this scheme is so…well, to be plain, unbelievable."

"Then I will go to Luxor and speak to him myself."

"That's a splendid idea!"

Varese smiled. "Do you think it will work?"

"If you can't do it," Grover said, "nobody can."

They sat morosely around the campfire, speaking little, occasionally glancing out at the guards. It was late afternoon. Earlier in the day, Pierce had questioned Ali Champs.

"What's happening?" he had asked, pointing to the troops.

"Nothing."

That was, quite literally, true. The guards stood about, rifles on their shoulders, smoking cigarettes, talking quietly. "Why are they here?"

"We are all awaiting orders."

"Orders? What orders?"

"From Cairo," Ali said, and then turned away. They could find out nothing more.

At sunset, another Land Rover rumbled into the camp and came to a halt. Still more guards clambered out.

"Christ," Pierce said. He counted them; the total was up to sixteen.

"And all I got is my trusty cobra pistol," Conway said.

Then, Lord Grover descended from the car, looking tired and sad. He was accompanied by a short man with white hair and a distinguished manner.

"Monsieur Varese," Barnaby said, leaping up.

"What is this action?" Conway whispered to Pierce.

"I don't know."

"This is an outrage," Barnaby was saying, "Why are these troops here? Why are we under guard?"

Varese pursed his lips and ignored the question. "I am here on business. Very serious business. I think we had best speak in private."

"Oh," Barnaby said.

"Christ," Pierce said. He caught Grover's eye. Grover shook his head sadly. He was leaning against a Land Rover, smoking a cigarette, his features drawn with fatigue. No one from the camp approached him; they had all separated, as if realizing that, to huddle together would appear suspicious. Actually, they looked even more suspicious now, standing apart, stiffly nonchalant.

"Come," Varese said to Barnaby. "We will talk in your tent."

An hour later, Barnaby made the formal announcement. The expedition would change its plans and search for the so-called tomb. The others in the group struggled to keep the shock and relief from their faces. Varese pretended to be delighted with the group's decision. He stayed for dinner at the camp, and Lord Grover, suddenly rejuvenated, produced a case of champagne to celebrate the new purpose of the expedition.

Pierce got him alone later. "You bastard," he said. "You enjoyed every minute of this."

"Not every minute," Grover said. "I was quite disturbed when Mr. Varese told me the robbers had been caught and shot."

"Then they don't think we did it?"

Grover smiled. "Mr. Varese," he said, "is a very clever man."

He would say no more. Pierce went back to Lisa and took her hand. She was smiling, radiantly happy.

"We're going to look for the tomb," she said laughing. "It's like a dream come true."

"Can you stand it out here in the desert?"

"We have to get married first."

"I can stand anything, as long as you're here."

"I know."

"You know?" he said.

"Yes," she said. "I know."

"We'll get an engagement ring," he said. "Alexandrite. Then we'll get married in—where would you like to get married?"

"In the embassy in Cairo."

"No. We'll get married in Athens. And for our honeymoon, we'll go—"

"To my uncle's villa in Capri."

"You're damned right you will," Lord Grover said, several yards away.

"Eavesdropper," Pierce said.

"Have some more champagne," Grover said, refilling their glasses.

Pierce thought: so that's why he bought champagne.

"Who's the best man?" Grover asked.

"Don't ask stupid questions," Conway said. "I have seniority."

Later that night, Varese moved around the fire, talking to each of the members of the expedition in turn.

"Tell me," Varese said to Nikos, "do you think this tomb really exists?"

"No," Nikos said.

"But the pictures were quite convincing."

"No," Nikos said. "We could spend ten years out here and never find anything."

"There's always a chance," Varese said. "The whole thing has been quite extraordinary. Do you know how we first became suspicious? A scarab beetle was traced to Aswan."

"Oh?"

"Yes. Our experts considered it fake but agreed it was unusually well made."

Varese took the beetle out of his pocket.

Nikos did not blink. "Pretty," he said.

"Yes," Varese said. He moved on. Conway bet him five dollars that the tomb didn't exist. Varese seemed to find this amusing.

When he came to Pierce, he stopped.

"Yes," he said, almost to himself. "You."

"Me?" Pierce was half drunk, giddy, with Lisa leaning on his shoulder.

"Yes," Varese said. "It was you. My congratulations."

"What for?"

"Your engagement, of course."

"Thank you."

"I admire you."

Pierce nodded.

"It must have been very difficult. But I think it will be better in the end."

"I don't think I understand," Pierce said slowly.

"If I may be permitted," Varese said. "A small gift for the new couple."

He nodded to a guard, who brought up a large cardboard box and handed it to Pierce.

"With my best wishes," Varese said. "You know, there was a time when I thought I might get killed. It was easy to be frightened."

Pierce frowned.

With a final nod, Varese walked away.

"What is it?" Lisa said. "Open it."

Pierce tore away the string and tape and lifted the lid. Inside, he found a black wig, a moustache, and a can of grease-paint.

Also, two cans of beans and two cans of chicken soup.

For a moment, he stared in stunned disbelief, and then he began to laugh. He laughed until the tears ran down his cheeks, and Lisa, clutching him, laughed too. Together, they walked out into the desert, away from the camp, until they were alone, still laughing under the dark sky, with Egypt all around them.

Starting in the early dawn light, he had driven up into the mountains, leaving the flat sprawl of Kingston behind him. He had cut through the tiny mountain villages, the native huts perched precariously beside the road; then down through lush valleys of tropical vegetation, damp in the misty morning wetness; and finally up once more to the cold air of the peaks which sheltered the north coast.

Now it was eight o'clock in the morning, and he was coming down, hunched over his bike, doing a hundred, with the sound of the engine in his ears, and the wind in his hair. In the distance, he could see blue water, with waves breaking across the inner reefs, and hotels lining the beachfront. A momentary glimpse: then he plunged into the final twisting green decline which led him to Ocho Rios.

McGregor hated Ocho Rios. Once a beautiful and elegant strip of coastline, it was now a long succession of gaudy hotels, ratty nightclubs, stud services and steel-band discos, all patronized by hordes of vacuous tourists who were seeking something a little more expensive but no different from Miami Beach.

It was to serve such tourists that the Plantation Inn had been built, an enormous complex on twenty acres of lavish grounds, phony colonial buildings, restaurants and snack bars. It was shielded from the road by a high fence. There was a guard in khakis at the gate, a smooth-faced native who saluted each limousine of tourists as it arrived from the airport.

The guard did not salute McGregor, however. Instead, he held up one hand, and rested the other on the butt of his holstered gun.

"You have business here?"

McGregor stopped, idling the bike. "I'm seeing Mr. Wayne."

"Mr. Who?"

"Wayne. W-A-Y-N-E."

The guard checked the guest register on a clipboard, made a mark against one name, and nodded. "Keep the noise down," he said, as he stood aside to let McGregor pass. "The guests are sleeping."

McGregor smiled, gunned his bike, and roared noisily into the compound. He passed manicured gardens, beds of bright flowers, carefully watered palms. At length he pulled up in front of the main hotel building, which was only three years old, but carefully constructed to resemble an old Jamaican plantation.

He parked the bike and went into the lobby. At the front desk, the clerk in a red jacket and tie stared at his greasy dungarees and dirty blue pullover. "May we help you, sir?" he asked, with an expression that was intended to be a smile, but was closer to a wince.

"Mr. Wayne."

"Is he, uh, expecting you?"

"Yes, he is uh expecting me," McGregor said.

The man winced a little more. "Your name, please?"

"James McGregor."

The clerk picked up the telephone, dialed, and spoke quietly for a moment before hanging up. He was clearly displeased, but managed to say, "Take the elevator to the right. Room four-two-three."

McGregor nodded, and said nothing.

❁

Despite the early hour, Arthur Wayne was up and dressed, sitting at a small table on which breakfast had been laid out. He was a lean man in his middle fifties, with a severe face and gray, cold eyes; despite the casual resort atmosphere, he wore a three-piece pinstripe suit.

"Sit down, McGregor," he said, buttering his toast. "You made good time. Want some breakfast?"

"Just coffee," McGregor said. He lit a cigarette and sat in a chair near the window. "How'd you know where to reach me?"

"You mean, at your…friend's?" Wayne smiled, and poured a cup of coffee. "We have our ways. I didn't really think you'd be here so fast, though."

"I told you, eight thirty."

"Yes, but we called at six, and it's four hours from Kingston to Ocho—"

"Not the way I do it."

"Clearly," Wayne said. "Clearly." He bit into the toast and glanced over at McGregor. A businessman's glance, steady, appraising. "You're older than I expected."

"So are you."

"How old are you, anyway?" He set down his toast, and started on the scrambled eggs. "Tell me a little about yourself."

"There's not much to tell," McGregor said. "I'm a diver. I'm thirty-nine. I've lived in Kingston fourteen years. Before that I did salvage work out of New York and Miami. It didn't pay, and I hated it, so I came down here."

"And before New York?"

"I was in the Pacific, clearing beaches for the Marines."

Wayne chewed his eggs. "What was that like?"

"Like a bad dream." McGregor puffed on the cigarette, and stared out of the window. He disliked this part: the early establishment of credentials with the client. You had to put on a good show. He hoped Wayne wouldn't get onto the leg business.

"I heard you were injured in the war," Wayne said.

"Yes. Nearly lost a leg. It took the medics three years afterward to get it back together."

"Remarkable," Wayne said, still chewing. "Remarkable. Well, I won't beat around the bush, Mr. McGregor. You come highly recommended to us. We're very eager to have you."

McGregor smiled slightly. "Especially since I'm the only one on the island equipped to do the job?"

"We are more concerned," Wayne said, "about finding the right man for the job."

"But your alternative is flying in a team from Florida or Nassau, and that costs. It costs plenty—all that heavy equipment."

"Are you telling me you're raising your rates?" Wayne said.

"Just thinking about it."

"I won't beat around the bush," Wayne said. "This is an important, very delicate job. We'll pay you anything you ask, within reason."

"Depends on the job."

"Then let me tell you," Wayne said, wiping his mouth with a napkin, "about the job."

He pushed away from the table, and, coughing slightly, lit a cigarette. He reached for a large briefcase and opened it, taking out maps, charts, and marine blueprints, which he spread across the floor.

Then he picked up a glossy photograph of a ship, and handed it to McGregor.

"This is the problem," he said. "The yacht *Grave Descend.*

One hundred twenty-three feet at the waterline, luxury fittings, five staterooms, each with bath—"

McGregor said, "Tonnage?"

"Forty-four twenty, I think."

"You think?"

Wayne checked his papers. "Yes…forty-four twenty."

"Where did it go down?"

"Five miles east of here, and three-quarters of a mile offshore, give or take. According to the best estimates, it's about here"—he gave McGregor a marine chart—"just outside the outer reefs. There's two reefs here, an inner reef of about twenty feet, and an outer reef that falls off to—"

"I know about the reefs," McGregor said. "When did it go down?"

"Yesterday."

McGregor paused. "Yesterday?"

Wayne sucked on his cigarette, and smiled. "You're wondering why I am here so soon. Marine insurance companies aren't usually so punctual in sending a representative—isn't that what you are thinking?"

"Roughly."

"I think you will understand as time goes on. The boat is insured for two million ten, so we are understandably concerned, but that is only part of the problem."

McGregor frowned. He had never heard of a marine insurance rep calling a ship a *boat* before. And Wayne was remarkably disorganized. He looked again at the map. "How does she lie?"

"We're not sure. We think the bow faces north, toward open water, and that the stern rests here. That would put the stern in about sixty-five feet, and the bow in about eighty. The drop-off is quite sharp here—"

"Fragmentation?"

"No. As far as we know, not. It is, we hope, intact."

"But you don't know."

"No. We don't."

McGregor frowned. "Whose is she?"

"She belongs to an American industrialist who made his fortune in steel. He bought it from an Australian nine months ago, and kept it in the Mediterranean until a few weeks ago. He brought it across to Miami—West Palm, actually, to a marina there—for repairs, and then had it sailed here."

"He wasn't aboard?"

"No. He lives outside Pittsburgh, and was planning to fly down, and take her from Ocho down to Aruba."

McGregor nodded. "And you want me to tell you if it can be raised?"

"Among other things," Wayne said. "But we have an additional concern, of great importance to us, from the insurance standpoint."

"What's that?"

"We want to know why it went down in the first place," Wayne said, and stubbed out his cigarette.

There was a short silence. McGregor waited for an explanation; when none came, he said, "I'm not sure I follow you."

"I'm not sure I'm making much sense, myself," Wayne said. "You see, something happened aboard that boat. There was an explosion—in the engine room, according to all accounts. The boat was outfitted with twin six-hundred-horsepower Caterpillar diesels—"

"Diesels?"

"Yes, why?"

"Go on."

"Twin six-hundreds. She cruised very nicely at fourteen knots. Those diesels were thoroughly checked out at West Palm. They were in perfect running order. Yet there was an explosion. And the boat sank very swiftly. It was down in a matter of minutes."

"Anybody hurt?"

If there had been a death or serious injury, it would be out of McGregor's hands. The Jamaican government would conduct its own inquiry, since the boat had sunk in Jamaican territorial waters.

"No," Wayne said. "That's the strange part of it. There were six crew members, including the skipper, Captain Loomis. And there was one passenger. They all made it off the boat safely, and were picked up by a native fishing boat."

"I see. Where is Captain Loomis now?"

"Here in town. He's staying at the Hotel Reserve."

McGregor nodded. He knew the Reserve, a cheap hotel back in the hills, where yacht owners traditionally put up their crews.

"I'd like to talk to him."

"Of course. I'll arrange it for later in the day—"

"Don't bother," McGregor said. "I'll do it myself."

Wayne shrugged. "As you wish."

"And the passenger? Who was he?"

"She, actually," Wayne said. "Monica Grant. Captain Loomis did very well as far as that was concerned."

"How do you mean?"

"I mean, publicity." Wayne picked up the day's copy of the *Gleaner*. "Not a word about the yacht and its sinking. Not a blessed word. Captain Loomis managed to keep everything quiet, and a good thing, too."

McGregor said nothing.

"You see, the owner of the *Grave Descend* is quite a good friend of Miss Grant. And the owner's wife…"

"Okay," McGregor said. "Got you."

"So there you have it," Wayne said. "The ship went down, and we don't know why. The owner is extremely eager to keep it quiet, and he doesn't want Miss Grant's name mentioned."

"You can't hope to conceal it forever," McGregor said.

"No. No, we wouldn't even try. What we intend is to announce the sinking as occurring this evening. That will allow us to safely remove Miss Grant from the scene of the action, away from the reporters and photographers. It is, after all, a very good story—bizarre sinking of a luxury yacht, with mysterious beautiful girl on board. A good enough story to make the Pittsburgh papers."

"Miss Grant is beautiful, is she?"

Wayne shrugged, and walked onto the balcony. "Have a look for yourself." He pointed down to the pool. "The blonde in the deck chair, reading the magazine."

McGregor looked down at a girl in a small bikini, lounging at the poolside.

"Beautiful," he nodded.

"She's registered as a guest of the hotel now," Wayne said. "She will have been registered for fully twenty-four hours before news of the sinking is released. No one will connect her to it."

McGregor frowned. "You seem," he said, "to be going to great lengths to protect the owner of this ship. Isn't that a little beyond the call of duty for an insurance agent?"

"I suppose," Wayne said, "but the circumstances are special."

"How's that?"

"The owner, Robert Wayne," he said, "is my brother."

❖

He let that sink in. McGregor didn't know exactly what to make of it, but he would decide later. Meantime, there were other problems.

"About money…"

Wayne said crisply: "We are prepared to offer you a hundred a day."

"Plus expenses," McGregor said.

"Yes. Plus expenses."

"I'll need a decent-size skiff, say thirty feet. Compressor, tanks, equipment—I have all that, but it goes on a per diem basis of a hundred dollars."

Wayne nodded. "All right."

"And my own rate is two hundred a day," McGregor said.

At this, Wayne paused. "I was given to understand," he said, "that you did not run quite so high—"

"I don't usually," McGregor said. He tapped the marine chart showing the position of the *Grave Descend*. "But this is powerhead country."

"I beg your pardon?"

McGregor smiled slightly. "Powerhead country. It means you don't go down there without a gas gun and a powerhead shaft. Especially outside the far reefs."

"I'm afraid I still don't—"

"Because," McGregor said, "that stretch of coast is the furthest Atlantic tip of the island, the most unprotected water. It's thick with hammerheads."

Wayne looked confused.

"A kind of shark," McGregor said. "One of the worst kinds."

"I see."

"Two hundred a day," McGregor said.

Wayne nodded. "Two hundred it is."

"I'll take care of getting the skiff, and paying the man. I'll have all my equipment over here by—by tomorrow morning."

"Very good."

"We can begin then."

"All right. You'll want something to get you started," Wayne said, and quickly wrote out a check for a thousand dollars, waved it dry, and handed it to McGregor. "Is that sufficient?"

"I think so."

"And I was going to suggest that perhaps later in the day you might want to fly over the site. We can charter an airplane quite easily from the Ocho airfield. Perhaps at two this afternoon?"

McGregor shook his head. "Sun's too high," he said. "You won't see shadows at two. Better three thirty or four."

"All right. Shall I arrange it?"

"Yes."

"Then we'll meet at the airfield?" Wayne said.

"Fine," McGregor said, and left, check in hand. He went down to the lobby, exchanged sneers with the desk clerk, and walked out to the pool to talk with Monica Grant.